Trails

of the

Heart

Trails
of the
Heart

Geneviève Montcombroux

© Copyright 2003 Geneviève Montcombroux
First published in abridged version by Zebra Books, an imprint of Kensington Books.

All rights reserved

No part may be reproduced in any form without permission in writing from the publisher except by a reviewer who wishes to quote brief passages for the purposes of review.

Canadian Cataloguing in Publication Data

Montcombroux, Geneviève

Trails of the heart

ISBN 0-9681675-4-3

If you purchased this book without a cover, you should be aware that this book is stolen property. It was reported as "unsold and destroyed" to the publisher and neither the Author nor the Publisher has received any payment for this stripped book.

Whippoorwill Press
Box 206, Inwood, MB R0C 1P0
Email info@whippoorwillpress.com
www.whippoorwillpress.com

Printed and bound in Canada by Hignell Book Printing

To my husband Michael, my greatest fan, my #1 critic, my inspiration.

Chapter 1

"Okay, Tyler Kade, where the devil are you?"

Kelly watched her breath form a plume in the still air. The bus had long since sped off down the unpaved road, swallowed up by the gathering October dusk. An icy cold cut through her parka and bit at her ears muffled in a blue wooly toque.

She wished now she could have spoken to Tyler on the phone before setting out. All she had got when she dialed his number was the impersonal whine of a fax machine.

Tapping one booted foot against the other in the hope of restoring the circulation to her numbed toes, she silently cursed her new boss. Maybe his reputation for being ornery was well deserved. She figured that if he'd been desperate enough to hire someone, he should be waiting for her at the bus depot.

In a nervous gesture, she tugged her collar over her ears. Serious second thoughts about this crazy adventure swirled through her mind. Whatever had possessed her to reply to the ad in the dog mushing magazine? *URGENT!* it had read, *Sled-dog handler wanted. Experience necessary. Able to take on Iditarod training responsibilities.*

The ad carried no name, only a phone-fax number and a post box address here in the Yukon, at a place so small she couldn't even find it on the map. Undeterred, she had sent him her resume. It had to do. Though how could the written word ever convey the passion she felt about working with dogs?

The reply had come back, and she thought she'd been given the chance of a lifetime. Learning the fine art of sled dog driving over long distances under the tutelage of a long distance musher was something she had planned to do ever since the death of her father.

After dispatching her application, days dragged by without a reply. Kelly had grown discouraged. Then one afternoon, right out of the blue, the office receptionist had dropped a fax on Kelly's desk.

"Here's your dream come true, Kelly!"

Hardly able to contain her excitement, Kelly had snatched up the message and read it over and over again.

The note was crisp to the point of being blunt: *Kelly. Hired. Meet October 18. Bus depot Fletcher Creek, Yukon Territory. Tyler Kade.* Tyler Kade! She could hardly contain her excitement at being hired by such a pro. Since no hour was mentioned, Kelly had assumed that in such a remote location there must be only one bus per day.

Now, as she stood on the edge of what passed for Fletcher Creek's main street, she felt very much alone, very much let down. She envied the handful of people who had got off the bus with her. By now each one of them would be toasting themselves in front of a roaring stove in the cosy cabins she had seen from the bus windows before the darkness had closed in. The light dusting of snow and the clumps of withered grass rendered the scene even bleaker. Her nostrils twitched as she sensed the peculiar smell in the air that precedes a heavy snowfall.

She looked around again at the scattered houses forming the settlement. *Trapper Jake's Lodge - Open 24 hours June 1 to Sept 10,* read the signboard of a bigger building set back from the road, its windows boarded up. The only bright lights in the town came from a ramshackle log building across the street, Ida's Diner. Oddly out of place in the semi-wilderness, its gaudy neon sign hung at a drunken angle above the door. Kelly was tempted to go in and inquire. A 'closed' sign on the door of a general store gave a forlorn look to the neatly kept building.

A shiver raked her body.

Then again, it might be better to walk down to the gas station and motel she could see on the other side of the street. But even if they knew Tyler Kade, what could they do? The damn man didn't answer his phone. There was little point in sending him another fax. Surely, he wouldn't forget, would he? Helplessness began to creep in. She wondered if she would regret coming all this way to try to fulfill a dream.

Had she stayed at home in New Hampshire right now she could be enjoying the resplendent fall colors and the rich smell of the quiet woods. The farmers would be hurrying to bring in the last of the crops. Here in this bleak northern land, the ground was already frozen. Only the dank odor of gloomy pine forests marching up the steep slopes alleviated the sterile chill in the air.

In her hurry to pack, Kelly had overlooked the fact that winter comes early to northern Canada. She'd gladly trade her fashionable light boots for some real snow boots. Shoulders hunched against the cold, she glanced up and down the street for a waiting man.

While she moved her shoulders in a circular motion to created muscle heat, she mentally tallied what she knew about her boss. Like her, Tyler Kade hailed from New England, and had moved to the Yukon, because it guaranteed him snow for eight months of the year. He was one of dog racing's greatest mushers. Tyler Kade was equally well-known for his fiery temper and his angry outbursts at the press and spectators.

Yet he had not always been a media bad boy. There was a time when he was their favorite, a man who won races. For the last several years he had only managed to scrape a finish "in the money", as they called it, but for some reason, he no longer took any of the big prizes. That meant an end to corporate sponsorship. Corporations demand winners.

Kelly was beginning to think that perhaps her scheme was not a good idea, after all. Not because of Kade's personality. That, she could handle. To race sled dogs stirred painful memories like the day her father, mother, aunt and uncle climbed into the truck with the dog-transporter on the back, to drive to a major sled dog race. Her father had been brimming with confidence when he set out on that fateful trip five years ago. Kelly had seen the race fever in his eyes. He was within a few points of the championship. Only, he didn't even reach the starting line. The truck was sideswiped by a car on an icy turn and ended up at the bottom of a steep ravine. Everyone was killed instantly along with ten of their fifteen dogs.

At the time, she had been starry-eyed and twenty. Her boyfriend shared her love of dogs and enjoyed the thrill of competition. After her parents' horrendous accident, the young man rapidly lost interest in her. Kelly didn't blame him. Not many young men could have coped with such a tragedy. Later, however, she came to realize he had been more attracted by the glory surrounding her celebrated father and how he could exploit it to his own advantage than any real interest in her as a person.

"So, Tyler Kade, you're letting me down." The sound of her own voice startled her. Only crazy people talk to themselves. Right now she needed to hear a human sound in this spooky darkness.

Her friends had hinted she was insane to go through with her plan. She didn't mind. They didn't understand the depth of her love for dogs, or why she should want to leave the comforts of the city to go to the frozen North. Could they ever appreciate what it felt like to run a superb team of huskies? To them it was merely being tugged along by a bunch of dogs. When she explained that her ambition was to enter the fabled Iditarod Race, their eyes started from their heads. Entering a thousand-mile sled dog race somewhere off at the wrong end of the North American continent was beyond their comprehension. And for a woman to think of doing it was sheer lunacy!

A pickup screeched to a halt in front of the gas pump. A door slammed. A man sprinted across the road to the diner. The scene passed in front of Kelly's eyes as if it were on a cinema screen.

A moment later, voices from the gloom broke into her thoughts. Kelly peered across the road. Two men were standing in the doorway of the eatery.

"Heck, Byron, I tell you that young guy I hired should've been on that bus!"

"Well, I tell you he wasn't," the other man replied. "I was here when it came in. The only person who got off that I didn't know was that young woman over there." He jerked his head in Kelly's direction. "I guess she's waiting for someone. She's been hanging around since the bus pulled out."

"Damn me! You just can't trust anyone these days. I'd never have thought the man would leave me stranded without a handler. What a lousy start to the race season. Who'd imagine that of a son of the great Guy Jefferies?"

At the mention of the name, Kelly snapped fully alert, her cold hands forgotten. *Guy Jefferies!* Her father! She stared at the man who spoke with so much anger in his voice.

By the light of a solitary street lamp, she made out the figure of the man waving his arms and speaking with much animation. He and his companion turned to cross the dusty thouroughfare to the waiting pickup at the gas station. A knife-edged gust of wind blew open his unzipped parka. Kelly caught a glimpse of a plaid wool shirt molded over a muscled chest. He was an inch or two taller than the man beside him and radiated an aura of strength and agility. By the way he walked - lightly, as though springing on the balls of his feet - Kelly recognized a conditioned athlete, which is what all top racing mushers are.

When the pair drew level with her, the man looked in her direction. In contrast to the other man, he wore no hat. A lock of dark hair fluttered over his forehead.

Kelly noted the knited brows and the complete absence of a smile from his eyes or from his full lips, drawn down at the corners. This and something about his resentful stare confirmed he must be the man she had come north to meet.

A tiny inner voice urged her to look away and to pretend that she was waiting for someone else. She ignored it. It was not too late to turn her back on this hostile place and the grim welcome she had received. Instead, she stepped forward as the men reached the curb of the rickety boardwalk.

"Hi, Mr. Kade? I'm Kelly Jefferies. You were supposed to meet me off the bus. I've been waiting over half an hour."

Kade halted in his tracks, one foot on the boardwalk. His jaw dropped. The dim light threw his features in sharp relief. Kelly couldn't suppress a smile when she saw the man's perplexed expression. She was also aware of even white teeth framed by the most sensual lips she had ever seen on a man, and of eyes that bore into her with disturbing intensity.

There was a moment of awkward silence while man and woman sized each other up.

Kelly moistened her lips with the tip of her tongue. Tyler Kade's gaze followed the tiny movement. Kelly pushed her toque further back on her head. Her gleaming chestnut hair spilled onto her shoulder.

"Kelly Jefferies? But you're a girl!"

Her laughter bubbled to the surface. "How wonderfully observant of you, Mr. Kade."

"I didn't hire a female!"

"It seems that's exactly what you've done."

"You didn't say you were a girl. And what the hell you're laughing for? It isn't funny!"

"I didn't hide anything. It was plain enough from my resume. Or didn't you read it carefully enough? Maybe you were only too glad to get someone, anyone, that you didn't even bother to look closely at my application." Kelly was enjoying his discomfort. It made up for the time he had made her wait out in the cold.

The man identified as Byron cut in. "Just a minute, Tyler. Don't get so het up. Kelly is a girl's name just as much as a boy's. Why the hell did you automatically assume she was a guy?"

"I never thought for one moment a female would bother to reply to my ad. That's why." His features hardened in a scowl.

"Well, maybe you should've spoken to her on the phone?"

"You know damn well I'm too busy with the dogs to come down to use your phone!" Tyler spoke defiantly. "It's bad enough having to trek to town to send a fax. I'm shorthanded. I've been working dawn to dusk."

He drew his hand over his face. Kelly saw that the glowering anger in his eyes had not diminished.

"And in the ad, Mr. Kade, you didn't specify what sex the applicant had to be," Kelly said.

"Of course not. It's understood—"

"No, it's not! There are a lot of women handlers and mushers today. I'm very sorry to disappoint you that I'm not a man, but you hired me in good faith. You're not going to rat on the agreement, are you?" She dropped the bantering tone. Kelly, too, was angry, and deadly serious.

"The problem is that a woman wouldn't be able to cope with the work."

"Why not? I have every confidence that I can do all that's required."

Byron interrupted an exchange which was rapidly becoming rancorous. He stepped with his carton of groceries between Tyler and Kelly. "Look, how about continuing this enlightened discussion in my kitchen? At least it's warmer there."

"Okay, let's go," Tyler said. "I'll move the truck."

Byron picked up one of Kelly's bags with his free hand, and strode toward a log house screened by a clump of pines. "Follow me."

Kelly snatched up the rest of her luggage and followed. She wondered what Kade would do now that he had found out she wasn't a man. For her part, she had no intention of quitting before she had even begun, not after traveling a few thousand miles. Besides, she had resigned her job at the office.

Once inside, Byron dumped his burden on the

table and went to the sink to fill the kettle. "I'll make some coffee then we can discuss this problem rationally." He held out his hand to Kelly. "Pleased to meet you, Kelly. I'm Byron Murdoch, the Government Wildlife Conservation Officer for the region."

Kelly shook his hand. As well as a comforting warmth, she detected an amused twinkle in his smoke-gray eyes.

Tyler Kade pushed in through the door and slammed it shut. Byron turned to his friend. "You know Tyler, I think Kelly's right when she says she can do the work. And it's true, what she says about women handlers and mushers. Some of them are darn'd good. Every bit as capable as a man. Aren't you forgetting that a couple of women have even won the Iditarod? You need a handler in a bad way."

"Okay. Maybe she can cope with the physical work. But there's another problem. She can't stay at the cabin."

"I knew I wasn't coming to a luxury condominium, Mr. Kade. As far as dog handling goes, I'm as good as anyone and probably better." She tilted her chin a fraction.

"Pretty modest, ain't she?" Tyler said.

His sarcastic tone was not lost on Kelly.

"If I don't say so, who's going to say it for me?" She stiffened her back and held her head up as a sign that she had no intention of letting this macho curmudgeon put her down.

Convulsed with laughter, Byron sank into an armchair.

Tyler grew red in the face. "Shut up, Murdoch." He swung round to face Kelly. "Don't be so hasty. You haven't seen the cabin. It's small. No running water. No electricity and only one bedroom. Mine!"

"You promised room and board in your ad. Therefore you must have arranged accommodation for whoever you hired."

Tyler mimicked a woman's voice. "Accommodation?" He dropped the silly tone. "Yeah, everyone who comes to the cabin bunks down in front of the stove. I don't have a fancy boudoir for you."

His gaze raked her slender body. A gleam lit his eyes for an instant, but he promptly lowered his eyelids. Still, she caught the glint and a strange tremor shook her.

"I don't expect a *fancy boudoir*, as you put it. So I'll just put up with what there is. I'd like to remind you it's not me that's making the fuss." Kelly reached to take one of the mugs of coffee Byron had just poured. As she did her fingers came into contact with Tyler's who was also reaching for a cup. They pulled back as if scorched, but not before Kelly felt a quiver of excitement shoot up her arm.

Kelly needed a deep breath to settle her nerves. This job was already more of a challenge than she had imagined. She could tolerate the stubborn attitude that had earned him his reputation. What she hadn't bargained on was reacting physically to him. An accidental touch of his fingers, and lightning had shot up her arm. Had Byron not been there, she felt Tyler might have completely lost his temper. Or would he have gone the other way and grabbed her to kiss her? He looked just as startled as she did.

Rumor had it Tyler hid himself away like a recluse between races. The smouldering look he had just given her was proof enough that he was no hermit and was far from being immune to feminine charm.

"You're maybe not making a fuss, but I happen to live in that cabin, and it's just not set up for visitors, let alone a woman." Tyler's growling tone exuded hostility.

"That's not a problem for me. Why should it be for you?" Kelly fought to keep her tone even.

Tyler looked toward Byron. "And she's opinionated too!"

"For goodness sake, Tyler, cut it out! You're acting like a mean old bear in one of my traps."

"I don't like company. I'm fixed in my ways."

"So am I, Mr. Kade. The difference is that I need a job. And you need a handler. Don't worry about me. I'll keep to myself. If I feel the need for conversation,

I'll talk to the dogs. You won't be bothered."

Tyler scowled. With his brows knitted, he both scared and fascinated Kelly. His clenched jaw sharpened the planes of his face. Yet she was determined not to be intimidated by his surly behavior.

Byron pounced on what he saw was a lull in the hostilities. "As far as I can see, you're both perfectly suited to each other. The dogs are going to improve their conversational skills and you two will live in harmonious silence. There are never any arguments in a Trappist monastery. But to make things easier, I suggest you let her have the bedroom, Kade. You can bed down in front of the stove."

"That suits me," Kelly said.

More than ever she was ready to put up with anything, his raw temper included, though she didn't know why. She threw him a rebellious glance. Despite her resolve, the warm current she had experienced earlier returned. Under his wool shirt she guessed there wasn't an ounce of fat on his athletic body. She longed to soothe away the lines etched around his mouth, and wondered what could have happened to fill him with so much bitterness?

She was thankful that Byron seemed to be on her side. He possessed the rugged frame of a man who spent his life outdoors. His black hair parted on the side and the way his mouth curled easily into a smile gave him a boyish air. He struck her as levelheaded and, in marked contrast to Tyler Kade, friendly.

Byron stood up and slapped Tyler on the shoulder. "You old rogue, Tyler, I reckon you've got no choice but to accept your new employee. Personally, I think Kelly is a terrific young lady." He grinned at her and added, "If he throws you out, honey, just come here. The door is never locked." He gave an exaggerated wink. His light gray eyes shone with warmth.

Kelly rewarded him with a smile. Her anxiety began to slip away. Tyler Kade drank his coffee in silence. This round was hers. But she was not fooled into thinking she'd won him over.

Tyler set down his empty cup. "I hope you've brought more suitable clothes than that citified parka."

"All my mushing gear is in my bag."

Kelly watched him pull a felt cap out of his pocket and jam it onto his head, a gesture of annoyance if ever she'd seen one.

"The truck's outside. Let's get going."

Byron plucked Kelly's sleeve as they followed Tyler out. "The old bruin is often grumpy," he whispered. He doesn't bite, though."

Tyler stopped, the door half open. "I heard that, Murdoch!" Tyler punched him in the ribs. "If it wasn't for the Iditarod..."

Once in the truck, neither she nor Tyler spoke. Kelly didn't mind. She was used to long journeys on the back of the sled where the only spoken words were commands to the dogs. If this was the way Tyler Kade wanted it, it was fine by her. At least they had one thing in common - their love of dogs.

She stole a glance at her new employer's chiseled features as he hunched over the wheel. His eyes remained riveted on the road. Not a hint showed of what was behind the shuttered face.

Eventually he must have become conscious of being watched, for he raked his fingers through his thick hair, but refrained from turning to look at her.

After several miles of empty road, he swerved off the main highway and gunned the truck up a rough trail that snaked steeply through the dense pines. Kelly may have been mistaken, but she felt Tyler was taking an evil pleasure in pushing his four-wheel drive to the maximum. Assuming he was doing it expressly to unnerve her, Kelly forced herself to remain unruffled.

After one ferocious bump, she turned to him. "I hate to mention it, Tyler, but I think we've just lost the box of things from the back of the truck."

"Hell!" Tyler slammed on the brakes, so hard that Kelly's seat belt locked and bit into her shoulder.

Tyler muttered another oath and backed up slowly. He jumped out and began gathering the cans of food scattered along the darkened path. Kelly opened the passenger door and slid out. Massaging her bruised shoulder, she walked back to help. A raw wind sapped her breath for a second.

Tyler didn't look up. "You don't have to. It was my stupid fault."

"I want to. From the look of it, that's also my dinner you've dropped in the dust. I figure I'd better lend a hand."

"I've found the cardboard box. Now, where on earth is the tarp?"

"Hooked on that tree. That's what caught my eye when it flew off."

"Thanks."

"You're welcome."

Tyler opened his mouth and shut it without saying anything more. Instead, he glared at the slender young woman.

Out of frustration he kicked at a stone, only to find it firmly embedded in the frozen ground. All he did was to hurt his toe. A muffled curse escaped his lips.

Kelly leaned against the side of the truck, content to observe Tyler's temper work itself out. From his distorted features, it was easy to see that a battle was raging inside him. Clearly, his stubbornness prevented him from telling her what troubled him. Something deep inside her stirred as she watched him effortlessly pitch the heavy box of canned goods and other spilled items into the back of the pickup.

The task completed, he went to climb back into the truck. Taut, powerful muscles on a deceptively lithe frame gave him the fluid movement of a mountain lion. She smiled at the wry association of wild cats and the big dogs he ran. But, yes, he did remind her of a cougar she had once seen. Close up, he was probably just as dangerous.

"Something funny?" he asked.

"This whole situation, I guess."

"Why did you come? You must have heard I was a loner."

"This late in the season, yours was the only want

ad in the magazine. Apart from that, I wasn't free earlier." She tried not to sound too flippant.

"You really know how to flatter a guy. D'you always have such pat answers for everything?" His tone was dry, a sharp contrast to his naturally deep mellow voice.

"Sorry. I didn't mean to sound smart. When I discovered it was you, I thought I was in luck. I would be learning from the best."

"Not the best anymore, not since..." He looked away. "Never mind. Get back in the truck."

"You have skills and experience—"

"Let's go. It's going to snow."

Unphased by his gruff tone, Kelly clambered into the warmth of the cab. This was not the time to ask questions. Tyler put the vehicle in gear, driving more carefully now. A strange feeling welled up from deep within her, a desire to comfort and appease, but she was loath to break the heavy silence. The moment for it slipped by.

Several bumpy miles up the road, Tyler stopped in front of a log cabin. A deafening chorus of howls greeted Kelly as she stepped down from the truck. Tyler switched off the lights and cut the engine.

Once Kelly's eyes became accustomed to the dark, she made out wolfish shapes all around her. Dogs, dozens of them, sat perched on their boxy log houses. She was startled by a shrill whistle from behind her. A sonorous voice called out to the dogs.

As if on cue, they stopped their serenade. Only the thump of tails on the flat wooden roofs continued. There was no mistaking the affection in Tyler's voice as he called out each dog's name in turn and told them to go back to sleep. Kelly was thankful of the shadows that hid her look of bewilderment. This man had two very different sides to him.

He switched on a flashlight, freed a big black dog from a nearby enclosure, and went into the cabin without saying a word to Kelly. Undismayed, she retrieved her bags from the pickup and followed him in, the dog at her heels. Inside, the animal shook his thick fur free of ice crystals. He turned to sniff at Kelly then wagged his bushy, curled up tail. She tickled him under the chin, obeying the rule never to approach an unknown dog from above to pat his head. Scratching gently, she let her fingers sink into the soft neck hair, so dense she couldn't feel his skin. The dog raised his muzzle and licked her face.

Kelly laughed. "Such a big, tough dog and you're as soft as my heart." She gazed into his eyes. "And you're so handsome with your black face and those two white spots above the eyes."

Tyler shot her an irritated glance from under knitted brows. He lit an oil lamp and hooked it to a nail in the low beam overhead. A warm glow bathed the cabin's interior. He then opened the grate of the cast iron cookstove and touched a match to the paper and kindling already laid in the firebox. The fire sprang to life and soon threw out a comforting heat.

Kelly trailed her fingers along the sturdy chinked logs that formed the walls of the cabin. Ignoring Tyler, she approached a small, curtainless windows looking out over what she determined was the kennel area. A few cupboards and a tiny counter with a sink devoid of faucets, with a white plastic pail underneath to catch the run off, made up the kitchen corner. The lack of running water didn't discourage her. In her history courses, she'd read with fascination about pioneer life. If those brave women could do it, so could she. On the other side of the cabin, a partition enclosed what was obviously the solitary bedroom, its doorway screened by a curtain. Another curtain concealed the door to an alcove, which Kelly presumed must be what passed for a bathroom. A plain wooden table, a few mismatched chairs, an armchair and a battered couch gave the place a lived-in appearance.

Tyler's black husky lay curled up on the couch, its tail over its nose, completely oblivious to the two humans staring at each other across the untidy room.

"Now that you've seen the palace I live in, I imagine you can't wait to get back to civilization," Tyler said. "The bus back to Whitehorse comes through Fletcher at seven-thirty in the morning."

"Fine. I'll be on it sometime next April or May. What's for dinner? I'm starving."

She noticed how her remark threw him off-guard. Did he really expect her, a refined young woman, to be horrified with his primitive living conditions? It would be like camping in a wooden tent. She remained calm in the face of his obvious annoyance.

"You'll find some frozen pizzas in that box I brought in."

"That sounds great. I presume you keep baking sheets under the counter." Kelly unwrapped a pizza and slid it onto a flat cookie sheet. Tyler fed more logs into the cookstove. A sense of compassion overcame her. Lit by the dancing flames, his handsome face was creased with bitterness and fatigue. An urge filled her to touch his knitted brows. She warned herself to rein in her emotions and decided to drop the attack-is-the-best-defense attitude she had adopted on first meeting him.

"How about if I put one in for you? There's room for another pizza next to mine."

"Thanks."

That concession, Kelly reckoned, must have cost the arrogant brute dear. His shoulders sagged under the burden of sadness and resentment he carried. On the road, while picking up the spilled groceries, Kelly's intuition told her he had been about to confess what bothered him. But he had changed his mind and retreated into silence. She quickly slid another pizza into the oven.

She guessed that Tyler must have suffered at the hands of a woman. Only an unhappy love affair could warp a man that way. She remembered once seeing a magazine photo of him crossing the finish line and being embraced by a woman. A wife or lover, maybe. Maybe not a wife. There's never any shortage of pretty women on hand to embrace the winner in the glare of the flash bulbs.

She wondered if she too could remain immune to such a good-looking man. With his bristling hostility there was little danger of anything romantic developing between them. And that was the way she wanted it. Kelly shook her head, amazed that she was even thinking such thoughts. Her cheeks reddened. She tried to convince herself that it was due to the heat of the stove, but she wasn't fooled. The need to settle, to claim her part of this territory, surged through her, and she busied herself with her bags. She hung her parka on one of the wooden pegs aligned along the log wall.

"I guess you'd better take the room."

"There's no need to-"

"I said you take the bedroom!" The words sliced through the air like a knife.

"Is that an order, boss?"

"I'll sleep on the couch. I'm an early riser."

"So am I."

Their eyes locked and they stared at each other. Silence persisted. Tyler shook off the torpor. "If we are going to work together, how about if we stop being at each other's throats? It's only fair you should enjoy the privacy of the bedroom. I'll move out my stuff tomorrow."

"I appreciate the gesture. Both the sleeping arrangements and the peace treaty. Judging by the smell, I'd say the pizzas are ready. Shall I make coffee?" Kelly struggled to keep her voice level despite the panicky feeling he was about to kiss her.

Perhaps easing hostilities was not such a good idea. She had to be on her guard and never let him think she was easy prey. It was too dangerous to feel sorry for a man who had been hurt by another woman. Why else would he be so miserable? Her curiosity had been piqued. In time he might ease his sorrow by confiding in her during the long nights of winter. Unfortunately, intimacy in front of a fire might just be too romantic for words. It was up to her to keep their relationship strictly on a business footing.

The effects of her long journey began to catch up with her. She tried to concentrate on her food, but her thoughts wandered back to him.

Before leaving home, she had checked the race results for the last couple of years. Tyler claimed he hadn't won a race in a long time, yet he finished moderately well in every event he entered. Though of course, finishing well didn't carry the thrill of winning first place. Some people just couldn't accept to be less than number one.

Could it be that he lacked that something extra that makes a top racer out of a merely competent one? He used to be the greatest of the great. If she could find out what was gnawing at him, she might be able to give him the right encouragement.

Right now, she was looking forward to sinking into a warm bed and closing her eyes. When she did retire to the tiny bedroom, all she could see was an empty road bordered by endless fir-covered mountains. Just as she was sinking into sleep, the dog pushed under the curtain and joined her on the bed.

"Ukiok! Get out here, boy." The dog ignored Tyler whispered command, stretched out on the bed and let out an enormous sigh of contentment. On Tyler's second more insistent call, the big black dog yawned, gave Kelly's face a friendly lick and went back to his master.

***

Tyler dropped on the couch. He couldn't understand how Kelly had managed to worm her way into his life so easily, so quickly. Now he was stuck with her for the next six or eight months. Why hadn't he inquired about what kids the late Guy Jefferies had? No matter how hotly she denied it, she had duped him. Despite all his efforts to keep women at arm's length, this smiling creature, who looked so innocent, had succeeded in slipping through his defenses.

He'd have to put up with her because nobody wanted to work for him anymore, not since word about his difficult character had become common knowledge in the dog mushing community. He had also given her a signed contract.

What a miserable start to the day! He had already made himself look foolish in front of this auburn-haired woman. Things were going from bad to worse. In addition, his body had suddenly woken up and was clamoring with want. Kelly Jefferies was just too damned attractive for her own good.

Tyler peered through the window at the rim of the valley, velvet black against the luminous dark of the sky. He tasted bilious anger in his mouth. Damn! He had almost emptied his heart, to a stranger, a woman at that!

What was she doing to him, anyway? He had only just met her and already was on the verge of confessing what he had been suppressing from his conscious memory for the last five years.

Ukiok thrust his wet nose against his hand. Tyler patted the broad head. "Okay, let's go out." Dog and man stepped into the cold night. Kelly's image in the golden light of the lamp came between him and the peaceful nature. His jaws tightened. Signed contract or not, she'd have to leave. His whole body tensed. The delicate profile of her face, the satiny skin glowing from a healthy outdoor life, and those steady green eyes had made his pulse quicken. Just thinking about her made him want to kiss her and bury himself in her. He gritted his teeth to ward off the wild familiar feeling. There was a time when he considered an attractive female fair game for his masculine prowess. But not this beautiful young woman who radiated a strong will, a determination that matched his own. Tyler checked himself and mentally corrected it to the will and determination *he used to have*.

He sighed and clipped a leash to Ukiok's collar to take him to his pen. He stared up at the stars until the cold drove him in. Back inside, he blew out the lamp and crawled under the covers. Sleep didn't come. This arrangment would never work.

Chapter 2

Kelly awoke with a start. For an instant she didn't know where she was. It was still dark. Then the vague shapes in the room and the dog howls from outside brought her back to reality.

Fascinated, she listened to the rising and falling song of the dogs. When it stopped the silence was all the more profound. From afar she heard an answering call. She strained her ears. Wolves! It had to be. There was an unearthly beauty in the sound. As if on cue, the dogs replied with the same primitive complaint. The wilderness seemed to be all-encompassing, swallowing her into its embrace. Kelly sighed with a sense of exhilaration that comes from being in an utterly isolated place.

The dogs ceased their moonlight serenade. A feeling of peace and solitude settled over her. She listened intently for sounds in the night. In the wilds, absolute silence does not exist. Scurrying animals, the splintering of ice in a stream and the creaking of the log cabin as its members contracted in the cold made up the thousand tiny noises of silence.

Kelly crept from under the covers and tiptoed over the rough-hewn floor to peer out of the window. In the predawn light she could make out a trail leading down through the pines to where a creek lay frozen under the fading light of the moon. As Tyler had predicted, snow had fallen during the night. A fresh mantle of sparkling white weighted the pine boughs. Kelly remained at the window, mesmerized by the growing band of orange in the eastern sky.

Her eyes caught the shadowy figure of a man half

hidden by a big tree. Tyler too was watching the birth of the day. After a few minutes, he shrugged as to shake off the spell of light weaving itself in the eastern sky and turned toward the kennels. The cold from the floor crept up her bare legs. She rummaged in her bag for her toiletries. It was time to get ready for work.

She stumbled across the dark room of the cabin. The bathroom, she had discovered the previous evening, was tiny, with a composting toilet taking up most of the space. Not the most practical arrangement for sharing with someone, but the bathing facilities were the last thing she was going to complain about. In the dark, she held out her hand, expecting to make contact with the curtain. Instead, she collided with a solid door.

Strange. This wasn't here last night. Yet a well-fitted door it was. Tyler must have got up early and noiselessly slipped it into the hinges she had noticed the night before. Inside, her hand found a box of matches and a candle in a holder. By the flickering light, she looked at a partially-built shower stall in one corner. The pipes suggested he intended to bring in running water. For a moment she wondered how. He'd have to dig a well and install a generator, which was probably why he hadn't. But for now, she was content to give herself a sponge bath in the enamel basin, using hot water from the stove's boiler.

Kelly was accustomed to starting the day with a good breakfast. Since Tyler was already out caring for the dogs, she felt she should be out too. Breakfast would have to wait. Taking down a can of whole milk powder from the kitchen shelf, she mixed herself a quick drink with water from a five-gallon container. Then she pulled on her parka and boots, drew the headband of her headlamp over her toque, and went outside to join him. The sharp air mingled with the subtle scent of pine assailed her nostrils.

Her arrival was greeted by a renewed chorus of howls. Ukiok came bounding to greet her, his pink tongue lolling from his black face. The powerful animal raised himself on his hind paws and licked her chin as a sign of acceptance.

"Good dog!" She scratched him under the collar.

A flash of light swept the ground in front of her. Tyler's voice drawled behind her. "You're making the others jealous."

"Oh, I intend to go round and say hello to them all. Isn't that what you to do every morning?"

"You have a quick tongue, young lady."

Kelly laughed. Among her office colleagues, she'd been the quiet one. Not so at the sled dog races, where the animation and the easy familiarity of the mushers made everyone feel like family.

"I'm only trying to get to know how things work around here."

"At least you've hit it off with old Ukiok."

It was a grudging admission.

Kelly started as his eyes roved over her figure revealed by the unfastened parka.

"Could you please explain the routine?"

"The routine? All right. First thing in the morning, I come out to greet the dogs and check that everything is okay. Then I have breakfast. Back to the kennel, I give a snack to those who are going out. After which it's clean up and feeding time for those teams not going out that day. By the time I finish, the outgoing dogs have digested their food and I hitch them to the sled. When there's no snow, I hitch the team to the ATV."

"So you really do visit with the dogs!"

"Yes, of course. Why wouldn't I? I love them." His voice softened over his last words.

Kelly was perplexed. Once again she had glimpsed the human side of the man whom the media had nicknamed *Old Grizzly* because of his rude refusal to cooperate.

She advanced among the dogs staked out on twelve-foot chains. The animals were quiet now, lying with their noses on their front paws.

"They're a pretty contented lot."

Tyler walked beside her.

"Uh? Oh, yes."

"I see you've made some enclosures over there."

"I'm building more. I'd rather have the dogs in pens than tethered."

"My father and uncle used to house their dogs in big pens. Many mushers simply stake out their dogs."

"Dog mushing sure isn't what it used to be!"

"Like everything else, it's evolving. I've attended several seminars on nutrition and athletic conditioning over the last couple of years. The technical advances alone are quite remarkable." Her enthusiastic tone was genuine.

Tyler raised a skeptical eyebrow. "I keep the pups in this big pen, along with the pack made up of their parents and the rest of the team. I only separate the pups from the adults at meal times to ensure they get enough to eat. They're six months old."

"They're beautiful! Huge for six months." Kelly crouched among the rowdy, jumping dogs. "Black and white, cinnamon and white, a gray one and a white one. How come there are so many different coat colors?"

"These are Inuit dogs from the Canadian High Arctic. They've been bred randomly in the North for thousands of years. The coat never got fixed as it did with other breeds."

The pups tugged at her clothes, licked her face, jumped on her and pushed her until she almost lost her balance.

"Okay, you pups, sit!"

Five of them obeyed Tyler's firm voice, two remained standing, looking at him cheekily. He repeated the command but they didn't budge. He put his hand to his pocket and instantly the two pups sat. They all craned their necks expectantly and took tiny pieces of dried meat from his fingers. He repeated the sit command to those who could not wait any longer and were trying to get served before their turn.

There was a great gentleness in his actions. A new sense of wonder came over Kelly. Finally, they left the pups to their play.

"Since Ukiok is allowed to run loose, I presume he

is the boss dog."

"Right. He's the Alpha male and the sire of the pups. Come over here and I'll show you the kennel building."

At a short distance from the main cabin stood another log structure. Inside, bags of dog food were stacked along one wall. An orderly array of harnesses, ropes, snow hooks and dog collars hung near the door. One corner of the room was fenced off to form two pens.

"Indoor pens?"

"The big one is a birthing pen. Pups stay there with their mother until they're ready to live outside. The other doubles as an infirmary, if necessary. Over here is where you'll prepare the food."

Kelly saw a propane stove used to prepare dog rations.

"I believe in strict hygiene. That's where you'll wash the bowls." He pointed to a sink with a tap set in a counter against the opposite wall. A heap of stainless steel bowls waited in readiness on the counter.

"Makes sense."

"If everything is clean, we have no bacterial problems. I'm one of few mushers who goes to such lengths. Everyone thinks I'm overly fussy, but I think it's worth it."

Kelly approached a kerosene heater in the middle of the room and tested its warmth.

"The heater is a nice luxury."

"Not a luxury, a necessity. It's kept on low heat. There's a well under the building and the heater is needed so the pressure tank doesn't freeze. The pump operates with a generator. This way we have running water year round. Otherwise, it takes too long to thaw blocks of ice each morning to water the dogs. In a pinch you can come and get water here for the house, but otherwise go down the creek."

"Perfect." Kelly was not in the least surprised to find more amenities for the dogs than for the humans. It fitted with Tyler's austere code too.

"Not asking why I carry water from the creek?"

"Let me think. The well water must be good or you wouldn't give it to the dogs. So, could it be the generator?"

He smiled. "Right. I'm trying to save on the gas. It's darned expensive up here."

"That's smart."

"Now you've seen everything, how about breakfast? Ours, that is."

"Wonderful! My stomach is clamoring for food. It's still dark. When does daylight appear?"

"About nine for the moment. Until the winter solstice, the days get shorter and shorter till there's no daylight at all. If the prospect of twenty-four hours of darkness is more than you can handle, you'd better pack. I'll drive you to town."

"Get off that old refrain, Tyler. I merely inquired about the time of day and night because I know it's the land of the midnight sun in summer and perpetual darkness in winter."

"Some people go crazy in the depths of winter."

"And I imagine plenty more don't. People go crazy everywhere. They don't need darkness to do it."

A grunt was the only answer she received as they made their way back to the cabin. Her arm brushed his as she stumbled on the rough ground. The jolt of electricity between them was almost tangible in the crisp morning air despite the heavy clothing. Touring the kennels with him, she had sensed the attachment he had to his dogs. In unguarded moments, she caught him looking intently at her. She was beginning to think she had judged him too harshly.

Obviously he was still in shock after discovering that Kelly Jefferies was a woman. He certainly was trying hard to make it difficult for her. However, relief settled over her, for they had similar ideas about dog care. So long as she confined herself to learning sledding techniques and dog handling in big races, everything should remain uncomplicated. No doubt she could squelch the physical attraction she couldn't help feeling for him since last night. He was a handsome man. It was normal for her to react like any other woman would.

"What's that small shed raised on wooden posts?"

"A food cache. We must keep all the meat up there out of reach of wild animals."

They walked on toward the cabin.

"Apart from the pens, I see you're planning to build something else." Kelly pointed to a stack of lumber dusted with snow.

For some unknown reason, her remark touched a raw nerve. He angrily growled something and hurried into the cabin. Baffled by his sudden change of mood, she ran to the door before it closed in her face. Ukiok pushed in behind her. Puzzled by Tyler's unexplained gruffness, she shrugged and closed the porch door behind her.

"Is Ukiok allowed in or not?"

"Let him stay. When he's too warm, he'll ask out." Tyler had his back to her and was busy loading wood into the stove.

Kelly set enamel plates and cups on the table and tried to be casual.

"What are you having for breakfast?"

"Let me see what there is." He opened a small hatch in the wall. "How about bacon and eggs with hash browns."

Looking over his shoulder, Kelly saw that the door opened onto a large cupboard. Tyler met her quizzical look.

"A cold larder built on the outside but within the porch. It's as good as a fridge, which you must have noticed we don't have." His tone was more amiable.

"How clever. I'll join you for bacon, eggs and hashbrowns. What do you want to drink? Milk or coffee?"

"Milk. It's powdered milk."

"I know, I found it."

"Powdered eggs too. I guess you're going to miss not having a convenience store round the corner where you can buy fresh stuff."

Instinctively, she'd raised her chin in defiance. "No. I've not always lived in the city. I know about life in the bush, even if mine was a little closer to civilization than this."

Tyler chuckled. "I'm glad you've got plenty of spirit. You'll need it. When I'm away, you'll have to cut the wood and haul water."

"That's no problem. I've used a chainsaw before." She spoke tartly, omitting to say that it had been at least five years ago and then only once under her father's supervision. "As for the water, I don't see that as a major inconvenience."

She found a jug and measured out the milk powder. As she worked, she felt Tyler's eyes boring into her back.

"Shall I cook? I'm no chef but I'm a wiz with a frying pan."

"Suits me." He stepped back from the cookstove. "Tell me, after the...accident, did you have to sell your father's dogs?"

"Most of them. Our racing friends offered to buy them. My cousin and I sold the young ones. We kept the older dogs and four one-year-olds that I had raised and trained myself."

"How many do you have now?"

"We still have eight, four eleven years of age and the pups. They're six but we still call them pups. We exercise them after work and on weekends."

"That must cut into your social life." Cynicism pierced his tone.

"I never even gave it a thought." Her reply was quick and sharp.

"You mean you live in a big city and never go out?" His tone now bordered on the sarcastic.

"We don't live in the city, only work there." Mentally she stuck out her tongue at him.

"I see."

"No you don't see." She felt the need to explain. "After my parents' death, I sold the house and bought a cottage on eighty acres an hour's drive outside the city. We commute." Her words carried a tinge of sadness.

"We?"

"My cousin and I."

"This cousin, is he very close to you?"

The sudden abruptness in his voice surprised her. Tyler didn't look pleased at the mention of her living with her cousin.

"She. Marcia's definitely a woman." A teasing laugh escaped her. What difference would it have been to him if her cousin had been a man? If the idea wasn't so patently absurd, she'd say he was jealous.

"Just the two of you out there? No man around?"

His growling tone startled her. She looked up from cooking the bacon and eggs.

"Marcia's parents died in the the accident, too."

"I'm sorry...You must miss your folks."

"Yes, I do, but life must go on. I had wanted to learn how to be a top ranking musher and a racer. My father insisted I go to college first before joining him on the racing circuit. So I missed out on a whole lot of his teaching while I was away. After that...well, it was too late." She tried to keep the grief she still carried out of her voice.

Tyler scowled and averted his gaze. She replaced the cups with glasses.

"You can have coffee if you want," Tyler said.

"No thanks, I've got to work outside. Coffee is too dehydrating."

"You mean it makes you run to the outhouse."

"Precisely."

The ghost of a smile that crossed his lips was not lost on Kelly. So he did have something of a sense of humor! They sat opposite each other at the table and ate in silence until the plates were cleared.

"We'll go back to the kennel room where I've got all the feeding instructions written out. I'll take care of the team I'm taking out this morning. I expect to be back in the early afternoon." Tyler stood up.

"Did you pack a lunch?"

"Lunch? No time for such niceties."

She didn't like the touch of scorn in his tone, but brushed it aside. "You nourish the dogs, you must do the same for yourself. Sled dogs are athletes, so is the musher. The body doesn't perform well on a deficit diet. Do you have an emergency pack?"

"What's this, Survival 101 exam?"

"I just hope you don't break a leg in the mountains and have to overnight until someone can go and rescue you."

Her casual tone didn't hide the underlying seriousness of her words. They stared at each other. Tyler blinked first.

"I've gone out for days on end without anyone caring whether or not I carried survival gear or extra rations. Why should you?"

"There are many different ways to kill yourself. This one seems awfully convoluted. You should know that even the best mushers can be stranded."

"How about if you mind your...?" Tyler clamped his jaw. "Oh, just forget it. Yes, I've got a survival pack. I'll toss it in the sled."

Kelly handed him a package.

"Lunch. Bacon sandwiches." She immediately turned and began clearing the table to head off any protest from Tyler.

"Uh...Thanks."

He stood as if hypnotized for a moment then followed her to the bedroom where she was retrieving her coveralls from her bag.

"What d'you...?"

He never finished his sentence, but Kelly heard the anger in his voice. She deliberately ignored him while she zipped up her overpants. He filled the door frame, a brooding giant of a man. Stormy brows contrasting with his full, sensitive lips.

"Excuse me, please. I have to go and work." She didn't feel as calm as she outwardly appeared. Had she pushed him too far in expressing what she felt were common sense ideas?

He responded by grabbing her arm as she brushed past him. Their bodies met. A tremor rippled down her spine. Instinctively, Kelly raised her face to his, her lips trembling in anticipation.

For one glorious moment she was oblivious of everything save the feel of his muscular chest pressing against the softness of her breast. She was filled with a yearning to have him hold her in his arms and kiss her. Warning signals went off in her head. Her breathing shortened. Feeling suddenly overheated, she wrenched her arm free.

Struggling to regain control of herself, Kelly took a step back. What on earth was happening to her? Tyler's gaze caressed the creamy smoothness of her cheek and neck. Her eyes dueled with his unwavering gray gaze. Finally, he stepped aside to let her pass, looking every bit as troubled as she did.

They grabbed their parkas and went outside. An uneasy silence hovered over them. In the kennel room, she read the instructions and pocketed a plan of the kennels with the dogs' names on it. Each animal received a specific amount of food, and she did not want to mix them up. Tyler busied himself rearranging the already orderly dog harnesses.

Kelly gave a low whistle.

"Something wrong?"

"Nope, just the complicated schedule. It looks like a battle plan."

"You can leave now if you think the work's too much for you."

"That's out of the question. Actually, I'm full of admiration for the mind that worked all this out."

Tyler was about to reply but checked himself. He took a deep breath and resumed the task of sorting his gear on the other side of the room. She gathered up the bowls, with the intention to feed the pups first.

Kelly wasted no time in attempting to get them to sit, without success. Around her the howls changed to a frenzy. She glanced over her shoulder. Tyler's sled was sitting in the middle of the path. Two dogs were already hitched to it. Tyler must have reckoned that the snow was thick enough for sledding. The pups were torn between running to the fence and the food bowls she was holding. Not wanting to distress the young dogs further, Kelly gave in. Their breakfast could wait. She put the bowls onto a plank shelf nailed to a post.

Accompanied by a hord of juvenile dogs, she went to the fence. Laughing, Kelly cuddled the two closest to her, so young and already so eager to run with the pack!

One of her duties was to take the pups out for an afternoon walk to begin teaching them trail commands. She would also have to sled with some of the adults. According to the schedule, dogs would be exercised on alternate days. From the look of it, she was going to enjoy her job.

She kept watching as Tyler hitched two more dogs and commanded them to sit. He pulled up a second sled behind the first and hitched four dogs to it.

"Come over here!" he shouted.

"Me?"

"Who else?"

Kelly hesitated. What was this, a test? She plucked the food bowls off the shelf and put them on the ground without getting the pups to sit. They rushed on them, slurping the meat hungrily.

"You're not trusting me with a team on my own, are you?"

"The dogs you'll help train are Inuit dogs. They're freighters, which as you know means they can pull huge loads effortlessly. You don't weigh much. I have to be sure you can handle them."

She bit her lip to prevent another curt reply. All he needed to do was to tell her then let her harness the dogs on her own. But no, this infuriating man had to go and hitch the sled for her. He made her feel like a rookie being checked out.

"Fair enough. What's the name of the lead dog?"

"Capitor."

Remembering fondly her father's first teaching, she didn't step on the sled runners immediately. Instead, she asked each dog's name. Then she patted the dogs and checked the harnesses and lines.

"All in order here," she said.

Kelly felt proud at the professional way in which

she had checked the equipment and acquainted herself with her team. But she was sure his male pride prevented him from complimenting her.

"You go on ahead. The trail slopes down for a short distance then up. After that it turns sharp right."

So he was checking her out! Calmly, she put her foot on the brake, pulled up the snow hook and wedged it into its holster. The dogs felt the movement and took up the slack on the lines. She released the brake and the team bounded forward. The sled shot over the fresh powdery snow. Although Kelly had expected the quick start, she had to cling to the sled's handlebar to maintain her balance. Tyler was probably disappointed that she hadn't fallen off.

In the exhilarating burst of speed, she forgot about him. The air rushed over her face, tugging at her long hair. A deep joy swept through her as trees became a mere blur on each side of the trail and the sled left a cloud of snow in its wake. The only sounds were the swish of the runners and the eager panting of the dogs. The sky had grown lighter, though the sun had not yet appeared over the mountains.

Turning her head, she caught sight of Tyler's sled following a few hundred yards behind. Kelly thought about their encounter this morning. Despite the cold, the memory of his touch brought a flush to her cheeks. Reason took over. So what if they felt some sexual attraction for each other? They were both adults. It was perfectly understandable, just like the harmless flirting and exchanges that took place among the young men and women at the races she used to attend. A deep friendship with Tyler might not be possible, at least not in the foreseeable future. She would treat the attraction in the same way as she did with her male friends: lightly.

Because she was wrapped in thought, she failed to pay attention to what the speeding sled was doing. Raising her eyes to the trail ahead, she was too late to avoid a big bump directly in her path. The sled's left runner hit it. Kelly gripped tight to stop herself being pitched off.

Damn! That's what came of letting her mind wander. She told herself again that if she wanted to make a success of her stay in the North, she'd better not think about Tyler in any other way than a man whose skills would be useful to her. All those other wayward ideas she had must be curbed. The job came first.

Soon after surviving the near spill, the tight bend in the trail was upon her. Kelly's foot missed the bar between the runners that lowered the two brake paddles with their sharp points. She yelled a command to the dogs, but they never slackened their pace. In their enthusiasm, they probably didn't even hear her. They were doing what they enjoyed most, and that was running in the crisp air with the wind in their fur.

Kelly bent her knees to give herself more leverage and leaned into the bend. Just as the sled was about to shoot off into the bush, she gave a powerful kick with her left foot, at the same time twisting the handlebar to her right.

The strength of the kick threw the sled back onto both runners. The dogs accelerated out of the turn, and Kelly let out the deep breath she had been holding.

That was too close for comfort! She bit her lip. Her heel smarted from striking the frozen ground. It would hurt for a few days. At least she hadn't lost the sled and plunged headlong into the snow. In the end, she relaxed, and hoped Tyler hadn't been near enough to see her stylish maneuver.

The rest of the outing was an anticlimax in comparison.

When she arrived back at the kennels, Kelly brought her team to a halt. She secured the sled with its snow hook and went up to her lead dog.

"Good dog, Capitor. That was great! I think we're going to get along just fine, you and I."

She straightened just as Tyler pulled into the yard.

"What the hell do you think you were doing back there?"

Even the dogs didn't snarl as nastily as he did.

"Back where?" He innocent look masked the agitation she felt. He was sure to chew her out.

"At the sharp bend."

"I didn't realize it was so close until I was right on it."

"You weren't focused on the task. It was obvious." Fury tainted his voice.

"Okay. So I got a little distracted." Kelly heated up. "I managed to stay on the runners, didn't I? Besides, it was my first time out on an unknown trail."

"Which brings me to the real question. Why did you want to come and learn with me?"

Anger flared in his eyes. His scowl etched deeper the rugged lines of his face. Kelly took a breath, refusing to be influenced by how magnificent he looked in his anger.

"Why? We seem to have been through this before, Tyler. It's getting kind of stale. I came because *you* hired me in response to *your* ad. How was I to know it was you? You didn't even put your name on it." Her heart was beating fast and not simply from the exhilaration of the ride. "Rather than criticize me, maybe you should tell me how I can improve my technique."

Tyler's features relaxed. His anger appeared to evaporate in the face of Kelly's unruffled logic. He glanced away for an instant. "First, you must constantly monitor the trail ahead. Watch the lead dogs. They're running more than twenty-four feet up front. When they begin to swing to one side, you know then you have to use the brake and keep the sled straight halfway into the turn before shifting your weight. You must be prepared for anything that's ahead."

Kelly nodded in agreement.

"Damn it all, woman! Tell me, what's your real reason for coming here?" His momentary calm dissipated in a blink of an eye.

"As I said before, I always wanted to take a handler's job and learn more about dog management and racing. One day I'll run the Iditarod." She did her best to ignore his angry outburst, and thought she saw a flicker of a smile hover on his lips.

"You don't fool me. Nobody gives up a good job to come and work for a pittance in what amounts to a slave labor camp."

Kelly laughed. "One person's labor camp is another person's professional development school. I love dogs and sledding and racing. I'm also aware that it's become big business. Nowadays, only competitors with solid training make the grade and win races. And with that comes the sponsorships. Fate decided I wasn't going to get that training from my dad."

A short silence followed her words.

"Yes. And I'm sorry about that. But, I'm not like your father."

"I'm well aware of that." Startled, she looked at him, thinking how different he was from any father figure she could imagine. And she certainly didn't react like a daughter when she was close to Tyler. Her breath rasped in her chest. Then for some reason she blushed and concentrated on unhitching the team.

"So why me?" he asked. "There are plenty of other mushers. Some of them are women."

"How many times to do we have to go over this? Yours was the only ad in the magazine."

"But I signed the fax. Once you knew it was me, why didn't you change your mind? Since you seem to know everything, you must have heard that I'm a difficult old cuss. Those jerks from the media are always going on about it."

"Why should I have changed my mind? You hired me. I saw no reason to back out. I'm here because of the dogs. Everything else is secondary, something I can work around. Now, if you'll excuse me, I have to feed my team."

She left him to stare at her as she moved to the wheel-dogs standing quietly in front of the curved brush bow of the sled.

"It wouldn't bother me if you decided to quit right now. I'm a loser anyway," he said.

"People are only losers if they believe they are."

"Very smart."

"Smart but true. If you want to turn things round, you must concentrate on your training. Like right now, not when the snow melts."

Tyler's jaw dropped. "This season's got off to a lousy start." Tyler grumbled loud enough to ensure Kelly heard him. "No snow till yesterday, and I've got myself a sassy female handler who's an expert in psychoanalysis."

Kelly choked back her laughter. She could see he wanted her to lose her temper and was determined not to let him have that satisfaction. He gave her every reason to hate him. No doubt he would derive some twisted pleasure from seeing her storm off to pack her things and leave him to his misery. She had no intention of letting herself be cowed in that way.

If it were possible to measure it, her stubbornness probably equaled his own. Never before had she backed down from a challenge, and she was not about to do so now. Yes, there were other mushers, mild-mannered ones, too, but something about Tyler Kade appealed to her. Underneath that churlish exterior was a strong vibrant man, a man she was drawn to despite everything, despite herself. For some reason she couldn't explain, she wanted to discover that other man.

She walked over to the kennel building and came back with four bowls filled with meat and fat.

Tyler finished loading his sled and headed down the trail in the direction of the creek on his routine run. Sunshine spilled over the mountains and valleys. The snow-laden pines sparkled with a million needlepoints of light, like so many diamonds carelessly thrown by an invisible hand.

Kelly watched Tyler disappear. The serene beauty began to appease the jumble of emotions he had left her with. To keep her mind off the turmoil of her thoughts, she threw herself into her new duties. She was here to do a job, to learn all she could, but it was difficult to concentrate.

After a few minutes work, she stopped and leaned on the shovel. What if she were to give in to Tyler's demands and return home? How could she admit to being a complete failure? True, she could buy fresh dogs and enter the racing circuit without the benefit of Tyler's instruction. It would take a while longer to get to the top, since she would doubtless make every mistake in the book, but she was confident she'd eventually work her way up to the Iditarod. Why, then was she so adamant about staying? She told herself it was because she had a contract to honor, but that was only fooling herself. Although she was reluctant to admit it, the real reason why she was still here was because of the man she had just seen disappear over the distant snow-covered ridge.

"Don't be stupid, Kelly!" Speaking aloud to herself delighted the dogs who barked a reply. She resumed her duties and got more acquainted with her charges then she played with the pups.

Early in the afternoon, the light rapidly dimmed and nightfall approached. Anxiety began to gnaw at her. Tyler had not returned. She finished giving broth water to all the dogs and went into the cabin to prepare dinner.

The kitchen tasks soothed her nerves, but the calm didn't last long. She soon found herself glancing out of the window, and straining to hear the sound of Tyler return.

***

Tyler tipped the dregs of his hot chocolate into the snow and looked up at the graying sky. No matter how he tried, he couldn't shake Kelly off his mind. Never before had he encountered such a stubbornly-opinionated young woman. Panic rose in him. He didn't want her here. She disturbed his peaceful existence. He had to accept the situation as he had no alternative. A musher can't race without a handler. The dogs responded to her as if she had always been there to take care of them, and that rankled. Her ease with the boisterous dogs served to remind him that lately he had been less than patient with them. A feeling akin to shame swept over him. He walked to the dogs laying in the snow and hugged each of them, murmuring soothing words. They responded eagerly. His love for his furry companions brought him a measure of contentment. He set off on the homeward trail.

Chapter 3

Tyler' return created a ruckus in the kennels. The cabin door opened, and light spilled out in the yard. He watched Kelly's slim silhouette as she shrugged into her parka. He hunched over the sled and applied the brake. She'd been waiting for him, but that was what a good handler was supposed to do, wasn't it?

She came forward to meet him.

"Hi there!"

He gulped cold air, and began unhitching the dogs. Only after the dogs were in their pens, watered and fed, did he mumble an acknowledgement of her presence. "Thanks for coming out to help."

"Don't mention it." Kelly headed for the cabin door. "Supper is on the go."

Her nerves were frayed he reckoned. He recognized a certain eloquence in her back. She must be biting her tongue to stop herself putting him in his place. Was she really concerned because he was late?

Tyler shuffled around the cabin, picking up items and setting them down again, as if looking for something to occupy his hands. He added wood to the stove and trimmed the wick in the oil lamp, anything to take his mind off the question that had gnawed at him all day. Why was he bothered by the presence of this woman?

He had spent most of the time he had been out sitting on a fallen tree by the creek. His mind had been trying to come up with the best way of telling Kelly Jefferies she must leave. Now that he was here with her, watching her bend her shapely back over the cookstove, and admiring how the lamplight fell on the coppery sheen of her hair, how was it he couldn't put the words together?

Was he really turning into the deadbeat musher the media painted him? When they discovered Kelly worked for him, they'd crucify him. Already he could hear taunts of "Tyler Kade is incapable of hiring a man to handle his dogs!"

He stole a glance at Kelly. His eyes were drawn to the graceful curves of her thighs, utterly feminine despite the thick wool pants she wore. It was all he could to curb the urge to reach out and touch the cascade of hair that fell to her shoulders. A craving to lose himself in her softness overwhelmed him. He fidgeted distractedly.

Still with her back to him, Kelly said, "Tyler, that's three times you've picked up that can of jam. Do you want me to open it for you?"

The unexpected sound of her voice jolted him.

"Uh?"

"Why don't you wash up? The dinner is almost ready. I hope you're hungry. I've made a mountain of hamburgers and mashed potatoes. There's a rice pudding in the oven. Unfortunately, I didn't find any raisins to put in it."

"I hate raisins."

"Funny. Me too."

He almost chuckled. They quickly set the table and they ate in silence for a while.

"You said you'd be gone two hours." She spoke casually. "Why so late?"

"Why so concerned?"

"I was beginning to think I might have to call out the Royal Canadian Mounted Police."

"Very clever." He threw her a dark look and returned his attention to his plate.

Tyler cleared his throat. "If you must know, I stopped awhile to think. We've got to talk."

"Whenever you feel like it." Her flippant tone hit home. His jaw contracted. Unphased, she went to the stove to refill their coffee cups.

The aromatic smell tantalized his nostrils. He took a sip. "I'll give you that, you make the best coffee this side of the Elias Range."

"Thank you for the compliment, sir."

Tyler focused his attention on the oil lamp, which threw their two strangely shaped shadows on the log wall behind them. A cloak of unhappiness settled over him. He was painfully aware that something was missing from his life. When was the last time he had held a woman in his arms? A powerful need to bury his face in the silken fragrance of her hair overwhelmed him. He wanted the velvety feel of her breasts against his chest.

In a gesture of irritation he ran his fingers through his hair and pushed back his chair. He was going soft. That's what domestication did to a man.

"Look, Kelly, I...I don't think this is going to work out."

"The job? I think it will."

"No. You don't understand. You're a woman."

"That, Tyler, I'm already aware of."

"And I am a man!"

"Yes. I noticed that too." Her eyes lighted on the growing bulge in his tight jeans.

His tanned face took on a darker shade.

"You're being deliberately awkward."

"No, I'm not. Not any more than you. If you mean we cannot live side by side in this cabin, you're mistaken. People to do it all the time. When Marcia and I were in our senior year at college we shared a house with two guys. Despite what you might think nothing happened. If doesn't bother me, I don't see why it should bother you."

"Sharing a big house in the city is one thing. How do you account for the needs of a male and female in a cramped cabin like this?"

"You think our base animal instincts will get the better of us? Are you assuming I won't be able to resist going to bed with you?"

"Perhaps. Or, if I want to go to bed with you."

"That's not part of my job description, Mr. Kade."

"You're a very attractive woman."

"Would you have preferred if I'd been lumpy and warty?"

"Frankly, yes."

"Well, I think you're a handsome man. Now that we've recognized that we're mutually attracted...I mean attractive, could we talk business?"

"Sure. I'll agree to pay your expenses and give you a month's salary. Get packed. I'll drive you to town. I'll even pay for a room at the motel. Like that you'll be right there when the bus comes through in the morning on its way back to Whitehorse."

Kelly blanched. "The motel is closed and I'm not leaving. There's absolutely no reason for me to go. You can't have any complaints about my ability to do the job, so you have no reason to fire me. Discrimination on sexual grounds is against the Constitution."

"We're in Canada. The U.S. Constitution doesn't apply here."

"How do you know it doesn't? Besides, I bet Canadians have a similar law on their books. And you're American and so am I."

"This is getting crazy!"

"Quite definitely. And as you've recognized already, I'm just as stubborn as you."

Tyler ran his fingers through his hair. "We're totally isolated here. There are no amenities nearby."

"There's Fletcher Creek down the road."

"Fletcher Creek is deader than dead in winter. It has one store and one *closed* motel."

"Anyway, who said I wanted amenities?"

"All women do."

"Really? On what does Professor Tyler Kade base such a scientific observation? You've made a lifelong study of women's needs, I presume?"

"It wasn't necessary. The reason is you're driving me mad!"

"I'm sorry. That was not my intention. And please, don't yell."

"What if something happens between us?" Tyler dropped his voice to a hoarse whisper.

Kelly remained silent for a full minute. Ukiok, unused to raised voices, got up and came to nuzzle her hand. To calm him, she stroked his rough-textured fur. "Nothing need happen between us, Tyler. I'll attend strictly to my duties and for the rest of the time, I'll keep out of your way. We can eat separately, if that would make you feel better."

Tyler stared at her and Ukiok at her side.

"Even my dog is siding with you. Since it looks as though you're staying...for the time being at any rate, we'd better work things out. We need to go over my training schedule."

"Good."

"I'll be away most of the time." He spoke quickly as if being away was the most appealing idea he'd had all day.

He took a sheaf of papers from a drawer. For the next half hour he and Kelly forgot their heated exchange and worked on the kennel routine. They discussed rotating the young dogs and experienced dogs on the teams and argued about various combinations. Ukiok sat at Tyler's side and put his paw on his thigh.

"Okay, pal, we're all friends again." Tyler stroke the dog's broad head.

In the end, Tyler threw down his pen in exasperation. "It's no good! I just don't have enough dogs to operate a real training program, let alone enter a big race."

"But the dogs you have are first-rate. Just select which race is most important for you to win, and forget about the others."

"Important for me to win?" He echoed her last words as if hearing the expression for the first time. "You expect me to win after the losing streak I've gone through?"

"Of course! Why else are we doing all this hard work?"

"If you must know, I haven't won a race in years." Tyler gave the sigh of a defeated man.

"You've got to believe in yourself and your dogs.

Otherwise they'll sense your lack of spirit and will just trot along mechanically."

"D'you charge extra for the pep-talks?" A grim smile stretched his lips.

"See, I knew you had the will! All you need to do now is get out of that negative groove you've gotten yourself into."

"What do you know about things like that?"

"How do you think I felt after burying my father and mother? Before the tragedy, I used to sing to my dog team when I took part in the junior races. And the dogs ran like the wind. The first time I stepped on the runners after the accident, I couldn't sing. The dogs didn't understand why, and turned to look at me. I saw the unconditional love in their eyes. Because of that I made the effort. I sang."

"Strange. I used to sing to my dogs. Haven't done so in a long time."

"Tomorrow, Tyler, take a team out and sing to them as you go along. Tell yourself and them over and over that you're going to win the Iditarod. I know you will. I have faith in you."

"It's not certain I can even enter the race. I've only got twelve huskies I can put in the race. Nowadays, mushers run sixteen."

"Can't your Inuit dogs run too? You have fourteen adults."

"Thirteen available actually. Arnavik has been bred. She'll have her pups in mid-December."

"Oh great! A whole bunch of new puppies!"

"Yeah. The problem is that Inuit dogs are much slower than Alaskans Huskies. They'll go on forever under even the worst conditions, but they aren't built for speed. I have them because I'd planned to establish an outfitting business. You know, taking tourists out by dog sled. People pay good money to come North for wilderness adventures."

"You sound like you've given up on the idea."

Tyler merely lifted his broad shoulders a fraction. "On my own? Another of my dreams was to run the Yukon Quest. That's got to be the toughest sleddog race on earth."

"Why don't you run both? The Yukon Quest is in February and the Iditarod starts the first weekend of March. You'd have two weeks rest in between."

"You make it sound so easy, Kelly, but I still only have twelve dogs and need sixteen."

It was the first time he had said her name, and it surprised him to find he liked it.

"Twelve good dogs are better than sixteen mediocre ones. My father always criticized mushers who start with a lot of dogs, just so they can drop off those who get injured or aren't running fast enough. Like that they finish with only those who can keep up the pace. In fact they're really wasting time at the beginning. A team goes only as fast as its slowest dog. But if you have high ranking dogs you don't need to drop any of them off and readjust the team."

"Your father taught you all that?" His admiration was sincere.

"Yes. And I've watched the Iditarod on Tv."

"What the hell to do you need me for? You can learn everything you want on your own. Like that you wouldn't have to put up with my grouchy moods." He'd said the same words before, but this time there was a touch of ironic humor in his voice. His repressed rage had faded.

"Forget about my going away, will you? I may have picked up a few useful ideas along the way, but nothing can replace hands-on experience."

"The dogs might be too tired to do both races."

"Why don't you take your Inuit dog team for the Yukon Quest?"

"Do you realize I'd be competing against mushers with the fastest Alaskan Huskies in the North?"

"It's a difficult race over rough terrain. Maybe the slower, more reliable Inuit dogs would do better in the long haul than the lightly-built huskies."

"Nobody has raced them before."

"Maybe not raced but generations of nomadic Inuit people used them to travel the Arctic. I think the dogs have all the stamina you need. When you're racing across a thousand miles of snow, endurance is often more important than speed. Isn't twelve the maximum on a team?"

"It's been brought up to fourteen."

"To cater to the less resistant huskies, I suppose."

"You're a pretty convincing talker, you know that, Ms. Jefferies? All the same, I can train one team thoroughly but not two."

"What about me? Isn't that why I'm here?"

"And who'd look after the pups and the older dogs? There aren't enough hours in the day."

"I can get up earlier in the mornings. According to your schedule, the pups are to run behind a sled pulled by the five veterans. You don't race those, correct?"

He nodded his head.

"Since we don't go very far, it doesn't take up too much time. On that day, the racing team can have a short run, with no weight in the sled. We can concentrate on speed. The next day, the pups and veterans rest, and I take the Alaskans for a long, fully loaded run."

"But I'll be away as much as one week at a time."

"Great! Like that we won't fight so much."

"You've got ready answers for everything!" Tyler gave a dry laugh.

"Somebody's got to make things happen. If not we may as well just content ourselves to giving sled rides down at the local seniors' home. It's about time you faced up to the situation and got to work."

"See what I mean!" This time there was a twinkle in his gray eyes.

"It's agreed, then? I train one team."

"How big a team can you manage?"

"That I don't know until I try."

"Until the huskies learn to obey the commands from you, you should start with only four at a time. I'll take your advice and enter the Inuit dogs in the Yukon Quest, since it's the first to be run. Hell! I'd like to see what those dogs can do. We'll give it all we've got."

"Alleluia!"

She stood up and moved away from the table. "Since we've agreed to start earlier, I guess I'd better turn in."

Tyler watched her disappear into her room. He was amazed at himself. For the first time in months his spirits were high. His blood tingled in his veins. A fire of want spread through his body. An insane desire to hold her in his arms swept over him. He knew she'd respond to him. He had read it in her sea-colored eyes.

He returned to the problem of racing the Yukon Quest. To no avail. A dull fury rose in him. This was impossible! He had to be able devote himself to nothing but strategy. And here he was dreaming about the auburn-haired woman in the other room! This was no way to win races. He had sworn never to fall again under the spell of a woman.

Yet it was a woman who had rekindled his excitement for racing. How could he send her away? Silently, he rolled her name on his lips. A name with a sharp edge to it, though belonging to a woman so soft it drove him wild.

He loaded the stove, then took Ukiok back outside to his pen. "Training, training," he repeated to himself. "Nothing else. Don't think, just train." When he settled down for the night, stretched out on the couch, he kept tossing and turning, repeating the mantra, "train, train." An hour later, his brain was finally numb enough to let him sink into a deep, dreamless sleep.

***

Sleep didn't come right away for Kelly. She was systematically reviewing the evening's conversation. Something had happened to Tyler and she wanted to figure it out. Had she overstepped the mark by taking over cooking duties? Tyler was clearly a man long used to living on his own. What else could she have done? It was absurd not to fix a meal for two, knowing he'd be back soon, ravenously hungry. No, that was not it. Nor was it because she had been so anxious about him. She'd hidden that feeling well, and he couldn't have seen how she had wanted to reach out and smooth away the creases marring his forehead. A tremor quivered deep inside her. But she had won a battle if not the war. The last thing she intended to do was quit or be forced out simply because she was a woman. She'd been here a mere twenty-four hours. For some unaccountable reason she felt she belonged. But if he made her name sound like a caress every time he'd call her, she might come undone. At the memory of the way he looked at her, heat suffused her skin. Her cheeks reddened. That was silly, stupid even. She was alone in the privacy of her bedroom.

With her provocative remarks, she had rekindled some fire in him. It was enough for her to hope he was finally accepting her. His enthusiastic talk about the races, his entrusting her with the race training of a team was a giant step toward a sound working arrangement.

Sleep finally blocked her thoughts.

Darkness still lingered over the mountains when Kelly and Tyler finished the first round of the kennels. They bumped into each other as together they reached the door of the cabin.

"After you," said Tyler.

The hoarseness in his voice didn't go unnoticed. Kelly hurried inside, and removed her battery-powered headlamp and her parka.

While she busied herself with the breakfast she searched for something neutral to say, something that would not break the fragile truce. Although Tyler had not yet spoken a word, he didn't appear to be having second thoughts after last night discussion.

Kelly put saussages in the pan and picked up the bread knife. She felt Tyler's eyes on her. Immediately, she was struck by the domesticity of the scene. Could she imagine herself living like this forever? When her brain responded with an unequivocal "*Yes*," she became frightened. She scolded herself, and asked silently, *What on earth am I doing?*

"Kelly, I've decided to do a short run with the Yukon Quest team. One day out, one day back."

That's not what he had agreed to last night, but Kelly sensed his agitation and didn't object. He wasn't talking about sending her away, but he doubtless felt the need to get away, to put some distance between them.

"Very well. While you're gone, I'll take teams of four Alaskan Huskies each day for two hours. Like that, all of them will run at least once. Which dogs can lead?"

"Singarnak and Pinghasuet, but only when they are together. Itirit is a smart little female but I haven't had time to try her out. There's Nunii. He shows leadership qualities, but he is a bit young to go in front of a team.

"What about Tioralak?"

"He's shy. He gets nervous when he's got dogs behind him. He likes being in the wheel position. Like that he has only the sled behind him."

"I guess I'll find out who's okay in front. Maybe I'll have to train more leaders."

"It's a big job training leaders."

"Not really. Dogs are always eager to please their teacher."

After a pensive silence, Tyler looked up. "True, but it doesn't mean they can all stand at the front for a long run."

"Let me try."

"Sure."

They sat in companionable silence. She noticed he kept stealing glances at her.

"Your hair...."

"My hair?"

"Is that your natural color?"

"Dark auburn? Yes of course. That's what I was born with. And I don't wear make up."

A repressed smile puckered his lips. Kelly burst out laughing.

Tyler looked abashed. "Alright, I'm a jerk, but it's so shiny, I was wondering..."

"It's usually women who want to know what brand I use to color it."

She expected him to say something about being beautiful. All men did. But not Tyler.

"I'll pack what I need. Go ahead and do your work."

About to say something tart, Kelly pursed her lips, remembering her promise to put up with anything, or almost anything.

"Let me prepare you two days' rations. I saw some dehydrated dinners in the cupboard. If you'd mentioned it last night, I could have opened some cans and frozen the contents in plastic bags."

"Plastic bags?"

"Much lighter and easier to pack than cans."

"Next time. Thanks all the same."

"Don't forget to leave me an itinerary of your trip."

"I'm not a kid, for hell's sake!"

But she was already outside. She zipped her parka and jammed her toque onto her head. Her heart beat faster. She was tempted to go back in and face him. For what reason? The man had been on his own for so long, he was not used to leaving an itinerary behind as a safety precaution, or to have someone care for his material welfare. She would ignore his outburst. The headlamp cord kept brushing her face. In annoyance, she removed the headband to untangle it. Momentarily blind, she tripped over Nunii's chain and sprawled ungracefully in the snow. The big dog jumped, pawing and licking her. Kelly laughed. "Okay, okay! Down boy! That'll teach me to keep my mind on task, right, Nunii?" She regain her feet, only to be caught in the glare of Tyler's headlamp.

"You hurt?"

"Of course not. I just didn't expect so much friendly attention."

"You're not heavy enough. The dogs can easily knock you down."

Kelly thought she detected a note of concern under the fierceness of his tone.

"I tripped, if you want to know. It could happen to anyone in the dark."

Gathering up her lamp, she stormed off to the kennel building. Inside its friendly warmth, she touched a match to the oil lamp and turned the wick up a notch to throw more light. In no time, she had water for the broth boiling on the propane stove.

The door opened and Tyler came in. He hung his parka on a nail and began collecting the food he intended taking for his dogs.

Despite herself, Kelly's eyes drifted to his tall, muscular frame. He scooped up the forty-pound box of frozen meat with the effortless grace of a well-coordinated athlete.

"Something the matter?"

His question made her flinch.

"Uh...I meant to ask about refilling the kerosene stove."

"The fuel is in the lean-to next door. There's a funnel on the peg above it. Switch off the stove first. One tank lasts thirty hours, but it's best to refill every night. And don't forget to check the gasoline level in the generator."

He showed her how to switch off and relight the stove as well as how to restart the generator. To avoid making a mistake, Kelly carefully wrote down the instructions.

When the necessary food and equipment were stowed in the sled bag, Tyler hitched the dogs and let them mill around at the end of their long lines.

"Why aren't you hitching them up two-by-two, in tandem?"

Tyler smiled. "They like the fan hitch better. The first seven dogs are hooked directly to the sled with different lengths of lines so they can regroup in twos when we're on a narrow trail and open up when we're on a lake or river. The other six are tied in the same fashion at the end of a long, central gangline."

"Don't they get tangled up?"

"Not too much. They stick to their places pretty well."

"That's the way the Inuit people hitch their dogs, isn't it?"

"Yes, but on the open tundra they don't have to worry about narrow trails so all the lines are tied directly to the sled and almost all are of equal length."

"I'm amazed they're not agitating to get going."

"That's the way they are. I've also reinforced that in their training. They know we're going. They also know how to conserve energy and pace themselves. When I give the signal, they'll give a burst of speed for about a quarter mile, then they'll settle into their cruising gait."

"That will carry them for miles and miles."

"You got it."

Tyler's pride in his dogs showed on his face. Kelly saw a fleeting happiness on his face at her admiration for his well-trained team.

He whistled twice. The dogs' ears pricked up and all of a sudden, snow was sprayed in all directions as they leaned into the harnesses. Excited yelps rose from those dogs not going out. The team of Inuit dogs never made a sound as they made their spectacular departure.

For a long while, Kelly stared down the empty trail, until the biting cold cut short her reverie. "I care for the man and yet he's the most obnoxious I've ever met. How d'you figure that out, dogs?" A few delighted throaty sounds answered her. The dogs kept up the conversation until they were all fed and watered.

When Kelly went into the cabin after running one team, she found Tyler's scribbled route on the table. She smiled at this small victory. Aware of the short daylight, she hurriedly snatched a sandwich and a glass of milk. Tomorrow, she'd pack herself a lunch so she wouldn't interrupt her day.

The next day, after she'd returned with the last team of huskies, she realized the cabin was low on firewood. She looked in the woodshed. Two chainsaws sat on a bench. Apart from that, the shed was empty. Outside, a tall stack of timber extended to the trees on the far side of the yard.

She took the smaller chainsaw and inspected it,

trying to recall the starting instructions. It was simple really. *Switch on the choke and pull the starter cord.* Nothing happened. She tried again, and again. Her arm became sore and sweat pearled on her forehead. The saw stubbornly refused to start. She repeated the operation with the other machine, with the same lack of success. Discouraged, Kelly leaned against the door frame to recover her breath and think of what to do next.

She unhooked the lantern and held it close to the ground, to examine the wood pile. Some small pieces lay here and there, not quite enough to fill the woodbox, though enough to burn for a few hours. The weather had turned relatively mild. As long as there was some heat, she'd survive. The smell of resin filled her nostrils.

Gathering the small pieces of wood took longer than she had expected. In the end, the supply in woodbox was still depressingly low. Finally, she took a small ax, her headlamp, and went into the woods. Surely she would find some dead wood. Luck was with her when she found a fallen tree with enough branches of a size she could cut. She was familiar enough with the use of an ax. Back home, she often cut the frozen meat for the dogs up in that way, just like it was here.

With a good store of wood, Kelly was just beginning to relax enough to think about making dinner, when a crackling sound came from the corner of the room. Puzzled, she noticed that the radiophone was switched on.

A voice came from the speaker. "Hi Boreal Kennels! Byron Murdoch calling, Omega Beta. Is anyone there? Over."

Kelly picked up the mike. "Oh, hi Byron! It's Kelly Jefferies here. Reading you loud and clear."

"I repeat. Boreal Kennels? This is Byron Murdoch calling, Omega Beta. Is anyone there? Over."

"Yes, Kelly here," she shouted.

"Kelly, if you can hear me, press the talk button on the microphone, then speak. Over."

Kelly pressed her finger on the button on the handpiece of the mike. "Hi Byron! It's me, Kelly. Sorry. I didn't know how to use the thing."

There was a moment of silence. "Byron, are you still there?"

"Well, howdy-do, Kelly! You've got to say 'over' when you've done speaking, otherwise I don't know when you're in receiving mode. Over."

"Okay, I get the hang of it now. Over."

"Good. What's the old bear doing? Over."

"Gone for two days. He's due back tonight, fortunately. Over."

"Why *fortunately*? Something wrong? Over."

"I've a confession to make. I don't know how to start the chainsaw."

"If you're out of wood, I'll come up and show you how to use the chainsaw."

"I was a girl scout in a previous life. I went into the forest and picked up dead wood."

"That's my girl! I knew you would manage no matter what. Have you heard from Charlie yet?"

"Who's Charlie?"

"He's our resident radio watchdog. A nice old guy who runs a regular sked. He calls every isolated cabin once a day to make sure no one's in need."

"He may have called last night when I was out watching the northern lights."

"It was quite a sight, wasn't it? If you need help with the wood, let me know."

"I sure will. Once you show me how the thing starts, I can do the rest. How do I work this radiophone?"

Byron gave her the instructions for operating the set. Still laughing at Byron's humorous parting remarks, she set down the microphone.

"That thing's not a toy!" Tyler's voice boomed across the room.

Kelly stiffened.

"If you miss gossiping on the phone, you better consider leaving. The radio is only used for essential calls and in emergencies."

"What's the good if I don't know how to use it?

Which is what I've just learnt from your friend Byron. Had a good trip, Tyler?"

Her honey-peppered-with-sarcasm tone was meant to combat his aggressive mood. Her heart rate sped up as she stared at his wind-tousled hair, ruddy cheeks and a two-day growth on his chin. His powerful presence dominated the room.

Tyler raked his hair with his hand. "The trip? Good, I guess." He abruptly crossed the room to the bathroom.

Kelly grinned and filled a jug from the stove's hot water tank. "I've got water for you to wash up."

Tyler's hand came out and took the jug from her. The door closed behind him.

"You're welcome!"

The door reopened. Wider this time. Tyler's head appeared. "Thanks." The door shut again.

Kelly added wood to the stove and went to the cold storeroom to see what she could prepare for dinner. If she wasn't mistaken, he had been overcome by the insane desire to kiss her, but obviously his willpower quenched it.

Chapter 4

Tyler splashed the water into the basin and set about removing two days' worth of trail grime and stubble. He washed vigorously as if wanting to erase his inner turmoil.

Kelly's taunting smile was imprinted on his mind. Try as he may, he couldn't suppress his arousal. She infuriated him, damn it! He had always been in control, that was until she arrived. It was a big mistake to let her stay on. Yet how could he possibly race if she wasn't there to help? He couldn't always rely on the kindness of Byron to look after the dogs while away on training runs. The local youths weren't interested in working for him, not since he was no longer the conquering hero.

Grudgingly, Tyler recognized that Kelly had revived long-dormant hopes in him. Her calm assurance that he could again win had shaken him out of his depressed state. She made him ashamed of his former negative attitude.

The melodious tones of her voice filtered through the door. For a second, Tyler thought she must be talking aloud. Then he remembered it must be the time for Charlie's sked. Opening the door intending to tell her about Charlie, Tyler suddenly realized he was naked. He closed the door none too gently, but not without getting a whiff of meat stew. Why bother to explain the radio calls to her? The woman worked everything out for herself as it was. And he mustn't forget that he was no longer the sole occupant of the cabin. His hunger growled in his stomach.

When her laughter reached his ears, he bit his lip and pressed his forehead against the wall, overcome by an ardent desire to throw the door open and seize her in his arms.

Tyler shook himself and looked at the unfinished shower stall. Perhaps he could fix a bucket of cold water to the top. He was going to need it if he had to live so close to such a tantalizing woman.

Kelly was setting the table when Tyler emerged from the bathroom.

"How did the team perform?"

"Just fine. The dogs didn't want to stop, and when we did, they were up and eager to go long before the rest period was over."

"Where are you going tomorrow?"

"Do I detect a wish to get rid of me?"

"Oh sure. I think I like my solitude better than your long face."

His features tightened. Though he didn't believe she meant to be unkind, it hurt. When she reached out, he expected her to caress his face. Instead she took the salt from salt shaker from the shelf beside him.

A strained silence followed while they ate their food. Kelly had to remind herself that this was precisely what she had accepted. In good time, Tyler would want to talk about his trip. For now, patience was going to be her most needed virtue. Well, maybe not the only one. A slow heat was spreading through her body setting it ablaze.

From under lowered lashes, she watched him get up from the table. She discreetly studied him, his wide-shoulders tapering to narrow hips above long legs. His raw sensuality made her quiver. She should gather the dishes and wash them, but she didn't trust herself to stand close to him.

The meal over, Tyler crouched by the sink, picked up the pail that caught the drain water and carried it outside. No point in starting the dishes until he brought it back.

When he returned, he had a tool box in one hand and a length of pipe in the other. Half his body disappeared under the sink. For the next half hour, there was only the clatter of a wrench coupled with grunts and the odd, muffled curse. Kelly thought it wise to remove herself to the couch. Strong fumes of adhesive filled the room. She stood up to open the window to let in the cool pine-scented night air.

Tyler came out grinning from under the sink.

"There we are! Connected to the outside drain. That's the end of carrying that damn slop pail."

"Wonderful! It's going to be more efficient and save me time."

"I should've done it a long time ago. Since I've got my tools here, I'll go and connect up the washbasin in the bathroom."

While he was fighting with plastic pipes and drain fittings, Kelly washed the dishes. She didn't pull the plug until Tyler had finished in the bathroom. A smudge of yellow glue streaked his hair.

"Can I use the drain now?"

"Go ahead, I'll check for leaks."

With some trepidation, Kelly removed the plug. The dishwater gurgled down the drain hole.

"Wow! No leak!" Tyler danced a few steps.

"Congratulations!"

They looked at each other and laughed at the absurdity of being so excited about a piece of plumbing. That instant imprinted itself on her mind.

"As a matter of fact, I'm staying here tomorrow. I reckon we need some wood cut. Did you hack those spindly pieces from the woodpile?"

"From the forest."

"Why didn't you cut some logs?

"The..."

"Oh! I bet you didn't know how to use the chainsaw." A smug smile flitted across his lips.

Nettled by his remark, Kelly fired back, "Neither of the confounded things would start!"

"Of course, you did check the gas?"

Kelly's face turned crimson. "Gas?" She mentally kicked herself for being so stupid.

"Never mind. I'll show you tomorrow."

Kelly nodded, unwilling to trust her voice. Their

gaze met and held. A fire danced in Tyler's eyes. Heat pervaded Kelly's core. Unable to trust herself, she rose to go to her room. Tyler stood up and blocked her path.

"Tell me, why are you doing all this for me?"

His caressing voice made her shiver.

"It's my job."

"That's not the whole of it." He put out his hand.

Panic seized Kelly. If he touched her, all her good resolutions would crumble like dry sand. But she didn't move away. His hand took her chin. His thumb gently stroked her smooth skin. Her breath came in short gasps. Without haste, he bent his head. His lips hovered close to hers.

Spellbound, she watched his eyelids grow heavy, his angular features soften. A trembling began deep within her. Alarm bells buzzed in her mind. She opened her lips and murmured against his, "This is not in the contract."

"To hell with the damn contract." His lips had barely grazed hers when he stopped and pressed his eyes closed. She saw him struggle against his mounting passion. With a supreme effort of will, he pulled back. "You're right. You're right." He was mumbling and made an effort to square his shoulders. "Though, I can see you want to kiss me as much as I want to kiss you."

"Maybe, but we must stop before..."

"What are you scared of?"

"The attraction between us. I'm here to do a job."

"You're right again. I apologize for trying to take advantage of you."

Astonished that he had caved in so readily, Kelly retired for the night. Her emotions drained, she sat in the center of the big bed. He was right. She had wanted that kiss as much as he did, but reason had to prevail.

***

Breakfast and morning chores passed in a neutral

atmosphere, without unecessary words. Only the throaty call of a jay and the harsh cry of a raven perched on the fence could be heard. Kelly watched as Tyler took his team on the trail heading north. Then directed her team toward the south.

A shallow depression in the snow indicated where the trail was. Kelly braced herself on the slender runners of the speeding sled. Up front, her six huskies, pulling an almost empty load, easily ate up the miles. Filled with the joy of being in the outdoors, she launched into a song. A few of the dogs turned their heads and gave her a curious look. Nunii in the lead with young Namatuk slackened the pace. Kelly laughed and called to them, "Good dog, Nunii. That's fine, Namatuk."

The huskies resumed the gallop, and Kelly took up her song once more. Later, she lapsed into a contended silence and let the team fall into a lope. Eventually, she ordered a halt.

She dug in the two snow hooks and secured the sled's snub rope to a nearby tree. Not wanting to leave anything to chance, she made doubly sure the knots were all secure. Next, she took stainless steel bowls from the sled bag, scooped virgin snow from beside the trail and half filled them. The dogs mouths drooled in anticipation as they watched her pour rich broth from the thermos into each bowl.

For several minutes, the dogs lapped the liquid. Once refreshed, they crouched in the snow, their heads resting on their outstretched paws. From away in the bushes came the animated chatter of whiskey jacks.

Kelly thought about Tyler, as she had done for most of the day. She hadn't slept well the previous night. It wasn't that she was shocked or even surprised that he had wanted to kiss her. What troubled her was why that should make her feel so vulnerable. Sitting close to him, her body had clamored for much more than a simple kiss. The emotions Tyler provoked were entirely new to her. Never before had a man had affected her this way. He wouldn't have been the first male to have made a pass at her, but no other man moved her so deeply as he did.

In the past, she had found it easy to deflect the often inept advances of the men she'd dated. This situation was different. Tyler was impossible to ignore. If only her insides wouldn't turn to mush each time he brushed against her or simply looked at her, she might be able to brazen it out. He seemed to sense how badly she wanted to be kissed.

Past experience was no help in knowing how she should react. If she had sex with him, should she simply treat it as a bonus on top of all the professional expertise he was teaching her? Kelly shook her head. That didn't sit well with her principles. Life had become very complicated.

She sighed and set about picking up the empty bowls. When everything was stowed in the sled bag, she pulled out the snow hooks and untied the snub rope. On the return journey, the sun had already dipped below the distant ridge. The once sharply-lit landscape dimmed to a world of blurred shapes.

Somehow, the dogs knew they were homeward bound and trotted briskly. Only the occasional hoot of a snowy owl and the steady swish of the runners over the packed snow broke the silence that had settled over the land.

Before the darkness finally closed about them, Kelly's attention was attracted by a dark shadow on the trail ahead. Out of caution she applied the brake. The dogs were already alerted and were slowing down. When the somber form moved toward them, Kelly realized it was a wolf. She put down a snow hook and pressed it into the snow with her foot, taking care not to make any sudden movement.

A wolf! She had never seen a real wolf before. Fear touched her. Would it attack the dogs? Her? No, she decided. She remembered reading that wolves stay away from humans, but the dogs might decide to take a run at it. Silently, she dropped the second hook for added security and stood with both feet on the brake.

The animal advanced to within twenty feet of her lead dogs. The majestic creature stopped and stared directly at her, regal and unblinking. This was his territory and he was king.

His gray and white muzzle was coated with frost. His eyes were unwavering. The wolf held his head high, unafraid and disdainful of the dogs. A feeling of joy bubbled up inside Kelly. An exhilaration set her pulse beating faster. The primeval beauty of the scene touched her deeply. Here in this vast wilderness, this lone wolf was welcoming her to his domain.

After several minutes of inspection, the wolf nonchalantly stepped off the trail and melted into the trees as silently as he had appeared. For a while longer, Kelly remained enthralled. For some unaccountable reason, she thought about Tyler. Her mind superimposed his image on the spot where the wolf had stood. The man, like the regal wolf, possessed a dark, untamed spirit, one that impressed her with its latent power.

Then, just as quickly, the spell was broken. As if at some hidden signal, the dogs strained in their harness. Kelly yanked out the snow hooks and the sled shot forward. When they reached the spot where the wolf had disappeared, the dogs swerved off the trail and would have followed its tracks had Kelly not yelled a straight ahead command. Her leader, Nunii, tossed her a mischievous glance, but obeyed. The team wavered and came back into line. The leader pulled on. The others followed his lead and kept up a furious pace until the dark shape of the cabin appeared in the distance. All the way home, Kelly's mind had been filled with the wonder of the encounter with her wolf.

Darkness had descended on the valley by the time she entered the yard to a chorus of envious howls from the dogs who had remained behind. Kelly tethered and watered her team, making sure she stroked and patted every dog in the kennel. Tyler's dogs were in the pen. He was back.

The steady whine of a chainsaw from beside the woodshed attracted her attention. Working by the eery light of the storm lantern, Tyler was stripped to his pants and undershirt despite the sub-zero temperature. The shrill noise of the power saw prevented him from realizing she had returned. Kelly watched him lift a log from the stack, muscles rippling across his broad chest. The chainsaw sent wood chips flying. Tyler's rebel lock of hair that she found so irresistible hung over his forehead. When the log was reduced to stove lengths, he put the chainsaw down and took up a long-handled splitting ax. Kelly's mouth went dry. An inferno raged within her as she watched him effortlessly split the logs. She was reminded again of the fiercely independent wolf she had seen earlier on the trail - a loner like Tyler.

When Tyler had finished, he threw down the ax and looked up. He grinned when he saw her watching him. "You're back! D'you want to learn how to use the saw?"

"Of course." Kelly dropped her backpack and stepped closer.

"Put it on the ground and grip the front handle with your left hand. Apply the choke, hold the saw firmly by putting the toe of your boot through the handle at the rear. Now pull on the starter cord."

Kelly did as he said. The chainsaw fired and stopped.

"Good. Take off the choke. It should start this time."

One more tug and the machine burst into life. The next ten minutes were spent in practicing under Tyler's critical eye.

"For a woman, you handle that thing darn'd well. Let's stack the wood in the shed."

Kelly swallowed the retort that came to her about being a capable woman as she looked in dismay at the mountain of wood he had cut. Her stomach rumbled with hunger. Her legs buckled beneath her.

"Have you watered the dogs?" She hoped he hadn't.

"Yes, all done. I also took the last of the meat out of the freezer."

"What freezer?"

"The one in the lean-to. It's plugged into the generator during the summer."

"I thought you kept the meat in the cache."

"Not in summer, we can't. That's why I have the freezer. Let's get that wood in."

"All right." Her words sounded just as weak as she was.

Steeling herself against the pangs of hunger, Kelly began picking up the cut wood. It was going to be a long job.

Beyond the circle of lantern light, night shrouded the earth in its mystery. The penetrating scent of the freshly-cut pine logs brought her a measure of comfort.

"What's the matter? You're slowing down." Tyler's voice penetrated the fog that was numbing her brain.

"Uh... I need to answer a call of nature."

"Well, you don't need to ask my permission." He was laughing at her.

Nettled, she tried hard to keep her tone light. "I was trying to finish the wood before making dinner."

"I've started it. Dried fish and potatoes. It's all in the oven."

"Good. I'll be back."

"I'll finish this."

"I'm not tired, really." The defiance in her tone wavered a fraction.

He smiled broadly. "I can see you're dropping with fatigue."

She shrugged, picked up her pack and ran to the cabin. On opening the door, she was welcomed by a savory smell. Near the stove, rising bread dough was almost overflowing its pan. *For a guy who claims he doesn't know how to cook, he does pretty well*. A fragrant steam escaped as she tore open the tinfoil to test the fish with a fork. Cooked to perfection. So were the potatoes. Kelly removed the crock and put it in the warming oven, then slid the bread pan in. Since bread needs a hot oven, she added more wood to the firebox.

Tyler was still stacking the logs in the shed when she joined him.

"I've taken the food out of the oven and put the bread in. I didn't know you made your own bread."

"Yes. Store-bought bread tastes like paste board. I like solid, well-risen slices for a sandwich. Unfortunately, I don't always have time to bake."

"If you teach me, I'll be willing to do it. My aunt used to make bread. It was always such a marvelous treat."

Tyler looked at her intently, and was about to say something when he changed his mind.

Kelly picked up a couple more logs, noting with relief that the heap was almost gone. In a matter of minutes, they brought the last piece of wood into the shed. She sighed when Tyler extinguished the lantern and closed the woodshed door.

He picked up his flannel shirt and cap, and placed his free hand on her shoulder. "Look at the northern lights."

Their bodies heated by the hard work drew together of their own accord. Kelly raised her eyes and gasped as waves of green, pink and white light swept the sky above the mountains. The rapidly moving light changed colors before spreading out to encompass the universe. The mystical dance of the skies with its fairytale display hypnotized the mere mortals below.

Kelly became conscious of Tyler's hand on her shoulder, almost a gesture of possession.

"I saw a wolf this afternoon out on the trail."

"And you were scared?" His voice betrayed a hint of amusement.

His tone annoyed her. "My only fear was that the dogs would attack it!"

"I didn't mean to sound sarcastic."

"It was impressive to see a wolf close up like that." Her quiet words made him look at her. "And yes, there was fear. Fear of something greater than me, greater than people or things. It was something I couldn't quite grasp. There was a beauty about that animal that words can't describe."

"This is the essence of the untamed North."

The eagerness in his voice told her he was being sincere and it conveyed his love of the land. In that instant, a tacit understanding bonded them. Kelly shivered. He slowly turned her in his arms. His lips searched for hers. His warm breath caressed her cool skin.

This time, she didn't move away. The aurora borealis wove its spell over them, the light framing his dark head in a halo of swirling color. Waves of delightful sensations coursed through her. Her breasts strained against her silk undershirt, tempting her to crush herself to his strong chest. The insistent swelling in his jeans intruded on her. Shockwaves rippled through her body. Luminous explosions happened behind her eyelids.

With eyes closed to retain forever the magical moment, she heard a faraway howl. A wolf. The eternal song of the North.

Close by, a dog rattled its chain. Kelly shuddered. Her reason fought against the attraction she felt for the man holding her. His lips barely touched hers but it was as if a million volts coursed through her body. The effort to speak came from some unknown recess of her mind.

"The bread's in the oven." What a lame way to break the spell!

Tyler grinned. He maintained his grasp for a second longer then released her. "Let's go inside."

Only too happy to come into the warmth of the cabin, Ukiok pushed past Kelly's legs. With the dog underfoot, Kelly found it difficult to serve dinner. She assigned Tyler the task of keeping the dog's nose out of the food on the table.

In Tyler's arms it had taken every scrap of her willpower to break the enchantment. Why had her body betrayed her so badly in the first place? Even now unbearable shafts of cravings stabbed her. Kelly glanced over her shoulder. His face, a closed mask, was bent over the dog he was petting.

The two humans ate in silence, their every move watched by the patient dog. Kelly didn't feel any resentment toward Tyler. What had happened out there in the woodyard was natural - the attraction of two healthy young people. Clearly the contact had troubled them both. She wasn't ready to give in to her clamoring body, not to a man like Tyler, a man who scorned any notion of commitment. Not that they had spoken of it. Kelly had only to consider his lifestyle and his belligerent attitude to know it.

Tyler interrupted her thoughts. "Look, we can't go on like this. I wanted to kiss you out there. Hell, I still do! It's just no good. I'll be honest with you. I don't want to be snared in the web of a relationship. I've had my fill of being pinned like a bug to a board."

Kelly steadied herself with a deep breath. The bitterness in his voice took her aback. "Who's talking about a relationship? I won't deny I expected you to kiss me, but it was me that broke away. In fact, the last thing I want is a relationship, and I don't go in for cheap sex."

To hide her confusion, she bit into a hot potato and burned her mouth. She forced herself to look into Tyler's eyes, while pretending nothing had happened.

A smile of amusement softened his lips. "I'm thankful you don't...go in for cheap sex, that is. You don't have to scald yourself to prove it."

His reply only riled Kelly further. "I'd like to point out that you made the first move."

"And I apologize. Any man would have difficulty to ignore a beautiful woman like you."

Kelly received the compliment with a grimace.

"But it's only physical. I'll get over it."

"Thanks! I'm just a worker, your employee. Don't forget it."

"How can I? Having you here has completely changed my life."

Kelly didn't answer. She wasn't sure whether to take his statement as a compliment or a criticism. She gripped the tip of her tongue between her teeth. *Keep busy*, she told herself, and stood up to clear the dishes.

The crackling of the radiophone came as a welcome diversion. Charlie's cheery voice rose above the static. While Tyler spoke to him, Kelly hurriedly washed the dishes, then took refuge in her room.

***

With Tyler away on a two-day training run, Kelly found she missed him. Working beside Tyler filled Kelly with contentment but made her wary. She was constantly on guard to avoid a repetition of their earlier intimacy, especially since she'd caught him stealing glances at her. More than once, she too was guilty of gazing in his direction. His handsome profile, the half smile that sometimes played on his lips, set her heart aflutter. At other less happy times he wore his old morose expression, tempting her to kiss him until he smiled.

That afternoon she intended to run the pups on foot to test their obedience. About to open the gate, she pushed back the bolt. A flash of white on the far side of the yard alerted her that something was wrong. Intuition told her it must be a dog on the loose. She walked over to see if all the dogs were in their enclosure. Her lips attempted to whistle the come-here command", but her whistling skills weren't up to it. A sharp little face poked from behind the compound fence close to the pine trees.

"Aqua! Come here, Aqua!"

The light-haired dog slunk toward Kelly, who promptly pulled a treat out of her pocket. Aqua came close enough to sniff it. As Kelly was reaching for her, the dog jumped back.

Kelly crouched, treat in hand, and called again. Three times Aqua came within touching distance, yet not close enough to be caught.

"Patience, patience." Kelly said to herself as much as to the dog. "The next time you almost touch my hand, I'm going to tackle you in the best football style. Now come on, dearest Aqua..."

The shy female approached, neck extended toward the treat. Kelly lunged...and missed, landing flat in the snow. Aqua scampered off toward the trees. Kelly picked herself up and brushed the crust of snow from her face. Hoping the escapee would join in, Kelly began to run the other way, calling, "Come'n Aqua. Where's your chasing spirit? Aqua! Here, girl!"

The dog had other priorities in mind. She

disappeared down the trail. With heart pounding in her chest, Kelly ran to the cabin and snatched up the microphone with shaking hands.

"Hi Charlie! This is Kelly, Alpha Dog. Do you read me? Over." *Please be there*, she prayed silently. She repeated the message and pushed the button to the listening mode. Static fizzled in the speaker and Charlie's voice came on.

"Hello, Kelly. I read you. D'you have a problem? Over."

"I've lost a dog. She ran onto the north trail and into the forest. Over."

"Okay. You want me to pass the word around? Over."

"Can you, please? It's young Aqua. She's white with some gray over her back."

"Oh, yes we know that little hound. She's always running off someplace. I'll get onto it and tell everyone to keep an eye out for her."

"Thank you so much, Charlie. I'll take a team and go after her. She might come to us and follow. Over and out."

Kelly pushed the button to the listening mode again, grabbed some food and a thermos of water. Methodically, she packed spare clothes and batteries. Not that she expected to be out long but she followed common sense safety rules. There were overflows on some creeks and if she had to take a ducking to round up her runaway Aqua, she wanted to have dry clothes in reserve.

The choice of dogs for the team was critical. She put dependable Itirit in the lead. Then Navut, as Aqua had a particular liking for him and was tethered next to him. Soon, she had six reliable dogs hitched up. Just as she was about to set off, a snowmobile driven by Byron roared into the yard.

"Byron! I don't have time to talk. I've got a missing dog."

"I know, I heard it over the radio. That's why I'm here. Did you want to go with me on the snowmobile?"

"I've got my team hitched. Aqua is likely to come to the dogs. The noisy machine might scare her off."

"You're right. I'll come with you. Can you spare a few dogs? If need be, we can split and cover two directions."

"Thanks. Take Pinghasuet and Singarnak in the lead, but leave Namatuk. She doesn't get along with Aqua."

"She doesn't get along with anybody."

"I ran her in front of three males and she went like the wind."

"Showing off for her admirers. The poor suckers. She's spayed." Byron's good humor eased some of Kelly's anxiety.

"Are you ready to go?"

"I've got my emergency pack and spare boots."

Between them, Kelly and Byron assembled a second team. Kelly returned to her own sled and pulled up the snow hook. "Search, Itirit. Search!" she called to her leader.

Kelly believed in varying the training and had been playing search games with some of the dogs. Smart Itirit had come through with flying colors. The game made the dogs sharper and wiser. But at this moment, she feared for Aqua's safety should she meet up with a pack of wolves or coyotes. A lone dog would be no match for them and could not outrun them even if she tried. Until now Kelly hadn't realized how attached she had grown to the dogs. A pang of nostalgia pierced her heart as thought of her faithful huskies back home in the care of her cousin. What would Tyler say if Aqua was not found? He loved every one of his dogs. Kelly felt guilty for not having checked her collar and chain more carefully.

"I have to find you Aqua. Aqua! Aqua! Search Itirit, good girl."

Itirit was running nose to the ground. The farther the team ran, the heavier Kelly's heart sank. Maybe Aqua had run deep into the thick forest. Itirit was perhaps following a false trail. The dogs had traveled the same trail only a few days ago. The light snowfall since then would not have obliterated the scent.

Byron was following. From time to time he gave a shrill whistle, the come-here signal Kelly wished she could master. In between, she called out Aqua's name and encouraged Itirit to search.

When she thought she may not find the young female, panic rose in Kelly's chest. Tyler couldn't afford to lose a dog, particularly a top-rate racer like Aqua, an ideal dog for the tough Iditarod race. Grief and anger at the unnecessary loss of one of his dogs might undo all the progress she had made since her arrival. Tears welled up in her eyes, blurring her vision.

Kelly braked the team to a halt when she came to a fork in the trail. One branch headed in a westerly direction, the other swung toward the north-east. She anchored the sled, and unhitched Itirit. Her lead dog sniffed both parts of the trail and grew excited on the north-east fork.

Byron drew up alongside.

"I guess, I'll follow Itirit's nose. I'm not sure if she can really find Aqua's track, but I'll give it a try," Kelly said.

"This north-east trail turns south farther on. I'll follow the other one. Turn home when it's dark, Kelly. There's no point in staying out all night."

Kelly sighed. "I know, but it's hard when you know there's one of your dogs out there somewhere."

"We'll find her. She won't go far. She knows where to get good food, not to mention lots of love."

"I hope you're right."

They parted. Kelly hooked Itirit back onto the line. Her fears came back in a rush. She felt very much alone without Byron's comforting presence behind her.

The sky was losing its brightness when Itirit gave a sharp yelp.

"Whoa!" ordered Kelly. The team stopped and Itirit yelped again. Her nose quivered in the direction of a clearing in the spruce forest. Navut sat and gave a series of short sad howls. A moment later, a small shape emerged from the dense bush. Kelly's heart leaped.

"Aqua, Aqua," she called softly. The young female approached cautiously, though not close enough to be caught. Kelly lifted the snow hook but kept her foot dragging the brake. The team started slowly. Navut made throaty sounds and turned his head toward his favorite mate. Aqua wagged her tail and fell into step next to him.

Kelly took a chance. She reckoned it was better to let Aqua run free next to her male companion rather than stop and try to snare her. She was confident that Aqua would now run alongside while they headed for home. But how to get home? Kelly realized that by concentrating on the search, she hadn't paid much attention to the fact she was heading into what for her was completely new terrain. A fraction second of panic hit her and she closed her eyes. Reason took over. The dogs always find their way home and Itirit was running with assurance. As long as Kelly refrained from giving any command, she trusted Itirit would lead them straight home.

Several miles later, Kelly breathed a sigh of relief when she recognized a familiar landmark. They were close to the cabin. Night was rapidly closing in when the team finally pulled into the yard. Kelly's first move was to secure Aqua to her picket with a new collar. The dog licked Kelly's face and pushed her nose inside the open parka, looking for a treat. Half laughing, half crying, Kelly cuddled her and gave her a biscuit.

The team was barely unhitched when Byron arrived.

A joyful shout erupted from Kelly. "I've got her!"

"I see that. Good for you!"

"I didn't do the work. Itirit and Navut did."

Byron and Kelly unhitched the second team and tethered the dogs. When the harness and equipment were returned to the kennel room, the dogs fed and watered, Kelly invited him into the cabin. Emotionally exhausted, Kelly dropped into a chair.

"Will you stay for dinner, Byron?"

"I should really go."

"And eat cold beans on your own? The least I can do to thank you for coming out is to share my stew with you."

Kelly jumped up and set the pan on the stove.

Byron laughed loudly. "Put like that, I can hardly refuse. Where's Old Grizzly?"

"I wish you wouldn't call him that."

"Sorry. Where's the boss, then?"

"Gone for two days."

"How is he these days?"

"We're getting along fine. We've got a working arrangement, a truce. And it's holding, if that's what you're asking."

"Darn. He's so lucky to have you around."

"I better call Charlie and tell him Aqua's back."

In no time everyone in the area would know the good news. The radiophone was anything but private.

Byron mopped up the last of the stew from his plate with a chunk of bread. He caught Kelly's eye. "Not the best manners, I know, but it's too good to waste. What did you tempt my palate with? Or shouldn't one ask?"

"I chopped up a piece of dark red meat I found in the storeroom and the last of the fresh potatoes. Since I don't know what kind of meat it is, I called the dish *Boeuf Bourguignon*."

"My, gourmet dishes in the wilds! Dark red meat, you say? It's got to be moose."

"Thanks, I didn't really want to know."

"Ah! But moose meat is delicious. As equally delicious as you." His impish tone made her smile.

The slamming of the cabin door startled them both. Tyler towered in the door frame. He dropped his bag noisily on the floor. His dark eyes fell on the remains of the meal on the table. "So busy entertaining were you, Kelly, you didn't even hear me come back? Don't worry, I took care of the dogs on my own."

"The kennel dogs never made a sound, except

when the wolves howled. And they didn't utter a peep when your team came back."

Kelly's protest was ignored.

"What are you doing here, Murdoch?" Tyler grumbled something else inaudible.

Byron stretched. "Having dinner. Kelly made Beef-something-or-other. A true culinary delight. We've left you some. Sit yourself down, Tyler, and tell us about your trip. And how come you're back so soon? Kelly said you were gone for a couple of days."

At his friend's bantering tone, Tyler's face darkened and his mood sank another notch.

Kelly bit the inside of her cheek.

"Did something go wrong? I wasn't expecting you back until tomorrow or the day after."

"Is that why you were throwing this dinner party?"

"Tyler, you sly old dog. If I didn't know any better, I'd say you're jealous."

An angry growl was Tyler's only answer to Byron's smirk.

"I believe this is my cue to exit," said Byron. "Kelly, I thank you for the best meal I've had in a year."

"And thanks for your help this afternoon." A smile floated on her lips.

Byron pulled on his parka and left. The door closed behind him. In the cabin, the tense atmosphere was almost palpable. Tyler still didn't move or say anything.

Kelly wondered why she should feel so guilty. Long-faced, Tyler sat at the table. She waited for him to ask her the reason for Byron's visit, but he didn't. Yet she could see conflicting emotions darkening his face. Jealous? A chuckle rose to her lips. No that couldn't be. Not Tyler.

To break the awkwardness of the moment, Kelly went to the stove and took the lid off the pot of stew.

Tyler's nostrils twitched at the rich aroma. "I see the lady's man has made a conquest."

Kelly dumped the pan on the table in front of him.

"Why should it bother you?"

Tyler's response caught her totally unprepared. Without warning, Tyler scraped back his chair and pulled her into his arms. His mouth descended on hers and plundered its softness. Kelly stiffened, but just as quickly, she relaxed under the onslaught. Her body sought his hard contours and molded itself to them.

Hands linked about his neck, her pliant lips opened to his urging. He drew her closer. Strong fingers burned a path down her spine and over the sensuous flare of her hips. Molten stars of heat burst inside her. He groaned and tightened his hold. Her fingers raked his hair, pulling him to her, harder still. Kelly tasted the male essence of him, the outdoors, the pine and woodsmoke. Tyler lifted his head to permit them to breathe. Hesitant fingers unfastened the clasp of her hair. The auburn glory tumbled to her shoulders. He sank his hands in its silken mass.

"I've wanted to do this for a long time," he said against her lips.

Kelly sighed. "But it doesn't lead us anywhere."

"Oh, no?" Tyler began to pull her toward the bedroom, but held back. Reluctance written over his face, he stepped away.

Flushed and troubled, Kelly wrapped her arms around herself. Heat still radiated between them. Belly taut with unfulfilled need, her breasts throbbing, she stumbled back, forcing her legs to move. With effort, she lifted her head to look at him. Heavy with repressed desire, his eyes bore into hers. For one sublime moment, time was suspended, during which she was aware that both she and Tyler were resisting the inexorable attraction which threatened to trap them in a web of passion.

"N-no..." Kelly stammered.

Tyler's hand paused in midair. His trembling fingers betrayed the violent battle raging within him. Abruptly, he lowered his hand and stalked out, slamming the cabin door behind him.

Kelly retrieved her clasp and fastened her hair.

Still shaking from the kiss, she replaced the pan on the stove. She poured herself a glass of ice-cold water and gulped it down. Slightly more composed, she debated whether to go to her room or face Tyler when he returned. It didn't matter which. There was no point in hiding what they both knew. They would kiss again. It seemed inevitable. She shrugged and resolved to cling to her resolution for as long as she could. Beyond that... she'd cross whatever bridges lay ahead when and if she reached them. She picked up some dog harnesses that needed repairs and began work.

When Tyler returned, she was sitting under the lamp, sewing a red strap on a harness. Kelly stood and took the food off the stove.

"I don't need to be served." His tone carried a trace of resentment.

"Suit yourself. I wanted to be friends but I suppose we aren't any more!" The pan clattered onto the stove and she threw him the oven glove.

"Look, I'm sorry."

"No, you aren't. I'm not either."

Tyler chuckled. "I don't know if we can be friends, but we could be lovers."

"Don't even think of it."

Their eyes met and held.

"Kelly, we have a problem."

"I know. As long as I have two ounces of brain in my head, I'll stay away from you and your kisses. And you can keep your distance too." She tried to appear nonchalant, though that was not how she felt inside.

"I'll do my best. By the way, this is delicious."

"Thank you."

Visibly fighting with himself, he asked, "Why did Byron come up?"

"Aqua escaped this morning. He came to help find her. We took two teams out."

Tyler's hand froze in the air.

"Is she...?"

"Itirit found her. Aqua followed us back home."

The relief in Tyler's voice was tangible. He gave

her a grateful smile and released the breath he'd been holding. "What do you mean Itirit found her?"

"I've been trying to teach the huskies to search. Just for fun. They aren't simply running machines, so..." She looked at him wondering if he approved.

"You mean search and rescue techniques?"

"Sort of. I take some dogs out. Then the next ones have to track them. Sometimes we go off the trail and around trees. Most of the dogs get the right idea, more or less. Itirit's the best, though."

"Interesting. But if you want that team to learn speed and long distance, they have to run to full capacity all the time."

"That's the theory. I'm sorry that you don't approve. From now on I'll drop the games."

A smile softened his lips. Crowfoot lines formed at the corners of his eyes. "No. Come to think of it, the dogs probably like it. Happy dogs put more effort into their work."

Nothing more was said. Tyler finished his meal. Eventually, Kelly spoke cautiously. "What made you come back today?"

"I don't rightly know. All of a sudden I didn't want to be away. I'll go out again tomorrow for the day."

His voice muted, he shook his head. Kelly wondered whether a strange kind of bond with his dogs made him feel something was amiss.

Unless...no, he surely didn't come back because of her? She'd assumed that once he was on the trail with the team, he no longer thought about anything else. Or did he?

Charlie's voice came booming from the speakers. Kelly went to the radio to answer and her sparkling voice filled the room until she signed off.

"Kelly...?"

"Good night, Tyler. It's early rising tomorrow."

His disappointed groan served as a goodnight. At least, that's what she guessed it meant. It had taken her all her strength to break his spell. She prepared for bed, taking care to make the least noise possible. Sleep should have taken over, but it didn't.

She heard Tyler move about to put wood in the stove. The couch creaked under his weight. Heat invaded her, right down to her toes when she pictured him undressing. One boot fell. Kelly waited for the other. It was a long time coming. Did he sleep naked? She visualized him standing, strong muscles flexing to spread the coverlet. Kelly pulled the pillow over her ears, more to dampen her wanton imagination than to muffle Tyler's sounds. Her tender breasts sent ripples of unfulfilled hunger through her body. "I'll survive," she whispered into the pillow.

Tyler's eyes drifted to the window focusing on the twinkling of the stars. A beam of white light shot through the dark sky. The aurora was playing. He sighed involuntarily murmuring, "Kelly". She was the reason he had cut short his trip. He needed to see her, to hear her. Now, he wished he was miles away for the sole reason that it was unbearable not being able to touch her.

He gritted his teeth. A long time ago he had vowed that no woman would ever again turn his life upside down. He'd better stick to that resolution. And starting right now.

He was impressed she had had the presence of mind to alert Charlie when Aqua took off. There was little habitation around these parts beyond the few oddball prospectors in the summer and those who lived off the land in remote cabins, but any of them would turn out to help.

There were also men like Byron, whose twin passions were nature and women, but would never sacrifice one for the other. Most of the other sled dog racers lived closer to the territory's capital. Tyler knew most of them, and met them from time to time while out training. Companionship was important, but he also dearly loved the quiet peace and isolation of his forest retreat.

Another sigh escaped his chest. There weren't two ways about it. He needed Kelly... for the kennel and the racing, he added mentally.

They completed the early morning chores while it was still dark. Afterwards, Tyler got ready to leave. This time he intended to finish the entire trip and not let his physical urges get the better of him.

"Here's my plan," he said. "I aim to do some night running while I'm out. I should be away three days at the most. Will you be okay?"

"Of course, I will." She smiled despite her misgivings. Three days was an awful long time to be without him.

"And Kelly..." He didn't finish his sentence. His face hardened. His shoulders tensed. Kelly waited beside the sled to see him off. Scattered snowflakes landed on her upturned face. Tyler turned his back abruptly, but almost as soon, reached for her and drew her tightly against him. He brushed the flakes off her eyelashes with his lips and trailed kisses down to her mouth.

"Do take care, Tyler," she whispered.

Kelly remained rooted to the spot as the thinning darkness swallowed him up. For a long time she watched the beam of his headlamp bob in the distance. Deep down, she knew Tyler had gone because if he hadn't he would have made love to her. And she would have been unable to say no. She asked herself if that would be so terribly immoral. People did it all the time. Other people, yes, but not her. Not unless she loved the man. That thought made her gasp. She had almost given in, but was it love? Her breath caught in her throat. She couldn't possibly love Tyler. She had compassion for his hurt, certainly, but she didn't love him. Love was something that was shared, wasn't it?

The unrelenting cold brought her back to reality. Somewhere behind her a pup gave a plaintive whine, a reminder that she had a training schedule to attend to.

It was past noon when she went back to the cabin for a bite to eat. A cursory inspection of the cupboards had revealed a dismal lack of food. The last of the meat for the dogs was in an insulated box. The cache was equally bare. She was not fussy, but food was a necessity. She made a list and estimated quantities for at least two weeks. Tyler had omitted to tell her what groceries she should get or whether she could use the truck. Since the track to the cabin hadn't been plowed, she was hesitant to drive. A sled dog team, however, would have no problem negotiating the path.

She didn't trust her memory to find the road to the village, and picked up the large scale map of the area from the bookshelf. It showed a trail from the cabin down to Fletcher Creek, and she decided to hitch up her veteran dogs to the toboggan sled. The team could easily pull her there and back with a load of groceries.

Her arrival in the community caused quite a stir. It was recess at the local one-room school and the kids flocked to her. The pretty woman teacher introduced herself.

"Hello. You must be Kelly Jefferies. I'm Vicky Peters. Nice to meet you."

"You know who I am!"

Vicky smiled. "Of course. In a small place like this everyone knows everyone else. You're a most talked about person for miles around."

"I am? Heavens! What for?"

"For daring to work for Tyler Kade. The bet was you wouldn't last three days. It was revised to three weeks, and now stands at three months." She shook with uncontrollable mirth as she tucked blond tresses back under her fake-fur hat.

"Then tell the gamblers to call the bet off. I'm staying till the end of the season, whether Tyler likes it or not."

"That's what Byron tried to tell them. Nice to see you come to town, and with the dogs."

"Town?" Kelly did her best to hide her amusement.

"I agree, it's funny to call this place a town. Like you, I come from the south. To the locals, Fletcher Creek is a big metropolis. It's home."

"Yes, I suppose it's home." A dreamy look crossed her face. "I came because we need groceries. I feel more confident driving a sled than the truck."

"Can't blame you. There must be quite a bit of snow around your place. Your road doesn't get plowed."

A dozen children had gathered to pet the panting dogs. Kelly had to answer a torrent of questions and explain how the harnesses and lines worked.

"The big red dog is called Palootok. He's ten years old and the boss. The others are also about the same age. That's old for a sled dog."

"Do you race them?" one child asked.

"Not any more. But this team has won many races." A little white lie wouldn't hurt, Kelly thought, since she didn't know whether those dogs did race or not.

The youngsters' eyes widened in admiration.

"All right, children, Vicky announced. "Recess over. Time to get back to class and let Kelly do her shopping." As she shepherded her charges back into the school building, she said, "I hope we can get together sometime soon, Kelly. I imagine you'd welcome a change of company from time to time."

Kelly laughed but felt saddened that the inhabitants of Fletcher Creek should have such a low opinion of Tyler. The dogs went willingly down the street to the grocery store. When she ordered them to halt, they immediately lay down, accustomed as they were to conserving their energy. Kelly secured the snub rope to a near by utility pole.

The store was unexpectedly large and stacked to the ceiling with goods. The odor of spices mingled with other unknown smells. A small woman, her white hair pulled into a tight bun, walked out from behind the counter.

"You must be Kelly. I'm Mary Foster. My husband over there is called Fred." She gave Kelly a broad smile. "Here's a letter for you. From a Marcia. Lovely handwriting she has. We're the post office as well as the general store. I was wondering when you'd get hungry enough to come in for supplies. I know Tyler doesn't believe in buying much food. It's about time somebody looked after him properly. So what do we need today?"

Overwhelmed by such a friendly welcome and amused at the lack of privacy, Kelly pocketed Marcia's letter. Small towns! Everyone knows everything about everybody. Next, the dear old lady would try to find out who Marcia was. She handed Mary her shopping list.

Mary's gray-haired husband joined them at the counter. "Don't bother with the dog food. I'll get Murdoch to bring it up tomorrow, since you say Kade's not home. Tell you what. Leave the flour, rice and potatoes too. No sense in burdening yourself down."

In no time, they had placed most of the two weeks' supply of groceries into the sled bag. Kelly secured the load with a tarpaulin and rope. The dogs stretched themselves, and Palootok turned round to sniff the sled.

"There, big boy." Fred came out of the store again to hand out a treat to each dog. "These are the nicest dogs I've ever known."

The dogs sat and took the treat delicately from the old man's fingers. "Some dogs take your fingers off with it, but not these."

Finally, Kelly and the team were ready to go. Under the watchful gaze of the patrons, looking on from the window, the dogs made a neat turn and headed up the street and out of town.

Darkness had already invaded the valley but a full moon illuminated the clear, starry sky. The snow reflected the silvery light. Kelly had no need of the headlamp to find the way. The sound of the sled runners skimming the snow and the panting of the dogs were magnified by the emptiness of the wilderness. She breathed in the pristine air with a deep sense of contentment. An owl hooted in the distance.

Kelly wondered if Tyler was also running his team in the moonlight. Behind her warm scarf, her lips tingled as though remembering his kiss. She sighed and shook her head to chase away the memory.

Back at the cabin, between the tasks of caring for the dogs, she snatched a moment to read Marcia's letter. Kelly felt a pang of remorse for not having given much thought to her cousin and their life together. Marcia's writing was full of longing. She had broken up with her boyfriend and was wishing she too had found an interesting job in some exotic location. Kelly smiled. Exotic location, indeed! With a tinge of nostalgia, she folded the letter and went outside to water the dogs. Time to write to her cousin later that evening.

The next day passed quickly. To sooth her impatience in waiting for Tyler's return, Kelly took old Tioralak for a walk with a couple of pups. Long before she did, the dogs heard the noise of the truck toiling in four-wheel drive up the slope toward the cabin. Perched on the flat roofs of their houses, the dogs sent up a combined howl of welcome while she was still some distance from the cabin. Hurrying, she arrived to see a man unloading a stack of heavy cartons at the foot of the cache ladder.

The red-faced man straightened his back "Hi, I'm Warren. I've brought the dogs' meat. All sixteen hundred pounds of it."

"Tyler didn't tell me about any meat delivery." Kelly eyed the cartons.

"Kade not around?"

"He's out on a training run. Won't be back till the day after tomorrow."

"This lot had better be put up into the cache before the coyotes or wolverines get at it."

"How many boxes are there?"

"Only forty. We're short at the moment. I'll be bringing out the rest of the order next week."

"Forty...that's forty pounds a carton!"

"Yep, that's right. They're our standard pack. I'd like to stay and give you a hand but I've got to make a delivery at Robertson's, an' that's another two hours drive north of here."

Kelly closed her eyes a moment, then smiled.

"That's all right, Warren. I'll manage just fine."

"Okay. Tell Kade he can pay me next week when I come back with the rest." Warren climbed into the cab of the truck, fired the motor and set off.

Kelly waved him goodbye. She took off her parka and hoisted the first carton onto her shoulder. Balancing herself, she carefully tackled the ladder. At the top, she realized it would have been easier if she had opened the cache door before climbing up. One sure thing, she was not going down again. Breathing steadily, she moved her free hand carefully to unhook the latch. She tottered on the last rung as the door swung open with a creak. A heave of her shoulder and she dumped the box of frozen meat onto the floor, then crawled in and pulled the carton to one side. Climbing down was a lot easier. As long as she took her time and moved cautiously, she would make it. Only thirty-nine to go. She corrected that to thirty-eight as she decided to drag one box into the kennel building.

After ten cartons, Kelly was shaking with fatigue and had to sit in the snow to recover. At this rate, the work was going to take the rest of the evening and probably most of the night. Perspiration streamed down her forehead. Her empty stomach rumbled. She'd have to eat before continuing her grueling task. Just then, the dogs signaled the arrival of another visitor.

Kelly groaned. *Not more heavy stuff to carry, I hope!* The unmistakable sound of a snowmobile pulling a loaded toboggan came closer and closer. It appeared and swung into the yard. Two men got off. Kelly went to meet them as they removed their helmets.

"Hey! What a welcome committee!" Byron made a theatrical gesture toward the second man. "Kelly, I'd like you to meet Conrad Windett, my fellow conservation officer."

The newcomer was as tall and as rugged as Byron. He brushed back a mane of dark blond hair. Blue eyes sparkled in his tanned face. *This North country certainly breeds big strong men*, thought Kelly, accepting Conrad's outstretched hand.

"Byron promised me I'd meet the most beautiful woman in the Yukon. And he wasn't kidding."

"You're embarrassing me."

"And you'll catch your death of cold if you don't put your parka on, Kelly," Byron said.

"There's no chance of that happening. I've got to get back to putting the meat away."

Byron placed an arm around her shoulder. "Why do you think we're here? I saw Warren's truck in town loaded with frozen dog chow. Then I remembered Tyler saying he'd ordered his regular supply of meat. Knowing the old rogue had skipped out and left you with the chores, I roped Conrad here into coming to help. And anyway, Mary threatened to cut my supply of mint drops if I didn't take some stuff to you. Now, get yourself something on and relax."

"This is really good of you both."

"You don't think we could leave a gorgeous lady like you wilt under all these boxes."

The gallant banter lifted Kelly's spirits. The two men didn't let her help. In short order all dog food was properly stowed in the high cache, and the groceries in the cabin.

"We were thinking we should celebrate," said Conrad. "You work too hard. You need some time off, some fun in your life."

Kelly's eyes brightened in the space of an instant. "Sounds good, but I'm awfully busy."

"We know how much of a slave driver old Tyler can be," said Byron. "One evening, after you've finished with your dogs, we'll throw you the welcoming party you never got."

"I can't say anything until I've talked to Tyler."

"Don't let him make a drudge out of you," Conrad said.

"He's got to share!" Byron said.

They all laughed.

"A party would do Tyler good too. Loosen up that serious mind of his. It's about time he came out of his shell." Although Byron spoke in a jocular way, he sounded serious.

"I'll try, but I can't promise anything."

"You must come and visit the conservation office," Conrad said.

"Unfortunately, we've got to go back now. We're after a poacher. Heard any shots today?" Byron asked.

"No. Not around here."

"I didn't think he'd come anywhere close because of the dogs. They sound the alarm as soon as someone's a mile away."

"Don't lots of people hunt for food?"

"They can only do so during the hunting season or in an emergency. But the poachers often hunt at night with a light and sell the meat in the city, and that we don't let pass."

"With a light?"

"A powerful flashlight. Animals are confused by the light and are easy to shoot."

"There's also trafficking of animals parts, antlers, gall bladders, bear paws and the like," Conrad said.

"That's terrible!"

"They only take the parts they need and leave the carcass to rot. It's big bucks for them, so these guys take risks." Byron shook his head. "We haven't half the manpower we need. We've got to rely on tips from the public."

"Tyler nailed one of them last summer when out with his team and a wheeled cart. He approached without noise. The dogs blocked the damn guy's ATV. He tried to run but Tyler tackled him. When the dogs jumped up, he was so scared he wetted his pants!" Conrad said .

Kelly shared their laughter but her heart still beat faster thinking about the danger Tyler might have been in while arresting the poacher.

"Won't you have a cup of coffee before you go?"

Byron's face lit up. "That'd be welcome."

Over coffee, time passed quickly in lighthearted conversation. Byron and Conrad stood up and zipped up their parkas.

"Stay in Kelly, you'll freeze," Conrad said.

"I've to water the dogs, anyhow. But I'm really grateful for your help."

"You were doing just fine, honey," Byron said.

Howls interrupted them. "Another visitor?" Kelly frowned. There had been no engine noise.

"Looks like Tyler's back," said Byron. "Hell, we could have left all those cartons for him to lug into the cache!"

"We could always take them down again," Conrad said.

They grinned and went to greet the incoming team. Tyler said hello his friends and turned back to the dogs.

"Okay, we're off!"

Tyler waved farewell. A moment later, Byron's snowmobile roared off. Kelly helped Tyler unharness the dogs and water them, as well as the other dogs. Happiness rose in her heart. Tyler was back two days earlier than expected. Her joy made her appreciate how much she really missed him.

Tyler glowered. "Can't wait to get your men friends up here as soon as I'm gone, can you?"

"Did something go wrong to make you grouchy like that?" Kelly pushed open the cabin door.

In a glance, Tyler took in the empty coffee cups and empty cookie dish on the table.

"I seemed to have interrupted a cosy gathering."

Her elation at his return slipped down a notch. Kelly shrugged his sarcasm and winced as pain shot through her shoulders. Jaws set hard, she lit the lamp and cleared the table. She kept her back to him and began to prepare the evening meal. Tyler stood and watched her. Catching sight of him reflected in the window glass, she smothered a sigh. Both Conrad and Byron, although big men, had not dwarfed the room the way Tyler did. Her heart pounded in her chest. She wasn't falling for him, was she?

After a lengthy silence, Tyler said, "I came back because I remembered Warren was to deliver the meat. I'm glad he didn't."

"For your information, Mr. Kade, Warren did make his delivery."

"Heck! Where's the meat, then?"

"All in the cache." Kelly spoke modestly with eyes lowered toward the floor, anticipating her punch line.

"In the...? You didn't get the whole lot up there on your own?"

"That's the cosy gathering I had with Byron and Conrad."

"Oh!" Tyler glanced away, shamefaced.

"There's no need to apologize for being so insensitive." Kelly savored her minor triumph.

Tyler took her by the shoulders. "I'm sorry if I act like a real rube sometimes."

Kelly flinched. His fingers were digging into her skin. She attempted a smile.

"What's the matter? Are you hurt?"

"I got ten of the cartons into the cache myself before Byron and Conrad showed up."

"You did what? You must be sore as hell. Here, let me massage you."

His strong hands began easing Kelly's aching muscles. A warmth invaded her that had nothing to do with her soreness. The circular motion of his thumbs soothed the pain but sent erotic shivers up and down her spine. His breath fanned her neck. Once or twice, his hands faltered. He bent his head. His lips touched her ear. A long pent-up moan she couldn't control escaped her lips. Tyler turned her in his arms, his lips trailed from her forehead to the end of her nose before kissing her waiting mouth. She let herself go against his hard frame and encircled his waist with her arms.

The pressure of his lips increased. Shivers of exquisite pleasure rippled through her body, while disturbing tremors ran through her. A tantalizing male scent clung to his skin and made her lightheaded. He lifted his head to look into her dreamy eyes. His hand found a way under her sweater and burnt a slow path up her back. Her taut young body shook. She didn't remember how her sweater came off or how she came to be standing in her silk camisole. Deftly, he brushed the straps of the filmy garment off her shoulders.

A low groan came from his parted lips. "You're so beautiful!"

She reddened with pleasure mixed with shyness, and moved her hands to his shirt buttons. In the golden glow of the lamp, she saw his muscles undulate. Her fingers trembled making her clumsy. A series of disconnected thoughts ran through her mind, but she couldn't stop what she was doing. She tugged his shirt from his jeans. Without losing contact, he shrugged off his undershirt. Her eyes feasted on the sinewy contours of his chest. She ran her fingers through the mat of dark hair and followed its line down to where it tapered to his waistband.

A slow, drawn out moan came from her throat as his mouth awoke a dormant volcano in her.

He lifted her in his arms and carried her to the bedroom, where he laid her gently on the quilt. He lowered her zip and removed her jeans. Heat from unknown fires steamed up her vision. The faint tremors that shook her soon became shock waves rocketing through her. She was caught in the vortex of a blaze burning out of control. A thousand pinpricks of light exploded behind her eyelids. She breathed in deeply the scent of his warm skin and tugged at his waistband.

With a wicked smile, he took her mouth again, while his hands played havoc with her senses. Tyler raised his head, and stayed her hand. "If we go one step more, I won't be able to stop." His voice, hoarse with pent-up desire, was barely audible.

She was desperate to assuage her craving, yet an unexpected wave of timidity assailed her. He watched a pink flush suffuse her cheeks. He pulled her to him, his hot breath fanning her cheeks. "Not your first time?"

"No, but I...I don't know...I don't have much experience..." Her murmur was barely perceptible, and she was suddenly terribly tongue-tied.

"We'll take it easy."

He kissed her lips lightly and let her explore him, guiding her hand till she grew bolder. The volcano inside her was out of control. She was panting, soaring to some dizzying heights, caught in a frenetic dance of the senses.

A feral need swept through them both as he shed his jeans. She tugged on his underwear, but he stopped her and gently dropped kisses over her satiny skin. He skillfully removed the lacy scrap of panty she wore, her only concession to feminine luxury in this active outdoor life she led.

Sharp, needlelike prickles spread to the tips of her limbs. As never before, she wanted to feel his masculine weight. When she thought she could no longer survive the onslaught of pleasurable sensations, he let her remove his last piece of clothing.

He took her a little at the time until she moaned in a delirium of joy. Shuddering pulses arced through her until an explosion as warm as a summer sun left her panting. Then moving faster, he brought her to another paroxysm of sensations before allowing his release.

He stood poised on his arms contemplating her radiant flushed face, then slowly lowered himself. In silence, they clung to each other for a long while without moving, savoring the intense spasms that still shook their bodies. Finally, Tyler moved to her side and kissed her love-bruised lips.

"I'm afraid I'm rather inexperienced," she murmured.

"And I've taken advantage of you." A sudden chill fell in the room. He rolled to the edge of the bed and sat, his head in his hands. "This is the last thing I meant to happen."

"But it did. I'm not sorry."

"Well, I am! I had no right to do that. Hell! It mustn't happen again. And it won't."

Kelly watched his back stiffen. She was tempted to caress the rigid set of his shoulders.

"You enjoyed it. I enjoyed it. There's no problem, Tyler." She yanked the sheet up to cover herself.

"There is. You just don't understand."

"Try me. I'm a mature adult."

A feeling of weariness settled over her. The enchantment had subsided, but she wanted to reach out and tell him she loved him. A shock made her start. Love him? No, she couldn't! It wasn't possible. It must be the glow of their lovemaking that made her mind hazy.

"I knew it wasn't going to work. I knew it!" he repeated.

Kelly cringed, hearing the anguish in his voice. "Let's put it behind us, then, and concentrate on the work of getting you to win races."

"Damn!" Tyler stood abruptly, picked up his clothes and strode out of her bedroom.

Kelly stemmed back the tears that flooded under her eyelids

Chapter 5

When Kelly awoke, she heard the dogs in the compound and reasoned that Tyler must be already outside. Through her window she could see the sky heavy with clouds. The early morning was opaque and gloomy.

She hesitated before swinging her legs over the edge of the bed. How should she behave toward him? How would he react? He had been furious and unhappy last night after they had made love. Last night... How tender and gentle he had been. So considerate, yet so passionate. The memory of it came rushing back. Her pulse quickened at the thought that she would have to face him today. Normal behavior was called for, but how can one behave normally after sharing what they had shared? They could never be the same with each other again.

The older dogs raised their heads and gave a brief howl of greeting but didn't come out of their houses. Only the younger dogs jumped eagerly to the fence before curling up on their springy beds of pine twigs. The pups made the most noise and played in their pen long after Tyler and Kelly had gone back to the cabin.

Strained silence presided over breakfast. The atmosphere in the cabin was so oppressive, Kelly sought a way to lighten it. Talking about dogs was neutral ground.

"Do you have a particular reason for checking on the dogs before you're ready to feed them?"

"Yes. I check if everyone is there. A dog could slip its collar or find a way through the fence, like Aqua did the other day. Something might have happened to one of the old veterans during the night. That would change the plans for the day."

She nodded. The heavy silence returned. By the time breakfast was over, Kelly noticed it was snowing hard.

Tyler jerked his head at the scene outside. "Do you fancy taking a team out in that?"

Surprised by the question, Kelly made a guarded answer. "I'm game for anything."

"We'll go up to the head of the valley, to Ashini Point. It's a two-hour round trip."

A rush of excitement lifted Kelly's mood. Not only was he now talking normally but had actually invited her to go with him. Floating on the edge of irreality, she prepared a bagged lunch and a thermos of cocoa.

They each readied their own team. The pleasurable anticipation of a rare outing with Tyler tingled in her veins like bubbles in champagne. It'd be tough going through deep virgin snow, though so exhilarating as they overcame the obstacles. Most of all, Tyler would be with her. Since he had made the invitation, perhaps he wasn't angry with her after all.

Tyler led the way with his sturdy Inuit dogs. Kelly was perfectly happy to follow in his tracks. Because of the worsening weather, it took them more than the hour to reach Ashini Point. They stopped to rest the dogs and give them some of the broth Kelly had prepared. Their strength restored, the dogs were soon eager to get back on the trail, but Tyler lingered. He served Kelly a hot drink.

"There's nothing better than a cup of hot chocolate on the trail," she said.

"Even better in a storm when the snowflakes fall right into the cup to cool it down."

They chuckled and put the cups and thermos back in the sled bag.

"You take the lead on the way home."

Kelly looked at him. "You mean that?"

"You'd better get some experience finding your way in a storm."

"I'd let the dogs find their way. I trust them."

"I do too, but it's a good idea to see if you agree

with them. But let's make it better. When you get to Lone Pine corner, you take the east trail and get us home from there."

"I'll have to turn south again, won't I?"

"Yes. See if you can find the trail. You've been on it once, and I've sledded over it a couple of times. Look at the snow, it'll be uneven compared with the undisturbed snow elsewhere."

The snow fell thicker now. Kelly could barely see her lead dogs. From time to time, she called out to Singarnak and Pinghasuet to keep heading home. The tracks of their outward passage had already filled with snow. Navigation wasn't difficult until they reached Lone Pine, a huge spruce standing by itself on the edge of a small frozen lake. After the turn, finding the right trail proved more difficult.

Her eyes strained to see the slight indentations left by earlier sleds and dogs. No matter where she looked, she was blinded by driving snow. She found a trail, even though it was nothing more than a space between the trees. By her estimate, it had to be the right one. It ran east or at least appeared to do so. Without the sun for orientation, she relied on the lie of the land that she remembered from studying the map. Tyler said she had been on this trail before but through the thick curtain of white, it was impossible to spot any familiar landmarks. The team turned just as she was giving the command. In fact, she could have sworn the lead dogs hadn't waited for her order. The trail twisted again and she assumed it was going south.

For no apparent reason, the team gave a spurt. From afar, Kelly heard faint howls. They were nearing home!

"Thanks, Tyler. That was a good exercise. In the south, we don't have this kind of weather." She spoke while unhitching her team.

"I know."

Of course! It was a trial run. That's why he had asked her out this morning. Not for the fun of sledding. Solely because he wanted to test her skills and her endurance. All the same, they had shared a companionable time. She sighed and watched him lead two dogs to their pen, his long legs slicing a path through the fresh blanket of snow, and sighed.

A spiral of longing began in the pit of her stomach and spread to the rest of her body. She released her breath and tried to ignore it by busying herself with her dogs.

Back in the cabin, she and Tyler ate a quick snack of bread and cheese. Tyler remained silent. Occasionally he looked through the window at the ever-falling snow. At other times, Kelly caught his eyes on her when he thought she wasn't aware.

Tyler left the table. "I'm going to chop up some frozen meat for tomorrow."

He was gone before she could reply. She shrugged and turned her attention to the bread she had started that morning. The dough was ready for kneading. She turned it onto the table, sprinkled it with flour, and folded it. Soon, she discovered how therapeutic pounding dough was. It was a welcome outlet for her frustration.

Tyler's businesslike attitude hurt her. After all, they had shared a wonderful moment of intimacy. It hurt her to see him treating it as a one-night stand. Kelly didn't expect him to love her. The only love he seemed capable of was the love for his precious dogs. But she expected him to treat her with respect, not like a woman he'd have picked up in a bar. If only she could find out what made him so angry, so defensive, she could help him overcome it. At least she thought she could.

When it came time to water the dogs, Tyler still hadn't returned to the cabin. Kelly pulled on her boots and zipped up her parka. She met him just outside the porch, shoveling a path to the dog pens and the kennel. The rhythmic bending of his powerful body that sent the snow flying triggered Kelly's longing once again. Closing her eyes, she took a deep breath and stepped forward. Ukiok leapt at her from out of the deep snow. She grabbed his head and rubbed her nose on his.

Tyler informed her curtly that he had already watered the dogs.

"Thanks. Dinner's ready whenever you are."

Ukiok took advantage of the partly-open door, and dashed into the comfort of the cabin. The big black dog shook the snow and ice from his coat in front of the stove.

"Ukiok, you infuriating dog! Couldn't you have done that outside?" Kelly couldn't be angry, seeing Ukiok smiling at her, a huge pink petal of a tongue lolling from his mouth. She laughed and patted his head, then set the table.

To occupy her hands until Tyler was ready to eat, she picked up a length of blue polypropylene rope and started on a new gangline by weaving the ends into a loop. A smile came to her lips as she held the aluminum fid in her hand. The basic design of the tool hadn't changed since the first sailors used the cone-shaped marlinespike to splice the ropes for sails several centuries earlier. Modern technology improved it by making it hollow and from light metal or plastic.

When Tyler came in, her hands wavered and dropped the fid. Why did he have to look so devastatingly handsome, with a crown of snow on his dark hair?

Her heart skipped a merry dance against her ribs. Around her the room was intimate and warm. The smell of fresh baked bread tickled her taste buds. For a fleeting moment, Kelly imagined she had stepped back in time to a simpler age.

Throughout the meal, Tyler brooded and limited his conversation to a curt "thank-you". When the meal was over, they washed the dishes. Kelly dried and put away.

Several times, Kelly opened her mouth to speak, then closed it again. Unable to break the impasse, she finally wished him goodnight and retired to her room. Stretched out under the covers, she remained awake, longing to go to him, to tell him she wanted him to make love to her. He would certainly reject her. Regret over their intimate encounter was written on his stern face.

Yet during those glorious moments, he had revealed a different Tyler beneath that forbidding exterior. She could easily love that other man. Perhaps she already did.

Persistent questions kept spinning in her mind, no matter how hard she tried to brush them aside. What were her real feelings for him? Maybe she really loved him, or maybe she merely succumbed to the effects of isolation. Cabin fever was what it was called.

In the morning, Tyler was still curt. When she opened the cabin door, she saw that the snow had stopped. It lay in a thick mantle over the yard, having erased the path Tyler had dug out the previous day. He handed Kelly a pair of snowshoes. She laughed at the novelty of wearing snowshoes to feed the dogs. The animals had dug tunnels from their houses and were busy playing in the snow. "If anyone ever doubted that they love the white stuff, they should see them now," Kelly said.

"Or when we bring harnesses out."

She hadn't realized he was so close. He had prepared a pack for his sledding run. The task of hitching the dogs was useful to calm her erratic heartbeat. The rebel lock of hair swept Tyler's forehead. Didn't the man ever wear a hat? A shiver traveled down her spine as she recalled how his soft hair caressed her skin when he'd kissed her.

Moments later, he was set to go. A ghost of a smile softened his lips. She suppressed a sigh. That's where all his love went, to his dogs and his wilderness. Unexpectedly, he took her in his arms. His fevered mouth kissed her trembling lips. Tyler groaned and deepened the kiss. Then, just as abruptly, he let her go. "Bye, sweetie." In no time, he and his team were gone.

For a long while, Kelly stood motionless and stared at the indentation in the snow where the sled and the dogs' feet had broken the powder snow. *Bye, sweetie.* Two little words that raced around and around her mind.

Thankfully, her morning duties absorbed most of her thoughts and energy. Kelly tried not to think about

Tyler, but that was an impossible task. He was an invisible presence, always at her side. When she paused, she could hear his voice, feel his talented hands on her responsive body. It was obvious he was fighting a battle between wanting to make love to her and keeping his distance. But why? She'd told him clearly enough they were two mature adults and should enjoy each other.

By the end of the morning the sky cleared and the sun came out. The frosty air smelled clean and new. The pine branches were bowed down under their load of snow. Kelly hummed to herself while preparing to take out a team of six huskies. They'd be challenged by the deep snow, but she didn't plan to go very far. She lashed the snowshoes on top of the sled bag, just in case she'd have to break a trail for her dogs.

For a while, she forgot everything but the delight of the huskies' panting as they plowed though the new snow. The sharp air turned her cheeks a healthy rose color. She adjusted her goggles to protect her eyes from the dazzling expanse of white.

The trail narrowed in a forest of mixed spruce and aspen. A great gray owl rose heavily from in front of the team, and the dogs sped up and jumped as one. In vain. The bird flew into a high branch. Her dreams took her back to Tyler. She was so absorbed that she didn't immediately hear the strident whine of an oncoming snowmobile. Not wanting to take any chances of having an accident, she ordered her team to the side and secured the snub rope to a tree. This was her first encounter with a snowmobile on the trail. She hurried to her lead dogs and held them by the collar. The machine slowed and stopped alongside. Even before the operator removed his helmet, she recognized Byron.

"Out on patrol, Byron?"

"Yes. We've had reports of our poacher in these parts, but no tracks. Since I'm here, would you like me to break a trail for you to the cabin?"

"That's good of you. I can manage, but since you're offering, how can I refuse?"

"It's on my way."

When they arrived back at the kennels, Byron helped her unhitch and care for the dogs.

"Want to come in for a cup of hot coffee?"

"I'd settle for a thank-you kiss."

"I don't have any to spare." It troubled her that Byron had grown very fond of her and she tried to keep her tone light.

"Saving them for Tyler?"

His forthright question caught her unawares. She flushed with embarrassment, knowing the truth must be plain on her face. Was she that transparent?

"Tyler's not interested in me." She hid her confusion with a nervous laugh.

"Don't try to fool me. Why else would he bite my head off every time he finds me here? He acts like one really jealous guy."

"It's not what you think, Byron. At the beginning, he was reluctant to accept me. You saw that for yourself. Now that I'm here, he's scared he might lose me. Not because I'm a woman but because he recognizes that I'm indispensable for his training program. He needs a handler."

Kelly tried to keep the sadness she felt from choking her words. That's what Tyler had become - a cold, calculating manipulator. He needed a handler, not a woman. Had she listened to her voice of reason, she'd have seen through him earlier. Tyler's lovemaking, with all its tenderness, was his way of keeping control of her. He wanted to ensure she didn't fall in love with some other man and leave. A cruel pain stabbed her heart. No matter that Tyler spurned her, she was unwilling to throw herself at another man. Kelly made a mental correction. She was unable to look at another man, not even someone as kind as Byron.

Byron stared at her. "You've got it bad, haven't you?"

She shook her head in a feeble denial while trying to conceal the tears welling up in her eyes. She brushed back her hair with her fingers. "It sounds crazy, I know. I tried reasoning with myself, without success."

"Look, honey, Tyler's been my friend since I came here four years ago. I've never seen him so positive and possessive at the same time." Byron placed a hand on her arm. "You've transformed him."

"But it doesn't lead anywhere."

"I hate to say this, Kelly, because I'm half crazy over you myself, but I think he really loves you. He's just too damned afraid to admit it."

"If I'd the slightest reason to believe that, I'd propose to him." A sad smile fluttered on her lips.

Byron squeezed her arm. "It'll come right in the end. You'll see. And, talking of the devil, look who's here!"

Tyler's team pulled to a stop in front of their enclosure.

"You again, Byron?"

Byron remained completely unperturbed by Tyler's bristling hostility. "Well, Tyler, still going round with a sore head?" He held the lead dogs while Tyler secured the sled.

"Are you looking for a fight or something? Anyway, what are you doing here?"

"I broke trail ahead of Kelly and her team."

"Why the hell did you do that for? If she takes a team out, she can snowshoe the trail!"

"My, I hadn't thought of that!" Kelly's taunt hardly masked her rising anger. Yet some other emotion drowned out her rage. Her eyes devoured Tyler's face, his rugged features contorted by some intense inner turmoil.

"I'd better go now. Talk to you later, Tyler." Byron turned to Kelly and dropped a light kiss on her nose. "I think this guy'll keep trying. I may be wrong after all."

The roar of the snowmobile shattered the stillness of the night. After the dogs had been cared for, Tyler stood aside to let Kelly enter the cabin. Inside, the soft lamplight heightened the somber expression in his eyes. He tossed his parka over a hook.

"So, what's going on? Secret rendezvous out in the wilds? Are you trying Byron out too?" The disdain in his voice cut her to the quick, though she wasn't going to admit it.

"It's a free country, isn't it?" Her sharp answer startled Tyler, but it didn't give her any satisfaction.

Tyler whirled and crushed her against him. His mouth came down possessively on hers. Faint tremors began in the pit of her stomach, growing in wider and wider circles.

A savage need to give herself to him possessed her. He put her through an ecstasy of torment. His hands roamed her body and tenderly cupped the swell of her breast. She moaned out her pleasure against his lips. He smelled of snow and the outdoors. His chin's incipient stubble rasped against her soft skin.

He pulled away. "Does he kiss any better?" There was a bitter challenge in his voice. Dazed from the sudden onslaught, Kelly stared at him in mute amazement. He raked his hand through his hair. Making a visible effort, he stepped back. "No. Forget I just said that."

"Why should I? That's a ridiculous question to ask. I wouldn't answer, anyway." Her breathing had steadied, but the desperate yearning inside persisted.

Tyler threw himself onto the couch and watched her pick up her backpack beside the door and disappear into her room.

Tyler fixed his gaze on the red glow of the woodstove. What the hell was he doing? Hadn't he sworn he wouldn't let another woman into his life? Not only had he let this one through his defenses, he had actually wanted to possess her so badly he couldn't stop himself. The memory of her firm but ever-so-sweet body made his loins ache. But more, he needed all of her, her vivacious personality, her sassy tongue. No, this wouldn't do. The auburn-haired woman in the other room was no different from the others in his life. True, she shared his passion for racing. So had Gloria. Only, her interest had been short-lived and a mere sham.

Nothing had been good enough for Gloria. He hadn't seen her for what she was until too late. She'd called him her diamond-in-the-rough, but the charm of living in the Northland quickly wore thin. He blamed himself for having driven her into another man's arms. Following her extramarital affair, it had been a mistake to take her back. To Tyler, she rapidly became an acid-tongued shrew. The ensuing custody battle over their baby son drained him financially and emotionally. No one, not even Kelly, was going to put him through that hell again.

Maybe he should just give up everything and go and live deeper in the mountains, the way old Hiram did. Tyler had met the white-haired hermit in the store one day. The old man came out of seclusion only once a year, driving his team of equally ancient dogs to buy his meager supplies.

Tyler smiled at the thought. Then his mind came back to Kelly. How different she was from Gloria! Kelly instilled a new confidence in him. Of course, she scoffed at the lack of modern conveniences because at season's end, she'd leave to go and get get her own team and disappear from his life. Full of knowledge and experience, she'd join the racing circuit and be a winner. She'd quickly forget about the ill-tempered man who had given her the break she needed. Why should she care for him? No sane woman would. One evening of great sex meant nothing to a hot-blooded woman like her. Determined as she was, she'd do anything to succeed. To women of her sort, sex was just another weapon to enslave men. That, he'd never ever allow to happen again.

Kelly stepped back into the room to prepare dinner. The thoughts churning through Tyler's mind vanished as his eyes followed her every movement.

Chapter 6

At breakfast, Kelly tried to find some way to bring Tyler out of the cloak of silence he had wrapped himself in. The only weak chink in his armor was his love of dogs.

"I don't want to disrupt your busy schedule, Tyler, but I think you should spend some time with the pups. If you don't, they'll grow up without knowing you."

Tyler flinched. His face hardened. He brought his hand down in a fist on the table, so hard he rattled the dishes. Without bothering with a coat, he strode out of the cabin.

Kelly stared at the closed door. His reaction to her suggestion surprised her. Why so angry? Usually, the mention of the pups was met with sympathetic understanding. She remembered the suffering etched on his face and regretted her choice of words, or maybe the tone she used. Had she injected a note of reproach in it, a challenge even? A sigh escaped her. Living with Tyler wasn't easy.

She put on her parka and took his over her arm. Outside, the sub-zero temperature hit her squarely in the face, but she knew where to find him. He was crouched among the pups, letting them jump all over him, pawing him, licking him. Kelly's heart beat faster to see how relaxed he was. Anxious not to break the fragile spell, she let herself into the pen. The pups turned their exuberant attention on her. Kelly handed the parka to Tyler. He took it with a brief thanks.

"Let's take them out to see what you have taught them," he said. "More games, I bet."

"Right."

Relief flooded Kelly at his change of mood.

Amazed, Tyler watched while she put the young dogs through their paces.

"Let's take them out on the trail," Tyler said.

It was Kelly's turn to admire as he ran and jumped with the pups. His tall, powerful frame was so agile, so vibrant, that she was filled with renewed hope. She wished she'd never have to leave this remote valley or leave the man presently making a fool of himself with a bunch of young dogs. A strong sense of belonging engulfed her.

For Kelly, the rest of the day passed like a dream. She sang as she worked with the dogs and refilled the wood box. With Tyler there, it was as if she were on vacation. The beautiful winter landscape around them was a picture postcard backdrop to her happiness.

After dinner, Tyler busied himself in sharpening the points of the sled brake. Kelly finished a new harness for one of the pups.

To avoid breaking the mood, she chose her words with care. "By the way, Conrad and Byron want to throw a party. They asked if you would come."

"A party! What's the matter? Missing the bright lights?"

Kelly quashed her sigh, realizing again that she'd chosen the wrong moment to speak.

"I couldn't care about the bright lights. Your friends have suggested a small gathering. You can't shun the rest of the world all the time." She bit her lip.

Tyler's face was a closed mask. "Fine. If you feel like that, you go. Take up with someone else, while you're at it."

"Grow up, will you?" Her face colored. "I'm talking about a social outing. One relaxed evening of fun wouldn't hurt you."

His voice hardened. "I've chosen my way of life. If it doesn't suit you, then go. All women are alike. All of them! I should never have let you stay on here."

Kelly refused to rise to his bait. Instead, she shrugged and went to her room. Once more she had blundered into forbidden territory. What further proof did she need that a woman had caused him grief? She hated that unknown woman who hadn't loved him enough.

Alone once more, Tyler sat staring at the glow of the stove. Bitter memories flooded his mind. Gloria had loved parties more than anything else. When the racing season was about to start, he had brought her north, with the promise he'd build her a big house fitted with all the luxuries of city life. By the time the baby was born, she'd have everything. Too impatient to wait, it hadn't taken her long to hate the cramped cabin and the simple lifestyle. In a few short months, she fled back to California leaving their baby to him.

At first, he'd thought Kelly was different. She claimed she liked the outdoors, the dogs, the routine of race training. Gloria, too, had claimed to have loved the dogs, but she later told him she didn't want anything to do with them.

The fact that Kelly wanted to go to a party was not, in itself, so awful. But it represented the first step down a slippery slope. Soon, he'd be enmeshed in a social whirl he wasn't prepared for. That would be the end of his rigorous training.

He didn't know why he should be so obsessed with her. He had to admit she worked well and his dogs adored her. She was truly a great cook and he was enjoying the best bread any man could wish for.

An unwelcome heat pooled in his loins. Damn her! Did she have to be beautiful as well? That deceptively soft feminine exterior hid a finely conditioned body. He ached to touch her again. Such delicate features and smooth skin didn't belong in the wilderness. Yet she fitted in here as if she'd been born to it. With her at his side, his days were brighter and the long hours of darkness were less somber.

Disturbed by thoughts of simmering passion and unfulfilled longing, he went outside into the frigid, starlit night.

When Kelly awoke in the morning, Tyler was

already out. That didn't surprise her. He often was first up. She hurried to the dog compound but saw no sign of him. There was no light in the kennel building. She glanced toward the pens and saw that one team of dogs was gone, so was a sled. Vexed that he had made a night start without telling her, and without breakfast, she went about her daily tasks, then took a team out. She was on her way back when she heard a deep baritone voice singing off key. Noises, particularly the human voice, she had discovered carry far in the cold, still air. She could hardly believe it was Tyler, but it had to be. There was probably no other musher within miles.

She stopped her team and waited. Her dogs had heard him too. Their ears turned as one toward the sound. He was closer now, and she thought it'd be unwise to surprise him on the trail. She resumed her way back to the cabin.

"Hike!" she commanded. Reluctantly, the huskies started for home. The singing had stopped. A moment later, Tyler's team broke from the cover of trees and drew alongside hers. Automatically, she called her team over to the side to permit Tyler to pass.

"No, no. We'll run together. It's good for the dogs. They're too isolated. We need to meet more teams."

"How about running some local races?"

"Too far to go for just a day's run. Anyway, my freighters wouldn't stand a chance in those races. I don't want to break their spirit by losing."

Kelly smiled to herself. Tyler could have easily taken the huskies to the local races, but he hadn't left any room for it in the training schedule. He'd made winning the Yukon Quest his goal and nothing was going to distract him from it. His pride had returned, and that she believed was an achievement.

They traveled in company. Close enough for Kelly to reach out and touch him. She had to breathe deeply to curb the urge. Aware of her scrutiny, he turned and smiled, a devastatingly winning smile. His eyes, grayer than the winter sky, brimmed with affection. Hope swelled in her heart.

Kelly's team, running parallel to his, paid scant attention to the other. Both teams strained to get ahead. The trail was almost too narrow for two teams abreast, but for a brief moment, Kelly imagined she was shoulder to shoulder with a rival, competing in the famed Iditarod. They were racing to the finish line in Nome, Alaska, with her sliding in under the burled arch, and the crowds going wild.

She burst into a yodeling song. Itirit in the lead pricked up her ears and leaned into her harness. The rest of the team members copied their leader and ran like demons. Kelly arrived home a whole length in front of Tyler. An impish smile on her lips, rosy and breathless, she greeted him. "I believe I won that heat."

"You did! Where the heck did you learn to yodel like that?"

"I haven't the faintest idea. Most times I just make a gargling noise. It doesn't seem to bother the dogs."

"Far from it! It makes 'em run like the wind."

She and Tyler laughed and went to take care of their respective teams. They did the evening chores together. Kelly promised herself to choose her words carefully from then on in case she damaged the wonderful yet fragile harmony that had so unexpectedly been established.

The dogs' howling, followed by a knock on the door interrupted their table talk. Byron entered, a broad grin on his face.

"There's a letter for you Kelly." He handed her an envelope.

"Thanks. You didn't come up especially to deliver this, did you?"

"I called in at the store and Mary badgered me into delivering it. I couldn't refuse. Besides, the Fletcher Creek singles' set has proposed we all celebrate Christmas Eve together at my place. Pot luck. Everyone brings something." Byron gave a smirk. "Tyler, you'll bring Kelly?"

"No. I won't be available," Tyler's terse tone chilled the air.

"Come on, you need a little R&R."

"I tell you, I will not be here."

Byron's coaxing had no effect. A pang of disappointment knifed through Kelly. Training was important, but she had hoped Tyler would stay home for Christmas. Home? She must stop making these associations, but there was no denying that the cabin had become just as much home to her as the big house she had grown up in.

Byron smiled at her said. "Then, if he's busy elsewhere, honey, I'll come and fetch you."

Kelly watched Tyler's expression turn sour. The relaxed atmosphere of before vanished. She almost groaned out loud, dismayed at how little it took to switch his mood back to the old bristling attitude.

"I've a letter to post," Kelly said. "Would you be so kind as to mail it for me?"

"My pleasure. Just give me a call whenever you have mail to pick up."

"She can go to town any time she wants. She doesn't need you to handle her mail."

"Well, thank you for telling me, Tyler." Kelly spoke with a touch of irony. "I wasn't planning a trip to Fletcher Creek for at least a couple of days."

"The keys are always in the truck."

"Actually, I'd prefer to take the team of older dogs to town. It's a nice run for them."

"Oh, you found the back trail to town." There was a hint of respect in Tyler's tone, yet he frowned as if annoyed.

Byron coughed. "Well, I have to be off. Give me your letter, Kelly, and I'll see it catches the next outgoing mail."

The noise of Byron's snowmobile faded into the distance, and the cabin settled back into silence. Kelly knew it was pointless to expect Tyler to revert to the happy state he was in before Byron's visit.

The vexed expression had returned. Kelly gave up hoping she could talk him out of it. She crossed the room and inspected the shelves of books.

"You don't mind if I read some of your books?"

Tyler face brightened. "Of course not. Try this book. It's *My Life of Adventure*, by Norman D. Vaughan. You'll discover he's quite a character. He was in his late eighties when he ran the Iditarod for the nth time."

She took the book from his hand, and read the first sentence three times over before realizing she couldn't concentrate.

Her eyes riveted on the page, though the familiar awareness of his gaze, a hungry gaze that expressed his primitive longing, crept on her. That familiar warmth of arousal spread from her inner core. If only she and Tyler could be honest and open with each other! It was plain that he wanted her as much as she wanted him. The tension between them rose a few more degrees.

When she did look at him, Tyler was writing in a notebook. Although he avoided meeting her eyes, she guessed he had been watching her. Exasperated, Kelly closed the book and wished him goodnight.

Tyler's self-control slipped when Kelly left the room. A surge of fire spread through his body already tense with unfulfilled need. His fingers gripped the pencil so hard the point broke. He stared at the only word he had written on the page: *Kelly*. Why did he tell her he wouldn't be there for Christmas? He didn't know whether Gloria would let him see his son. The number of times he had requested a visit was too numerous to remember. After having raised the child in his first year, his son Glenn was now growing up without a father.

He brushed his hand over his face. A knot caught in his throat. Why was he taking it out on Kelly? She'd come to do a job and would be gone at the end of the season. At the same time as craving her touch, her kiss, he wanted her miles away. The turbulent feelings that tortured him whenever she was close threatened to drive him out of his mind..

In the days that followed, Kelly and Tyler behaved like two boxers in the ring, each wary of making the first contact. If they happened to collide while handling the dogs, they recoiled with mumbled apologies.

Before setting off with his team, Tyler finally exploded. "Damn it, Kelly! This pussyfooting around is killing me. I want you."

Without letting her reply, he took her in his arms and invaded her willing mouth. A jealous dog thrust itself between the two humans and quickly brought them back to the present reality. As unexpectedly as it had begun, the kiss ended.

Tyler struggled with himself to behave as if nothing had happened. He looked to his team. "Can you take Arnavik to the maternity ward? She's due any time from now on." His voice, heavy with thinly controlled passion, wavered.

"Certainly."

She watched him depart. His kiss had set her body afire, although the trembling had subsided. No doubt he would come back early. Arnavik came and nuzzled her hand, just as she always did. The once trim dog waddled ungainly at Kelly's side as they walked to the kennel building. Kelly put more straw in the pen and let the pregnant female in. Arnavik walked around and around until the straw was flattened to her satisfaction. Then she settled down and went to sleep.

After dinner that evening, Tyler and Kelly went to check on Arnavik's progress. They sat together on a bale of straw in one corner of the pen and observed the canine mother-to-be. Tyler talked gently, and Arnavik responded by rubbing her head against his hand. The dog's heavy panting was the only sign that something was about to happen.

Several minutes later, the dog turned and brought her first puppy out. Well licked but still damp, and protesting vigorously, it found its way to a teat to suckle greedily. Tyler pulled a notebook from his pocket and recorded the birth. When a second pup appeared, Tyler picked up the first one, weighed it and placed it in the open front of his jacket to keep it warm, while its mother was busy. Then he put it back to nurse alongside the second pup.

The pups, all seven of them, arrived at intervals. Kelly marveled at Tyler's gentle manner. There was an expression of quiet on his face, as though this was the first time he had seen the miracle of birth. He placed a black and white pup in her hands. Kelly looked down at the tiny creature, blind, deaf and so utterly dependent. She kissed its moist little head and put it back to suckle.

When the new mother ceased labor, Tyler checked her thoroughly and left food and water for her in the pen. Smiling with satisfaction, he extended his hand to Kelly to help her up. Taking it sent millions of delightful miniature shocks up her arm. She stretched her cramped limbs and turned off the lamp. Closing the door securely, they walked to the cabin.

As she removed her outer clothes, Kelly threw him an affectionate glance. "It's always wonderful to be present at a birth, isn't it?"

"It never fails." He loaded wood into the stove. "I always feel privileged to see the creation of new life."

The softness in his voice tugged at Kelly's heart strings. Would he have the same sense of wonderment at the birth of his own child? Better not think about that since she would never know the answer. Standing side by side with him at the kitchen counter was enough to send shivers down her spine. For the moment, a sense of having truly come home flooded her with a happy feeling.

She poured milk into a saucepan. Tyler picked up the can of cocoa. Their eyes met. His head tilted slowly toward her and his lips touched hers. The pressure on her lips increased. She raised herself on tiptoe to press closer to him. He let the cocoa can fall as he encircled her waist.

"Tyler, the cocoa..."

"Who the hell needs cocoa?"

Kelly molded her body to his. He teased her lips

till she allowed him to probe the sweet moistness within. A wild, primeval force swelled between them. His male scent, so redolent of this mysterious northern land, intoxicated her. He pulled the clasp from her hair and let the silken tresses tumble over his face.

"Your body's too tempting for a sane man, your skin too velvety and your beauty is utterly irresistible. You smell wonderful. I have to make love to you." He breathed with relish the wildflower fragrance of her hair.

She smoothed the anxious lines on his brow. "I want you too."

His passion rising, he lifted her in his arms and carried her to the bed. In a crisis of want, she clung to him, her fingers unmercifully gouging his shoulders. Just as savagely, he claimed her mouth. An untamed need was unleashed within her. Clothes became a hindrance to be hastily removed. The heat of their naked bodies fused them together. Legs intertwined, their hands searched and explored the hidden contours of the other. Man and woman were consumed by a fever of primal lust.

"I.. need you," she whispered.

They pressed themselves together to heighten the sensation. Kelly arched her back. He made her his. Deeper and deeper he branded her as they writhed on the bed.

For the longest time their arms held the other close. With soft caresses, he elicited sighs of pleasure. He took her again, this time slowly with infinite tenderness.

At last they lay sated in the warm shadows of the room. Lulled by the distant cry of wolves, they drifted into sleep, only to awaken with renewed thirst for each other.

They rose late next morning. Gentleness expressed itself in his every gesture. They set about the day's work. Tyler announced he didn't want to be away. They would run the teams together and arrange to have their two teams meet and pass on the same trail, so the dogs would get used to passing.

As his sled passed hers in the opposite direction, Tyler stole a frozen kiss from Kelly. Laughter echoed among the pines. Gray jays sat on the end of branches and looked on with curiosity.

Back in the cabin, they cooked their meal. Mirth and happiness filled the air.

Kelly pulled a sticky mess of dough and apples from the oven. "I reckon I wasn't concentrating." She grimaced. "I'd best throw it away."

Tyler stayed her arm just as she was about to empty the pan's contents into the trash pail. "Don't. It's perfectly edible! All good ingredients." He tried his best to suppress a smile.

"Even though my mom kept saying there's nothing to cooking, I still create regular disasters."

"Don't put yourself down. You're a great cook." His eyes shone.

Kelly's sparkled with humor. "At least the dogs don't complain about my cooking. But then, with raw meat and bagged food, I can hardly go wrong."

"Your broth is delicious," Tyler said, his face a deadpan.

"You haven't tried it, so don't speak."

"Oh but I did. One day, I'd spilled my thermos. I was too lazy to set up the stove to melt snow, so I drank some of the dogs' broth."

They shared a moment of carefree laughter.

"You must miss not having your dogs around."

"I've got plenty others here."

"That's not the same."

"Agreed. I do miss those old dogs of mine. But it's only a temporary absence."

A silence fell. *A temporary absence*! Suddenly she realized that eventually she'd have to leave. Not to see Tyler again would quell the flame of happiness she had kindled with such care.

She loved him. Of that she had no longer had doubt. For the first time, she freely admitted it to herself.

That all encompassing feeling which submerged her could be nothing else but love. It was love that made her watch anxiously at the window when he was late returning. Love for him overflowed into such wondrous excitement when he smiled.

The flipside of being in love with Tyler was that he didn't love her. Lust, yes. Love, no. Last night they had glimpsed paradise. But during those idyllic moments, he had not been able to say the magic words *I love you.*

"How about getting your dogs up here? There's room for them."

"That's very nice of you to offer, Tyler, but then Marcia would also miss them. Besides, I can't afford the cost of transport."

"We could arrange that. I've got a friend, Jerome is his name, who comes up every year to race the Yukon Quest. He could bring them."

"I'd feel a heel taking them from Marcia. Anyway, two of them are hers, and we couldn't possibly separate the dogs. They'd die of grief."

"Yes. I know how they get so attached to one another. Sometimes they don't even survive the death of a lifelong companion."

Charlie's sked, on cue as usual, interrupted them. While Tyler talked to him, Kelly occupied herself by tidying the cabin. Her mind kept returning to the question of whether she and Tyler would again share a night of passion. The very idea kept her tingling. Was this the beginning of a relationship? Could he learn to love her? So many questions without answers. It took very little to throw him back into a bleak mood. She ought not to be dreaming, but she'd take all she could in the meantime, starting with a goodnight kiss.

Tyler watched the curtain fall back, and almost jumped up to follow her. Her beautiful body drove him crazy, but more than that, he needed her to keep up his spirits, keep him centered on the task of preparing for the big race. Her quiet assertiveness and her feminine presence had become indispensable. Her jauntiness spiced up their daily life. There had to be a way to keep her with him at the end of the season. He shook his head. No need to think about it yet, but ideas crowded his brain.

A smile lingered on his lips while he loaded the stove for the night. A quick look around to make sure everything was in order and he blew out the lamp.

A feeble light shone through the curtain to the bedroom. Half-undressed, Kelly turned round and smiled at him. The soft light of the oil lamp threw a golden glow over her skin and set sparkles of fire in her hair. Mesmerized, Tyler stood still a moment before slowly reaching to finish undressing her.

Without haste, she peeled off his shirt and feasted her eyes on his athletic frame, his muscles bulging under the closely fitted thermal shirt. Her fingers lingered on the contours of his chest while he sighed with impatience. Finally, she lifted his shirt above his head and combed her fingers through the mat of chest hair down to the zipper of his jeans. His uncontrolled sighs made her chuckle. Her wandering fingers rolled down his soft wool drawers, eliciting little gasps from his lips.

All barriers removed, they stood together and let their bodies burn with the heat of anticipation. They joined hands and leaned back, arms stretched between them, as they admired the beauty of their well-made bodies. A groan escaped Tyler's throat and he scooped her up to continue the voyage of discovery on the bed.

The days passed in a haze of bliss. Lulled by the steady pace of the huskies up front, Kelly breathed the cold air as it rushed past her face. Darkness had already crept over the valley. A shimmering white mantle of snow reflected the tranquil light of the moon and stars.

It was only days to Christmas. A genuine friendship had blossomed between her and Tyler, but she was preoccupied with how she could change Tyler's mind about the party at Byron's. She breathed deeply and murmured to the wind. "Lovemaking it was, but not love." Tyler had made no further mention of going away, and the training was going well. Surely he could skip one day?

When she pulled into the dog yard, she saw immediately that Tyler was back. Her heart leapt with joy. She quickly finished her duties so that she could sit for a while with the new puppies. They'd grown. Their eyes had now opened onto the world.

Tyler was talking on the radiophone when she entered the cabin.

A line creased his forehead and his smile was strained as he set down the mike. "Had a good run?"

"Yes, it was fine, thanks. You're back early?" She wasn't really surprised.

"The dogs were impatient to turn back."

"Were they? Just the dogs?"

"Well, their musher too. Don't think I'd push my dogs just because I want to kiss you."

"I hope not, Mr. Kade." She went and raised herself on tiptoe, offering him her lips.

"I've missed you." He engulfed her in his powerful arms. His stubbled chin rasped her cheek as the kiss lengthened. A tremor shook her and warm sensations rippled to her extremities before he lifted his head for a breath. Her lips still trembling, Kelly reluctantly pulled apart.

"I must go and water the dogs."

"Don't take too long. I'll wash and shave."

Dressing rapidly, Kelly let herself out. She was hardly out when she thought she heard the call on the radiophone. Charlie must be early.

Once the dogs were checked and watered, she hurried back to the cabin. A smile floated on her lips as she watched the northern lights dancing in the sky. The rattle of a dog chain, the subtle scent of pine smoke drifting skyward, Tyler waiting in the cosy cabin, their common goal and the dogs, all that was home. Home wasn't a house or any place. Home was where the heart found love.

During the dinner, Kelly sensed Tyler's mood had changed. The old shuttered look was back. Her heart sank. Why? They'd shared some beautiful moments over the past few weeks. She was careful not to make any demands on him. He went on with his usual training program, being away for two or three days at a time, coming back impatient and ardent.

At the beginning of the evening, he'd been happy, carefree, almost. What happened that he couldn't confide in her? Unless it was something Charlie had passed on, but then if something had happened in the far-ranging community, surely he'd share it with her?

"I've got to catch the bus tomorrow morning. Will you drive me to town?" Tyler asked.

Only with the utmost willpower did Kelly prevent her jaw from dropping.

"The bus...? Yes, of course. While I'm in Fletcher Creek, I'll get some groceries. It'll save me a trip later." She was babbling but the silence still hung heavily.

Since he wasn't willing to share his travel plans, Kelly wasn't going to ask in case it completely broke the magic that had enchanted them earlier in the evening. His face showed signs of the old hostility. Standing by the window and looking out into the night, he still hadn't said a word.

More puzzled than annoyed, she quickly dealt with the domestic chores, then retired to her room. The certainty he wouldn't be joining her tonight weighed heavily on her. A sudden weariness tinged with sadness crept into her bones. As she had often done of late, she wondered where this relationship was going. He had responded, if not with love, at least with passion. Hostility had given way to tenderness. Yet, tonight, he'd once again withdrawn into his shell. At the heart of the sublime emotion she felt for Tyler was the numbing realization that she had given herself to a man incapable of making a commitment. Her earlier happines clutched at her heart as it disintegrated.

Evidently, their recent intimacy meant little to him. In that respect, he was a typical male. He took what he wanted and walked away. Now he was seeking to put distance between them, literally and figuratively, by taking the bus to goodness knows where, at Christmas, of all times. A need to paint him dark gnawed at her and in a strange way absolved her.

Kelly bit her lip. She had failed miserably to follow her own advice and resist the sexual attraction between them. It was too late now to undo the past and just as useless to regret it. Though regret it she would, and bitterly. What if she discovered she were pregnant? Contraception had not even crossed their minds. She shrugged. *Que Sera Sera*. She hummed the tune.

Black thoughts swirled in her mind and prevented her from sleeping, but eventually, she sank into an abyss of oblivion.

The night was short. She awoke to the sound of Tyler moving about the cabin. Tyler! A sudden rush of emotion caught in her throat. He was preparing to leave. Leaving without confiding in her! For no reason she could think of, he had shut her out of his life.

Despite the thick comforter, the cold crept around her and brought an acute sense of abandon. So different this was from the previous departures with their joyful teams of huskies. Of course, he said he was going for a few days only. Then he'd be back because of the dogs and the race training. Now she was sure it wasn't because of her, or maybe just to satisfy his sexual needs.

Tyler looked up when she came out of her room. His face registered nothing, but she read the signs.

"Good-morning," he said. His voice sounded awkward, stilted. He resumed packing his bag.

Kelly put the frying pan on the stove and took the last two eggs out of the larder.

"I don't need breakfast. We should get going."

"Well, I need to eat. I'm not driving on an empty stomach."

Kelly refused to be cowed by his aggressive manner. Tyler shrugged and went outside. As before, he took refuge with the dogs. She prepared the food for them both and served two plates. When he came back in, she waved him to a chair.

"There's no need to sulk. Eat."

Tyler grumbled about wanting to be away, but ate. "You sure you can take care of things while I'm away?"

"Of course, that's why you hired me, isn't it?" A faint trace of mockery tinged her voice.

He frowned but made no reply.

Kelly glanced at the clock. Tyler was right. There was no time to waste if he was to catch the seven-thirty bus. She climbed into the truck. Tyler already had the motor running. He drove the four-by-four in low gear through the deep snow until they reached the main highway. Kelly breathed easier and wished she didn't have to come back alone to tackle their snow-filled track.

She didn't wait for the bus to arrive. There was no point in a lingering goodbye, not when Tyler was morose and silent. He didn't even look at her. Despite the hour, the store was open since it also served as bus depot. Her shopping didn't take long. When she came out, the bus had come and gone. So had Tyler.

On the return trip up to the cabin, the fight to keep the truck on the road took her mind off her sorrows. Once home, she resolved not to give Tyler another thought. Maybe it wasn't being realistic, but from now on, it was going to be strictly a business relationship.

The work took her mind off the hurt she felt, but it troubled her that Tyler had left, a man bristling with suppressed anger. She wanted to share his worries, to soothe and encourage him, but he wouldn't let her near him.

Later in the day, the dogs signaled the approach of someone on the track. Kelly listened. The noise of an engine made her anxious. It couldn't be a delivery truck. The rest of the dog meat order had been stored in the cache while Tyler was home. She remembered wistfully how their laughter had lightened the task of carrying the heavy cartons. The vehicle eventually came into view. A huge snowplow blasted its way into the yard. It stopped and a man jumped down from the cab. Kelly went out to meet him.

"Hi! I'm Devon Santoni. Byron said I'd better plow your road so you could get to the Christmas celebrations in town. Is Old Grizzly here?"

"He caught the bus out this morning."

"Darn! I wanted to know if he'd sell me a couple of pups. When will he be back?"

"That I don't know."

Tall, dark eyed, and broad-shouldered, black hair protuding from under a wool toque, Devon looked as though he'd stepped off the cover of a men's fashion magazine.

"Do you mind if I take a look at the dogs? I never come up without visiting them." He flashed her a devastating smile.

"Sure. Did you want a couple of the nine-month-old pups?"

"Yes, that's right. I got rid of my wife," he said. "I want to rebuild my sledding team. Recreational only, I'm not into racing."

It took Kelly a moment to absorb his off-the-cuff remark. "What do you mean you got rid of your wife?"

"The wife didn't like my dogs. I gave them away and regretted it ever after. Then she decided she hated it up here. She left and went back south." Devon pointed out a lively pup. "This black male is a beauty. Do you think Tyler would part with him?"

"Quite possibly. I noticed this particular pup stays on the edge of the pack. He never seems to join in with the others. He'd make an excellent sled dog in a small team."

"Would he get along with my old Bruno? The guy who took him has offered to give him back to me."

Kelly could see the emotion in his dark eyes. She guessed the pain he suffered when he had to give away his faithful companions.

"I'm sure he would. He gets along fine with our older dogs. And he's got a very friendly nature."

"Good. By the way while I'm here, would you like me to clear your yard? I see you're getting a little choked up with snow."

"That would be great. I find it hard to move about

and there's too much to clear with a shovel."

"Your road isn't on the schedule to be plowed, but what the Public Works Department don't know won't hurt them."

They shared an easy chuckle. Kelly watched as he skilfully maneuvered the big machine, removing several weeks' accumulation of snow and dumping it on the edge of the compound. He waved goodbye to her from the cab, and sent the powerful machine down the incline and back along the track.

Overwhelmed by the noise and Devon's whirlwind visit, Kelly walked to the forest edge and gathered spruce boughs to make a Christmas wreath. Back in the cabin, she cut a length of tin foil into narrow strips and wove them through the clumps of fragrant green needles.

The result was so pleasing she decided to do some more decorating. By the end of the evening, she'd made garlands of spruce and small tin-foil bells to lend a festive touch to the cabin.

It was totally dark when she went out to check on the dogs and let Ukiok out of the pen.

"Come along, big fellow," she said. "You miss Tyler, and so do I. We'll keep each other company."

The black dog bounded inside and ran straight to the couch Tyler used as a bed. Though when Kelly went to her room, Ukiok had no hesitation in following her in and curling up on the mat beside the bed. After a moment, he stood and put his muzzle on the bed cover. Kelly reached over and scratched him behind his ears. By way of thanks, he held out his paw. Laughing softly, Kelly shook it, then kissed his broad head. The dog lay back down and gave a sigh of sheer contentment.

Chapter 7

In a fit of mild exasperation, Kelly dumped the contents of her bag on the bed. Makeup! It was unthinkable to go to a party without makeup, even here in the back of beyond.

After a long search, she located the few items that made up her cosmetic kit and placed them in readiness by the mirror. She then turned her attention to the old-fashioned flat iron heating up on the stove. Gingerly, she tested the heavy iron by holding it close to her cheek. With even greater caution she touched it to the damp cloth laid over her one and only party dress, a pretty outfit in fine viridian wool.

Before dressing, she applied soft brown eye shadow to her eyelids and enhanced her long eyelashes with dark mascara. Pink gloss outlined her lips.

Kelly wriggled into the sleeveless dress. The clinging fabric with its elegantly simple cut outlined her slender figure. In the cramped bathroom, she performed a pirouette to flare the skirt. "What a pity there's nothing better than Tyler's wretched shaving mirror to view myself in." Mention of Tyler made her wonder what he would say if he could see her now, dressed in all her finery. Would that be enough to jolt him out of his touchy mood? From her bag, she took a gold-mounted topaz pendant that had been her mother's favorite. Kelly fastened the thin gold chain around her neck. The lamplight glittered on the jewel lying in the gentle valley of her breasts.

Just as she finished, the lights of Byron's truck lit up the windows. A knock followed, and Byron himself filled the door frame. His mouth gaped.

"Wow! Princess, where have you been hiding all this time? You look absolutely gorgeous."

"Thank you, sir."

"That dress does wonders for you. You should wear it more often."

"Can you imagine me sledding in this get up?"

"Why not? Right now, my imagination is running wild."

Kelly laughed. "In that case, you should go outside and cool it off in the snow."

"Won't I just gloat when the guys see me with you on my arm. Seriously, I'm the luckiest man this side of the mountains."

"Have you been lacking feminine company by any chance?"

"You can say that again! Shall we go?"

"Give me a minute to get my outdoor gear on and I'll be right with you." Kelly pulled on her insulated snow boots and zipped her down-filled parka. In one hand she carried her silver high-heeled sandals and in the other the plastic container of cookies, her contribution to the party. "Okay, Byron, I'm ready."

Byron didn't react immediately. His eyes traveled down her body from head to toe and back again.

"A man could die for a touch of that long hair of yours," he said at last.

"It seems like the night for compliments. I suppose I should be happy to hear them."

"Aren't you?"

Her eyes met his. "Don't take me wrong, I love it. I'm just out of practice. Now let's move if we're going to the party."

"I could think of some alternatives." Byron gave a devilish grin.

"So could I. There's meat to be chopped up for tomorrow's dog chow, and a whole stack of wood waiting to be split."

Byron laughed at her quick wit. He walked her to the truck.

The noise of the party hit them the moment they climbed down in front Byron's log house, one of

Fletcher Creek's finer residences. Smiling faces greeted her as she entered and made a bee line for Vicky Peters.

"Hi Kelly! I'm so glad you could come," Vicky said.

Conrad came forward to greet her. "And isn't she elegant?"

Vicky dug him in the ribs. "How can you judge? You spend your life in the backwoods, so I don't think you know what a woman looks like."

"I'd recognize a nice pair of legs anywhere."

Vicky took Kelly by the arm. "Come along. Let me rescue you from these uncouth men. I'll show you were you can leave your coat."

Back in the living room, Vicky introduced Kelly to a number of the other guests. Among them was a petite brunette by the name of Nicole Lantell.

"Make yourself at home, Kelly. Here, have some of the punch the men made. It's supposed to be non-alcoholic, but it's got a terrific kick to it."

Conrad leaned over and whispered in Kelly's ear. "The secret is the half-bottle of Tabasco sauce I threw in."

Like the punch, the party proved to be lively. Devon was in high spirits and cranked up the music to dance. Byron dragged Kelly, laughing and smiling, over to the space that had been cleared at the end of the room. Other couples soon joined them. For a good part of the evening, Kelly found herself dancing almost nonstop.

"My feet!" Kelly groaned as she sank onto a sofa.

"What else do you expect in a place where men outnumber the women by three to one?" Byron said.

After only a short respite, Byron pleaded with her to dance with him again. While she swayed to the music and chatted with him, Kelly's thoughts were with Tyler. Where was he at that precise moment? And why the puzzling and abrupt coldness after such wonderful intimacy?

In spite of the carefree laughter and talk all around her, a dull pain settled in Kelly's heart. If she had to fall in love, she should have done so with an uncomplicated man like Byron. He was happily flirting with her. His adoring eyes followed her whenever she wasn't at his side. Unfortunately, when he held her on the dance floor, his touch didn't bring her alive the way Tyler's did.

"Are you enjoying yourself, Kelly?" Byron asked. They were filling their plates at the buffet table.

"Terrific. I just hope I can get up tomorrow, or rather later this morning, to care for the dogs."

"When you're ready to go, just say the word. I'll drive you home."

Several dances later, Kelly noticed that almost everyone was dropping with fatigue. "I guess it's time we went," she said to Byron.

The farewells were warm and the feelings genuine. The guests exchanged promises to meet again soon. Byron made a point of helping Kelly on with her parka. In doing so, he failed to see Vicky's wistful gaze on him. Kelly noticed it, though, and immediately felt like an intruder.

Kelly wished she'd thought about leaving a light burning. In the dark, the cabin appeared deserted were it not for the chorus that greeted them the moment the dogs heard the approach of the truck.

"Just a minute, before you get out," Byron said. "I've got a flashlight here someplace. I don't want you to fall in the snow."

He helped her light the lamp in the cool cabin and coax the embers into a roaring fire.

"Would you care for something to drink? Since Fletcher Creek is a dry community, you'll not be surprised that the choice here runs to coffee, tea or hot chocolate. We do have good water too."

"Coffee would be nice. And Kelly..."

Something in the way he said her name sent a jolt of alarm through her mind. She finished preparing the coffee before turning round.

"How is it going with Tyler?"

"Professionally, very well."

"Emotionally?"

Kelly knew where the conversation was leading but couldn't find the words to deflect it. "It's all right. I had a great time tonight. Thanks for a lovely party."

"You didn't answer my question. I asked because I've grown more than fond of you. Since I met you, my heart has been turning sommersaults."

Kelly bit her lip and attempted to make light of Byron's words. "I'm not a heart specialist so can't give you any advice for that serious condition of yours."

Byron had the good grace to smile. "I know you don't want to hear this, but I love you. I did the moment I saw you standing on the road in the twighlight."

Shaking her head, Kelly looked down. "I'm so sorry."

"I know. I've just been hoping that maybe you didn't really love him."

Her voice strained. "For all the good it does!"

A long silence fell between them.

"I'd better go and let you catch some sleep. Unlike the rest of us, you have work to do in the morning."

Kelly stood and gave him a shaky smile.

"Actually, I should come up and help you feed the dogs."

"Thanks, Byron, but you don't have to. It isn't a difficult task and the busier I'm the better I like it."

"Okay, I've got my marching orders."

"Can I still count on you to be my friend?"

"You bet. Any time you need me, I'll be here for you."

He'd already donned his parka and set his fur cap on his head when he bent his head toward Kelly. The kiss was light but burning.

A moment later he was gone. Kelly stood by the window until the glare of the headlights disappeared down the hill. She wiped the tears from her eyes and felt the emptiness of the cabin close in around her.

After a few hours of sleep, she got up surprised how fresh she was. Following a simple breakfast, she was deciding which dogs she would take out for a run, when she was alerted by the approach of a vehicle.

Her heart leapt in her chest in the hope that it might be Tyler. It wouldn't have been the first time he had returned unexpectedly. But, no, it wasn't Tyler. It was a snowmobile, with another one coming up behind it. Both drivers had a passenger on the seat, and the second machine was pulling a toboggan with two children. They drew to a halt in the yard. Kelly went out to meet the visitors.

"Season's greetings!" Byron said, pulling off his helmet. "Meet Cindy and Mike. Cindy's Mary and Fred's daughter. And, Conrad needs no introduction. These two scamps, Jack and Danny, are Mike and Cindy's kids. They've never seen sled dogs before, so I thought it might be fun for them. I hope you don't mind our impromptu visit."

"Merry Christmas, everybody! I'm delighted to have company, even though I've nothing much in the house to offer you."

"Don't worry, Mom sent a Christmas cake for you," Cindy said.

"Thank you. How about a sled ride? I was about to take a team out."

"The kids would love that, if it's not too much trouble."

"Not at all. It's good training for the dogs. Do you want to take a team and come along, Byron?"

"Okay. I'll take Conrad and the kids in my sled. You take Jack and Cindy. That should equalize the weight."

Conrad gave a good-natured growl. "Hey! I'm not riding in one of those!"

"Yes, you are. I need the ballast. These freighting dogs can really pull."

"You didn't warn me about this when you dragged me up here. Right now, I could be sleeping in."

"The fresh air will do you good." Byron laughed while preparing the gangline and the sled bag.

Soon, seven Inuit dogs were hitched to Byron's sled and six to Kelly's. The passengers settled themselves in. The dogs turned round and came to inspect the helpless travelers, generously kissing them with wet tongues. Satisfied with their cargo, the dogs tightened the lines and waited for the order to "hike".

The dogs sensed this was a special run. They started at top speed, kicking up the snow behind them. Shrieks of laughter burst from the children. A short way down the trail, the dogs settled into their cruising speed.

The impressive silence of the wild nature awed the young visitors, and no one wanted to spoil it with a human voice. Kelly watched the children closely in case they were cooling down, but saw only happy smiles. The party arrived back at the kennel with cries of excitement.

Conrad joked and rubbed his backside with exaggerated gestures. "That damned sled needs its shock absorbers testing."

"Bring a cushion next time."

Conrad adopted a more serious tone. "Is it hard to drive that bunch of dogs?"

"Easy enough," Kelly replied.

"I think I could like that."

"See, I told you. We'll give it a try some time," Byron said.

The men took care of the dogs. After Kelly petted them all then she showed the new puppies to the children. Later, she made hot chocolate for everyone and even discovered some leftover party cookies in the cupboard.

Conrad regaled the visitors with outlandish tales of the wilderness. Long after her guests disappeared down the road, Kelly stood in the yard.

It had been a fun day, and for a while, her mind hadn't been filled with disturbing thoughts of Tyler. The pain came back quickly enough. She recalled the conversation she'd had with Byron, in which she'd almost admitted that Tyler must have exploited her feelings for him to keep her here. That wouldn't have been fair as at no time had she even thought about leaving. She chewed her lip. *Well, Kelly, old girl, it's too late now to think about curbing your sex drive. You did behave like an adolescent with runaway hormones.* She sighed and went into the cabin to make more cookies, just in case she had other holiday visitors. The task would keep her from worrying about Tyler.

Next day, Kelly was shouldering her day-pack when the radiophone crackled.

"Hello Boreal Kennels. Are you there, Kelly? Over"

She ran to the microphone.

"Hi Byron. I'm about to take a team out. What's up?"

"Would you be willing to take some out-of-season tourists on sledding excursions into the wilderness?"

"You're serious?"

"Of course. I'm not joking."

"I haven't done it before."

"There's nothing to it. You have the dogs, and you know the trails. It's the same as taking Mary's grandkids."

"Tourists usually don't have winter clothes that are warm enough for this sort of activity."

"We'll scrounge something."

"But when and how would you get them?"

"That's my secret."

"Alright. Let's do it."

"That's my girl. Over and out."

Kelly pursed her lips. It would be futile to press Byron to find out what he had in mind. When that man focused on something, he went for it until he got it. If he said he'd bring tourists, he would. In the meantime, she should think about how to feed those potential visitors. This was a rare opportunity to earn some money, and almost as important, it would take her mind off Tyler.

Two days after Christmas, Kelly came back into the cabin to pick up her pack before taking a team out. The faint smell of fresh baking floated in the air and made her hungry. The radiophone crackled.

"Listen, Kelly. There's couple of American tourists in town. I reckon they must have gotten lost to be up here at this time of year. They really would love to see something of the back-country. It would make a memorable stay if you'd take them for a sled ride. Over."

Kelly chuckled. In his round about way, Byron announced her visitors without informing the whole neighborhood about their attempt to start a tour business. She played his hand.

"That sounds like fun. Bring them up, but make sure you find them some warm clothes. Over."

"Don't worry, hon, we're outfitting them with parkas and boots. I'll bring along the bear skin too."

"Great. We could take them to Ashini Point and back."

"Splendid. See you in a half-hour or so. Over and out."

Kelly laughed as she replace the microphone in its cradle. She welcomed the unexpected diversion. She packed a thermos and her still warm cookies, then went to prepare the sleds.

The tourists, an older couple from Texas, climbed down from Byron's truck.

"Ms. Jefferies? People call me Rex the Texan and here is Daphne, my wife of forty years."

The jovial Texan shook Kelly's hand vigorously. Tall and slim, he swam in his borrowed parka. Daphne's fitted better. She was beaming.

"We must look the height of fashion, but I'm sure the dogs won't mind. Can we see them?"

"Certainly. Come with me."

Kelly gave the visitors a tour of the kennel. She explained about the training and racing.

"So if you're entering that thousand-mile race, you have to run the dogs a thousand miles before?" Daphne asked.

"Not in one go. First we run the dogs for a few hours, then progressively we increase the time and distance. One day we train for speed, so we have a light sled and encourage the dogs to go as fast as they are willing."

"What if they aren't?" Rex asked.

"We go back home and try to figure out why

they're not willing and correct the cause. Those dogs love nothing better than to run. When they don't we have to find out if they're ailing or something."

"Of course, it's just like with kids. Then, after that?" Daphne, intensely curious, was impatient with her husband.

"The next day, we load the sled with all the stuff we'd need in the race plus some, and we run at a steady pace. As the date approaches, we camp out more and more to simulate the race schedule."

"Marvelous dedication!" Rex looked impressed.

When they got to see the puppies, Kelly thought they might not get anywhere soon until Byron reminded the visitors that the days were short.

After the couple learned how to put a harness on a dog, the party was finally on its way. Byron drove the second sled. On the return, both Rex and Daphne had to try standing on the runners. There were some hilarious moments, but they made it back without tipping the sleds.

They enjoyed themselves so much they pressed a generous check into Kelly's hand for their outing. Kelly began to protest. Byron waved her into silence.

"They're happy," he whispered. The couple went to look at the pups once more. "You can easily do this for a business, if you had a mind to, and charge twice that amount."

"I guess you're right. Tyler had thought about developing something on those lines."

"Yeah, I remember him saying so. A long time ago. Never did anything about it, though."

"Thank you, Miss Jefferies." The Texan gave her a broad smile. "You've been most hospitable. I can't wait to tell the folks back home. This is going to make them green with envy."

Alone again, Kelly hid the check in the empty dog-shaped crock Tyler used for keeping his money. Danny and Jack had excitedly dropped a few coins in it, "to help with the dog food". For some strange reason, she felt proud having earned some money from dog sledding. It had been fun too.

As if wanting to boost that pride, Byron brought a young family out for a short tour the next day. They too left a contribution in the crock. The family was followed the day after by others. The stream of visitors didn't end till New Year's Eve.

"How did you manage to find all those people wanting sled rides, Byron?"

"Nothing to it. We just spread the rumor that a former Miss America was willing to take people out on sledding excursions. The phone didn't stop ringing."

"Miss America indeed! And I thought my cookies were the attraction!"

Byron departed with the last guests, and Kelly's mind drifted back to the void created by Tyler's absence. Her throat tightened. Shaking the gloom from her mind, she finished her chores.

Somehow, seeing in the New Year without Tyler didn't feel right. She had become far too emotionally dependent on him. One of her New Year's resolutions was going to be to break free of this psychological reliance. It wouldn't be easy, but if she didn't, she was going to be hurt. Ukiok, lounging on the couch pricked up his ears and jumped down. She looked up from the dishes she was washing. "What do you want... Oh! someome's coming. Not more visitors?"

Three snowmobiles came to a halt at the cabin door. Five people in all climbed off the machines and stretched. Through the kitchen window, Kelly immediately recognized Byron and Conrad. She dried her hands and went to welcome them.

"Hello, Byron. Come in out of the cold. And who have you brought this time?"

"Friends," Byron said.

Smiling, Vicky and Nicole came up behind him.

"Since you're stuck out here on your own, we all thought we'd bring the New Year to you," Vicky said.

"My goodness! I'd forgotten it was New Year's Eve." That was a lie but she wasn't about to tell them how despondent she'd felt earlier on.

"How about a cookout?" Devon asked. "We've got steak, potatoes, wieners, marshmallows and I don't know what else."

"That's a great idea! Let me put on my parka." Kelly dressed warmly, and the group filed outside. In no time, they had a fire going. Kelly found an iron grill in the shed to use as a makeshift barbecue for the steaks and wieners. She brought a huge pot of steaming coffee from the cabin. Ukiok made off with a mouthfull of wienners. Peels of laughter rose to the overhanging pine branches and was echoed by a howl from the dogs. Kelly tied the thief by the door.

"I hope you don't mind, but we've invited two other guys along," Byron said. "They should be here soon. Andy and Garth. You probably remember them from the Christmas party."

"The two Wildlife officers from the region south of here, right?"

"Correct. They had to attend a meeting in the capital, otherwise they'd have been here already. Poor suckers! Can you imagine anyone scheduling a meeting on New Year's Eve?"

He had barely spoken when the dogs announced the arrival of the missing guests.

"What a racket the dogs make!" Nicole put her hands over her ears hidden by a wooly toque.

"It takes some getting used to," Conrad yelled over the din. "But they sure make an excellent early warning system."

A government truck appeared over the crest of the hill and parked between the cabin and the dogs' compound. Two men Kelly recognized as Andy and Garth jumped out.

Kelly gasped in surprise when a third man emerged from the truck and shot an angry glance at the group around the fire. "Tyler!" she shouted. "You're back."

Tyler acknowledged her presence with an awkward wave of the hand. He turned and yanked his bag from the back of the truck. Without giving her or the revelers a second glance, he strode toward the cabin. Kelly ran and caught up with him. When she was level with him, he stopped suddenly.

"Is this what you've been doing while I've been away, entertaining the entire neighborhood?" He left her dumbfounded in the snow. At the cabin door, he bent down and released Ukiok. Master and dog disappeared inside. Undeterred, Kelly pushed her way in.

"Tyler, it's New Year's Eve! I don't know why you're getting so hot under the collar. Our friends decided to come up and spend it with me. There's lots of good food." She placed her hand on his sleeve. "Please, Tyler, come and join us." She regretted the words the moment they escaped. It sounded so absurd, inviting him in his own home.

He tossed his parka on the couch. "I've got things to attend to."

"Attend to them next year. You can't stay in the cabin while your friends are outside."

Tyler whirled on her. "Just watch me!" He ripped off his shirt.

The sight of muscles cording across his broad back as he bent to unzip his bag sent a liquid shiver over her skin. Kelly shook her head in disbelief and leaned against the doorjamb. All the joy that Byron and the others had brought was snuffed out.

Despite her misery, her body clamored for his touch. Her heart cried out for the buoyant and carefree days before his departure. She craved a kind word, a look from him, anything that could give her hope. He ignored her pleading eyes and stomped off to the bathroom. The door slammed shut behind him.

Kelly smoothed her palms over her eyes in a desperate gesture to ease her wretchedness. Sensing that it was pointless to wait for Tyler, she rejoined the merrymakers around the fire. As the laughter and welcoming cheers to the New Year exploded around her, she watched the northern lights dance frenetically in the dark sky.

"It's too bad we don't have mistletoe," Byron said in her ear

"Mistletoe is for Christmas, Byron. We're celebrating the New Year."

"Who cares? You're evading me." His casual tone carried an underlying streak of seriousness.

"We're not back on that, are we?"

"You can't fault a guy for trying. What's got into old Kade?"

"Have you ever seen him relaxed and ready to enjoy life?"

"Yes. Just before he went off, he really seemed to be happy."

"As you can see, it didn't last long, did it?"

"How come Tyler isn't out here?" Conrad asked.

"A bit tired, that's all," Byron replied.

"Is he giving you a rough time, Kelly? Maybe Andy should have left him at the bus depot in the capital."

"I'm glad your friend gave him a ride," Kelly said. "It saved me a trip." Mentally, she added, *I think I prefer to put up with his black moods as long as I can breathe the same air as he does.*

When the friends concluded they had truly welcomed in the new year, the men doused the fire. Kelly and the other women carried the leftover food into the cabin. She opened the door cautiously. There on the couch lay Tyler's inert form, shrouded in a comforter. Vicky and Nicole looked at each other and shook their heads. Kelly motioned them not to leave the food on the table, pointing to Ukiok's expectant face.

After everyone had gone, Kelly took Ukiok back to his pen. He licked her face and curled up in the snow while the other dogs poked their noses out of their houses. Seeing that no food was offered, the noses disappeared. When Kelly went inside again, Tyler hadn't moved. Without noise, she got ready for bed, hoping Tyler would be in a more reasonable state of mind in the morning.

Kelly willed herself to wake before Tyler. For the first time ever, she was successful. She soundlessly went outside to check on the dogs. On her return, Tyler was up, slouched on the edge of the sofa. His hair was awry and his chin sported two days of growth. The sight of him, disheveled as he was sent Kelly's heart turning somersaults.

"Good morning, Tyler. Do you have any plans for today?"

"Maybe I should ask you what social events you've got organized?"

His belligerent tone distressed her. She was tempted to lash out at him in an equally bad-tempered way, but refrained. Instead, a wicked smile lit up her face. "As a matter of fact, I've arranged to take all twelve Huskies right around Mount McKinley and party with some real hunks of Alaskan mushers."

The look he gave her altered subtly while the silence stretched.

"Okay, okay. You win. I'm sorry I'm such lousy company. You know, it's not too late to change your mind about working for me. If you want to go, you can. You don't have to put up with my surly moods."

Kelly watched him wrestle with some powerful emotion. "I thought you'd learned by now I'm not the kind of person who reneges on a promise, let alone a contract. In some funny, twisted way, I've got used to you by now."

Her remark was met by a flicker of amusement in his eyes. Just as suddenly, it vanished. He propped his chin on his hands. "I just don't think I can run those races." He didn't look at her. "It would be too much for the Inuit dogs."

"No way, Tyler! They're raring to go. You can't give up now. There are only four weeks before the Yukon Quest."

"In which case, I'll take the Huskies. The maximum allowed is fourteen. And I'll scrap the Iditarod."

"That's not right. You need to enter both races. Your two teams are ready." Resolve heightened her voice.

Tyler shook his head. "No. I won't be able to run both. I never discussed it with you before, but I don't have enough money to afford the expenses of both races. If I cancel now, I'll get back some of the registration fees. You've got wages coming to you."

For a brief instant, Kelly was too surprised to speak. "Wages? You don't need to worry about paying me! I live here free, as it is."

"Handlers are supposed to get paid for their work."

"Well, I'm not your average handler."

"Don't I know that!" A touch of grim laughter colored his voice.

"If you forget about paying me, you can cover the race expenses, correct?"

"Wrong."

Kelly dropped to his side. She caressed his hands, his hair, and drew his face toward her, touching his lips with hers. Reluctantly, his mouth moved to possess hers. He stood up. Kelly fell back, confused.

"No, we can't-" His words were cut short by the radiophone. He made no move to answer the call.

Hurt by his rejection, Kelly went to the phone as Byron's voice boomed from the speaker. "Hi, anyone home? It's Byron, here. Over."

"Yes. Kelly speaking."

"Great. Sweetheart, there are two parties of southerners in town. Can I bring them up?"

"Certainly. Give me an hour to prepare. How many?"

"Six in all. They'd like to have a taste of the wilds."

"We could take them to the old Indian encampment and back. We'd return by five or six o'clock tonight. I'll pack some food."

"Good. We've rounded up some clothes for them. See you in an hour. Over and out."

Kelly put the microphone back in place and smiled.

"What the hell's all that about?" Even the dogs didn't snarl the way Tyler did.

"Boreal Sled Dog Adventures and Company. Your new business venture."

"Are you crazy? I've got training to do. And what d'you think you're doing, feeding six people?" His brows knitted fiercely.

"They pay." Kelly grabbed the old earthenware crock from the counter and slammed it on the table harder than she had intended to. "Take a peek inside!"

With a quizzical look in her direction, Tyler removed the lid. A pile of checks and bills spilled onto the table. Tyler's jaw sagged. "Where did all this money come from?"

"From satisfied customers."

"We're training dogs to race. Pleasure excursions will ruin them." Despite his outburst, his eyes remained fixed on the money. An expression of disbelief spread over his rugged features.

Kelly remained unperturbed. "I think we agreed before that the dogs are not merely running machines. They need variety to keep in top form. I don't see what's the problem. Their training is not suffering. They go out with a full weight, more than you'd carry in the race, so it certainly helps build up their stamina. The money from the tourists will pay for the race expenses."

"What about the dogs' speed?"

"The freighters keep going at the same pace. I think we should take a team of huskies on today's outing and see how they handle it. I presume you'll want to drive a sled. Byron will drive one and I'll take another."

Tyler raked his hands through his hair, looked at the money again, and shook his head. "I don't know what to think."

"Then, don't bother to think. Just accept it. Oh, by the way, I've sold two of the older pups to Devon Santoni. That is, unless you disapprove. Get dressed. I'll cook us some breakfast."

Tyler hesitated, then picked up his gear and disappeared into the bathroom.

Neither of them lingered over breakfast. Out in the compound, Tyler didn't protest when she told him what to do. An air of amazement still marked his face.

One hour after the call, Byron's truck, closely followed by a car full of visitors, pulled into the yard. Tyler fumed silently to see the camaraderie between

Kelly and his best friend, although his respect for her soared as he watched how graciously she welcomed the visitors and took them on a tour of the kennel.

"Murdoch, whose damned idea was it, these tours?"

"Nobody's. It happened quite by accident. First it was Mary and Fred's grandkids wanting to go for a little outing, then a couple of Texans."

"She didn't make Mary's grandkids pay, did she?"

"Of course not. The kids enjoyed themselves so much, they wanted to help buy food for the dogs. We couldn't stop them dropping their allowance in the pot. As for the other people, they were only too happy to pay for the excursions."

"They pay well."

"They sure do. There was no question of them not wanting to. Kelly sure knows how to operate an efficient business. Customer satisfaction all the way."

"What about you? You've got your own job to attend to. You can't come and drive a sled for nothing." Tyler's dry tone resonated in the cool air.

Byron suppressed a laugh. "I love being out with the dogs. We're not too busy right now at the office. I don't mind using some of my free time and days off to help out here."

Tyler still seething, had no doubt about the reason his friend was so eager to help Kelly, but he composed himself.

"How do you manage to round up all these people?

"Trade secret. Actually, my brother and his wife run a travel agency. I just happened to mention sled rides to them."

"You're taken with her, aren't you?" Tyler couldn't disguise the anguish that gripped him.

"Kelly? Of course I am. Who wouldn't be?" His smug look provoked Tyler, who, with teeth clenched, shook his head.

Everything was ready, and the passengers installed

in the sleds. Kelly flushed with pleasure when Tyler motioned her to take the lead. Driving the team of twelve huskies, she kept a close eye on their performance. Mostly, she thought about Tyler bringing up the rear with half the freighters. He was smiling again, a marked contrast to the night before.

She hadn't realized that part of his problem was a shortage of funds, so much that he had thought to pull out of the Iditarod. With the money she was making from the tourist excursions, optimism blossomed once more.

By Lake Tootkoo, the halfway point in the tour, the party stopped and built a huge fire of dead pine branches.

"What are those big tracks? Is that a bear?" asked a visitor, anxiety in her voice.

A half smile lit up Tyler's face. "Bears hibernate in winter. This is a wolf following close in the tracks of a moose."

A woman shrieked and everyone turned round.

"I'm sorry, but you said there are wolves. That's dangerous. I read about them in *Call of the Wild.*"

"You mustn't believe the stories Jack London wrote. Wolves are actually shy of people and will run away as soon as they sense you, long before you can see them. In fact, sighting a wolf is a rare occurrence."

"Still, I don't think I'd like to camp out."

Her companions chuckled and her husband put his arm around her. She sighed with relief. Byron pointed to the far shore of the lake. All eyes focused on the brown shape.

"Caribou," Tyler said.

Kelly pulled out a pair of binoculars and passed it to the guests. For a long while, they watched the heavily antlered animals paw the snow to reach lichens and grasses beneath.

Kelly's heart beat with renewed pride as Tyler willingly shared his love of nature. This was a side of him she'd not seen before. She had only guessed at its existence. Along with the pride, there was another feeling, that of quiet desperation. If only he would love her the way she loved him, unreservedly and unconditionally. For now, she had to settle for the heady pleasure of being with him.

Later that evening, when Byron had left to escort the tired but contented tourists back to town, Tyler sat at the kitchen table. His eyes were glued to the check in front of him. He could hardly believe the figure. Long ago, he'd vaguely sensed that a winter tourism business could be developed. That was as far as he had taken the idea. Now, almost without effort, Kelly had started it, right under his nose. Next spring, though, she'd be gone, and he would slide back into his old negative rut.

"Is there enough to cover both races?" Kelly's voice interrupted his thoughts.

"Just about."

"Good. I'll bet we get a few more tourists in the next couple of weeks."

"The travel agent will be wanting a cut of the profits."

"Not at the moment. All the sister-in-law does is give out Byron's phone number. If we go one step further and set up a formal business, then she'd treat us just like any other holiday package and charge a commission. The man reckons the market is unlimited."

"What would setting up properly entail?" Tyler was testing her, wanting to hear her describe the dream he himself had relinquished.

"Print brochures, offer tours of various lengths and so on. Naturally, we'd have to supply warm clothes, boots and other equipment. Some tourists might like to ski alongside the sled. Then there are those people who might want to try skijoring. The idea of being hauled on skis by a dog or two really appeals to some people. Everything involves planning and a wise investment of capital. It can only help finance the racing. Down the road, we might think about providing accommodation by building a few log cabins for the guests."

"You're saying we should go into the hotel business?" His face became genuinely alarmed.

Kelly laughed. "Not right away. At first, we could get a couple of wall tents and put woodstoves in them. It wouldn't suit everybody, but a lot of people like to feel close to nature. They don't expect a real hotel. More of a wilderness lodge."

He loved it each time she used the word "we" in her plans. This fascinating woman had a way of weaving her spell about him, enmeshing him with soft words. The craving for her flared again in his loins. She must have read his mind, for he saw a pink blush invade her smooth cheeks. They fell silent, each looking into the eyes of the other. He speculated on whether she was gripped by the same urge as he was. Memories of their lovemaking surged into his brain. He clenched his fists to prevent himself from reaching out to her. In the morning, they would both regret their actions. But how he loved to see her smile.

Tenseness twisted his stomach. The old yearning for the sweet warmth of her body rolled over him. And she was there, vibrantly close yet so distant. He had to keep her at arm's length otherwise, he'd make a fool of himself. Now that he had admitted the fact that racing didn't provide enough of an income, reason was telling him to push it aside and get a job somewhere in a city. Then he'd be able to claim his son for the holidays. The judge made himself clear on the matter. If he couldn't pay child support, he couldn't visit either.

He couldn't drag Kelly into all this mess. She had to go on with her racing career. The beautiful dream of a sledding tour business remained just that, a dream. He couldn't give up his child. Something indefinable pulled him toward the little tyke. It was just like bonding with a puppy. The moment he had held the infant in his arms a strange feeling had overpowered him. For the first year, it was he who had fed, changed, smiled and talked to the baby. Tyler grasped his forehead. He pressed hard on his eyeballs, remembering how gentle the dogs had been when they had licked Glenn's face, and how much he had laughed. The year had been one of tremendous happiness. With his young friend Jerome acting as a handler and babysitter, Tyler had won a few major races.

Everything came crashing down when Gloria had reappeared. She couldn't live in the cabin, didn't even try. One day she was gone and took their son with her. He shook his head to clear the bitterness of the long battle that ensued, one that he had lost.

One day his son would grow up and question why his father wasn't there for him. Tyler wanted to be part of his life and watch him grow to manhood. This Christmas visit he'd wrenched out of his ex had been a revelation for him. The joy of having his son cling to him, and the overpowering emotion of holding his hand in his, flooded back into his brain. That was worth any sacrifice. Maybe he could keep a few dogs?

For now, he had to tell Kelly about his lightning trip to California, tell her this was his last season, tell her there'd never be a Boreal Sled Dog Adventures Company. The pain gouged a raw path through his heart.

He closed his eyes and held his breath. The only sounds were the ticking of the clock and the logs shifting in the stove.

He stiffled his yearning, enven though it took all the willpower he could muster. As much as he tried, he couldn't subdue his needs. He had to make sure that she didn't get attached to him. The first thing to do was to put an end to the short training runs that permitted him to be back by early evening. That was a perfectly legitimate excuse. Close to the big race, he could ill afford any distraction from his schedule. It was true of course, as true that he had to distance himself from Kelly. Then he must stop lusting for her and stop making love to her.

Tyler closed his eyes for a long while, then threw off his stupor. He needed to go outside in the cold to clear his mind and body. That was the northern version of a cold shower. Kelly stood up at the same time. With a few inches between them, the heat rose to an unbearable degree. By some deep instinct, he pulled her to him. One last time, he told himself. His mouth came down hard on hers. She gave a meek cry of protest, even though she parted her lips to permit him to invade her moistness. Tyler groaned.

Their bodies molded one against the other. His hands explored her back and the swell of her buttocks. He lifted his head. His heavy-lidded eyes burned with unspoken passion.

A sharp gasp broke the heavy silence. Tyler dropped his hands and stepped back. Kelly swayed.

With a will she didn't know she possessed, she stumbled to her room with a soft "Good night."

Abandoned and unfulfilled, her thirst for him flushed red on her skin. The sting of his rebuff wounded her, but a wild hope that he'd relent slowed her few steps even more.

After a moment of hesitation, she lifted the doorcurtain. Unable to comprehend his rejection, her mind reasoned that it was better not to indulge in lovemaking. Her body felt otherwise. She hungered for him. Not just his body. She wanted to possess his heart. Love, she'd discovered, was a terrible torment when it wasn't returned.

Awakened from an uneasy sleep, Kelly had already slipped out to check on the dogs. She prepared breakfast and wondered whether she should speak. A look at Tyler's troubled features discouraged her. Silent and somber, Tyler bolted his food, grabbed his pack and left the cabin.

A long sigh, almost a sob in its intensity, relieved the pressure in Kelly's chest. She admonished herself. Something upsetting had happened to him during his brief absence. It must have been traumatic for him to take her in his arms and then recoil. Since he didn't want to discuss the problem, she could do nothing more than treat him as her boss. The jolt of that resolution shook her to the core. She wasn't one to turn love on and off, and that was exactly what she was trying to do. Fortunately, he'd only seen the physical attraction, not suspecting for one moment she harbored deep feelings for him. It might be difficult, but she knew she could restrain the impulses and desire to make love.

For the time being, the pups required her attention and she gave herself fully to her furry companions and the tasks in the kennel.

Three days later, Tyler returned. The dark stubble on his chin made Kelly forget her resolve for one short moment. An aroma of woodsmoke pervaded the room as he removed his parka. A picture of the solitary man, brooding by a campfire passed through Kelly's mind, but she dismissed it. Only a log crackling in the stove and the bubbling of the cooking pot broke the silence. Soon, the smell of butter and garlic invaded the cabin mingling oddly with outdoor scents.

Kelly served moose stew and the pasta she had made earlier in the day. After a few days on the trail, a musher is ready to down a healthy serving of solid food. Tyler's first words were to thank her. For the first time, he appeared to relax. Kelly began clearing the dishes. Tyler got to his feet.

"I'll wash."

"Thanks, I'll dry."

She didn't know whether to laugh or cry. At least he was being civil. Maybe he'd talk when they sat down after stoking the fire.

He examined the ganglines that Kelly had made.

"Pretty fancy handiwork!" His approval was genuine. He opened his old race notebooks and appeared to concentrate on comparing the race strategies he had used. Kelly picked up a book.

On the couch, Ukiok rolled over and snuggled with consummate enjoyment deeper into the bed comforter. Of everyone in the cabin, only the dog was perfectly at ease. The humans both sensed the tension in the air.

Tyler was chewing the end of his pen, but still he didn't talk. He bit the pen so hard the plastic cracked in his mouth. In disgust, Tyler spat out the fragments.

Kelly looked up from her book. "Anything I can help with?"

He hesitated. "Not at the moment."

Palpable stress filled the room. Kelly had to curb her spontaneous nature which wanted to tell him to spit out what was troubling him. Instead, she went to her bedroom.

Training came to an end one week before the start of the Yukon Quest Race, which this year started in Fairbanks, Alaska, and ended in Whitehorse, Yukon Territory. During that time, the dogs were allowed to frolic and play, running free in small groups or sledding just a few miles a day. The dogs chased each other and cavorted in the fresh snow, but the sight of a harness attracted them to the gate raring to go.

Tyler and Kelly spent all their time packaging food for both canines and humans. Then he drove the load to Whitehorse. From there it would be flown to the various checkpoints.

Although the atmosphere had been one of companionable work, Kelly sensed a reserve in Tyler she couldn't explain. A whole day without him was a welcome respite. He had not long gone when she heard a snowmobile rush up the trail. Her mood lifted. She darted ouside to greet her visitor.

"Hello Byron! Have you been hiding?"

"The territory we have to cover is huge. How's the big man?"

"Gone to the capital."

"Ah! Getting the food out. Is he still grouchy?"

"It's a guarded peace. He's making an effort to be sociable."

"He baffles me."

"I think he has a problem but he won't share it."

"I don't know how you put up with him when you could have a guy like me."

Kelly laughed and opened her mouth to speak.

Byron cut her off. "No don't say it. I know, but I

can't help wondering if love doesn't wear a little thin when it's always brushed off."

A long sigh was her only reply.

"Anyway, I'll be here to help with the tourists on Saturday."

"Thanks. Since you're here, come see the pups. I was about to take them a little way down the trail before it gets dark."

"How can I refuse?"

Carefree laughter and yipping sounds echoed among the pines. Snowballs made good toys for pups to run after, grab and then drop it in disgust. Back in their pen with the reward of a biscuit, they scooped big mouthful of snow.

A nostalgic look in his eyes, Byron took his leave.

The day of Tyler's departure for the big race arrived. He and Kelly drove the Inuit dogs to Whitehorse. His friend Andy had offered to fly him and the dogs from Whitehorse to Fairbanks in his private Cessna.

When the dogs were loaded, Andy closed the cargo door. There, all set."

"You be careful, now," Kelly said.

"I sure will. Your precious dogs are safe with me. That's what you're concerned about, isn't it?"

His teasing brought a smile to Kelly's lips. "Right."

"I've been part of the Iditarod Air Force for years."

They laughed.

"Who decided on the name?" Kelly asked.

"I don't really know. One of those things that starts as a joke and then sticks."

"It's well named for the number of planes that help the racers."

"I treat it as my vacation. You know what they say in Alaska?"

"Tell me."

"There are three holidays: Christmas, New Year and the Iditarod."

"What exactly do you do after you get there?"

"Myself and the other volunteers fly in the

supplies. We patrol the length of the race trail checking on racers and teams. We fly out injured or tired dogs. We carry the media types. You name it, I've done it."

"It makes you wonder how they coped in the early years of the race."

"You could say they were like acrobats without a safety net."

"Do you do the same for the Yukon Quest?"

"No. We make food drops, that's all. We're on stand-by, though, in case of emergency. The Quest is still a rugged, no-frills race. Man against untamed nature."

"What about woman against untamed nature?"

Andy gave a sheepish grin. "That too, Kelly. A few women have taken part in that race. But as far as I know, no woman has come close to winning."

"Well, there's always a first time, isn't there?"

"So there should be." He glanced at a figure leaving the terminal. "Here's Tyler coming now." Andy climbed into the cockpit and fired up the motor.

Kelly stepped back. Her pulse fluttered as she watched Tyler stride across the tarmac. As usual, he was bareheaded, his coat open to the wind. He came up to her and pulled her against him. The wash from the propeller blew her hair in his face. Quivering with anticipation she waited for his kiss. He hungrily took her offered lips. For one exquisite moment, time and the outside world stood still. "Good luck!" she whispered.

"Thanks. See you back here in Whitehorse."

"I'll expect to greet a winner."

Tyler smiled. Kelly's heart leaped in her chest, the runway suddenly illuminated. He put a finger on her lips then on his and clambered aboard. The door slammed shut and the plane taxied to the end of the runway. From the windswept observation deck, she watched the plane carrying Tyler and the Inuit dogs she was so fond of, gather speed and lift into the air. It banked steeply and pointed his nose toward Alaska. She remained until the tiny speck disappeared into the clear northern sky.

It was just a good luck kiss. The refrain went around in her head. Just a good luck kiss. He meant nothing by it.

On her way back home, she stopped at Fletcher Creek for supplies, and called on Byron.

"The race will be covered on radio, won't it?" she asked.

"Sure thing. It's a big event up here."

"The only problem up at the cabin is that we get such lousy reception. Tyler says it's due to the shielding effect of the mountains. And we have only a battery-operated receiver." Kelly reddened, realizing how easily she used "we"' to describe her life with Tyler.

Byron must have noticed for he gave her a grin. "You can always come down here to take in the coverage."

"Thanks, I might do that."

With her thoughts focused on Tyler, Kelly adapted to her new routine. In the evenings, her duties done, she'd drive to Fletcher Creek to listen to the race reports with Byron. Some nights when the temperatures plummeted and the truck refused to start, she covered the distance by dog sled.

"How is this cold weather affecting the race?" she asked.

Byron pulled a face. "It's not a happy picture. Two mushers scratched today. A few others are about to."

"The race won't be canceled, will it?"

"Unlikely. Most teams are doing well. Tyler is still among the front runners. There are about ten of them, all jockeying for position."

The special race report came on the radio. Kelly glued her ear to the speaker, impatient to catch any mention of Tyler. There was good news and bad. The front racers had left Eagle, Alaska, the last checkpoint before Dawson City, and were toiling over Eagle Summit before winding their way down to the ice-covered Yukon River. From there, the race trail followed the river to the Canadian border. The bad news was that the fierce blizzard sweeping the area showed no sign of abating. Part way along the lonely trail was a cabin, whose occupants served the mushers hot drinks as they passed through. Otherwise, it was pure wilderness all the way.

In the swirling snow, Tyler had trouble seeing the red trail markers. Only occasionally would a scrap of fluorescent ribbon assure him he was on track. Without slackening their pace, the dogs kept their noses to the ground. He wondered what Kelly would say under such conditions. *Keep awake and put your trust in the dogs,* most likely. The image of her smiling green eyes danced before him like a beautiful mirage.

Heartened by the thought that she was possibly thinking of him at that very moment, he drove on into the worsening storm. He came upon a team halted on the side. Tyler slowed his dogs to a crawl. "Everything okay?" His voice hardly carried above the shriek of the wind.

The other musher raised a hand in recognition. "Yeah, Tyler. I reckon I'm going to bivouac down right here until it eases off. My dogs are protesting."

"You're probably smarter than I am. I feel the urge to push on. My dogs are eager to run." Tyler lifted his foot off the brake. His dogs bent once more into their harnesses.

An hour later Tyler was forced to stop again when he came across a team blocking the way. He anchored his sled and ordered the dogs to lie down. He stepped off the runners and approached the musher.

"Trouble?"

The other musher's face was haggard with fatigue. "Got to take a rest. Can't get my tent up in this wind."

"Let's secure the dogs first. I'll help."

Words translated themselves into immediate action.

"Thanks, Kade. Do you want to share with me until this crazy storm dies out?"

"Thanks, no." He tugged his parka hood to

protect his face, climbed back onto the runners of his sled and set off again. It dawned on him that the man he'd just helped was Hans Reesink. Hans had been out in front. Tyler could hardly believe that there was now nobody left between him and the Dawson City checkpoint.

Smiling at his dogs, he called out, "All right, my friends, we're up in front!" Capitor and Tekoone, his leaders, were barely visible through the curtain of thick snow. For the race, he ran the dogs two-by-two in tandem formation. He'd found that by doing away with necklines, and having the dogs linked to the center gangline only by the traces attached to their harnesses, they were less restricted and pulled harder. It wasn't the accepted practice but nobody had complained.

His lack of sleep eventually began to take its toll. A long-distance dog musher has many tasks to accomplish during the short rest periods. The race schedule must be adapted to the dogs' requirements, not his own. Tyler could hear Kelly telling him, "When you feed the dogs, feed yourself." Shamefully, he had not followed that advice over the last two days. Now the effects of lack of nourishment and rest were showing. He removed one hand from its mitten, and fumbled in the sled bag in search of the cookies and dried bananas. The high-sugar food gave him a new burst of energy. He even sang to his team above the roaring tempest.

The dogs' sudden change of direction almost pitched him off the sled. As if of one mind, the entire team swerved off the trail and hurtled down a steep slope. Tyler's shouts were futile to stop the runaway dogs. In the deep snow, the sled brake had minimal effect.

Out of desperation, he was about to flip the sled over to drag the team to a halt, when he saw the dark shape of a man laying face down in the snow. The dogs slackened their stride and stopped a few yards from the motionless figure. Tyler recognized that the man was not a race competitor. There no signs of a team or sled tracks. Tyler jumped off and ran to him.

"Hey! Wake up! Are you hurt?"

"I dunno," the man groaned. "I'm god-awful tired."

"You're freezing to death!"

"I got lost in the storm. Say, you're Tyler Kade! Remember me? I'm Rob Larter, photojournalist with Federated Press."

"You won't be much good to them frozen solid. I seem to recall we've exchanged a few choice words in the past. Let's get you back on your feet. How come you're here at the bottom of a ravine?"

"Stupid snowmobile broke down."

"Where is it?"

"I abandoned the piece of junk back a ways. Figured I'd hike to the next checkpoint."

"Have you the slightest idea how far it is to Dawson City?"

Larter smiled lamely, his speech slurring. "I was hoping to hitch a ride."

Tyler groaned. The damned fool! His former irritation toward the media flared briefly. He went to his sled and rearranged the load. "Get in the sled bag. You've got hypothermia."

The man did as he was told and stumbled onto the sled. Tyler made him drink from one of the thermos bottles he carried.

"That's good. Warms me up already!"

"Now don't fall asleep. Talk, or sing, but keep up the noise."

Now Tyler turned his attention to getting his team and their load out of the ravine. The dogs were fully responsive to his commands. They stretched themselves, and with Tyler pushing from behind, they dragged the heavy sled back up the slope.

Chapter 8

To fill the void left by Tyler's absence Kelly spent more time than perhaps she ought playing with the young pups. No one could feel depressed when surrounded by seven exuberant little dogs.

The chores finished, Kelly was about to go in when pitiful cries reached her ears. "The pups!" She turned and ran to the kennel house. The cries came from behind the swinging door to the outside. Laughing, Kelly lifted the door and scooped up the puppy.

He wriggled in her arms as Kelly returned him to his concerned mother. "You're almost big enough to live outside, but we'll wait until the weather warms up a bit. In the meantime, try not to get stuck again in the exit tunnel." Disregarding her injunction, the pup dashed back into the tunnel followed by his littermates. Kelly laughed. Nine weeks old and already so independent and cocky! Arnavik made guttural sounds to call her offspring. They pushed on the swinging door and rushed to nuzzle her mouth in the hope she'd regurgitate some food for them. With a wistful sigh, Kelly left them to their play. She could spend the whole day amused by their antics.

In the cabin, someone was trying to get through on the radiophone. Kelly picked up the mike. "Hello. This is Boreal Kennel, Alpha Dog. Over."

A shrill feminine voice came though. "Who am I speaking to? Over."

"Kelly Jefferies. Tyler's dog handler. Over."

"Put Tyler on."

"Who's calling?" Kelly made an effort to be polite,

despite the woman's hostile tone.

There was a throaty laugh at the other end. "Gloria. Tyler's wife, that's who."

Kelly's jaw dropped. She gripped the edge of the counter, unable to believe what she'd just heard.

"Hello? Are you still there? Press the talk button."

Kelly took a deep breath. "I'm sorry. I'm not used to this machine."

"Yeah. Stupid contraption. I never got the hang of it, either. Now let me speak to Tyler."

"Tyler's away in a race. May I take a message?" Kelly was amazed she could still talk. Tyler, married! Shock wrapped itself around her in an icy cloud.

"You sound young. You must be his latest girlfriend."

"No, I'm not!" Kelly yelled before she realized she hadn't pressed the send button. A steel vise tightened around her chest. "No, I'm not his girlfriend," she said in a strained voice. "I only work for him."

"All the same, Tyler has quite an eye for a cute little behind. Too bad he isn't here with me tonight. Funny, over Christmas he didn't mention anyone called Kelly or that he'd got himself a new handler."

"He didn't? He must have had other things on his mind." Kelly leaned against the cabin wall. Another piece of the Tyler Kade jigsaw puzzle just dropped into place. She'd solved the mystery of where he'd spent Christmas.

"You can say that again! I have to speak to him to tell him that I'm sending Glenn. It'll do the kid good to spend some time with him."

"Glenn?"

"Our kid. Tyler's son."

The restriction cramping Kelly's ribs tightened another notch. Tyler's son!

"Does Tyler know about the arrangement?" The effort to be polite brought beads of perspiration to Kelly's forehead. "He didn't mention anything."

"I wouldn't expect him to discuss his private life with you. But, no, he doesn't. I've changed my mind about Glenn not visiting his father."

"When are you sending the child? It may be some time before Tyler gets back."

"He's on a flight north tomorrow. He's due in Whitehorse at three in the afternoon. Tell Tyler he's got to meet him at the airport."

"Impossible! Tyler's running the Yukon Quest. He's still on the trail in the middle of nowhere."

"Quit stalling, won't you, girl? Get a message to him. They've got planes for an emergency. That's what this is. Tyler's got to accept his responsibilities. I'm flying off to New York with a good friend an hour after Glenn boards his plane."

Kelly was at a loss. If she put up an objection, Tyler's wife would start phoning the race organizers. There was no saying what might happen then. The rancor in the woman's voice hinted that she was capable of anything.

Hurriedly and hiding her panic, she articulated, "Don't worry. I'll meet Glenn at the airport."

"Are you capable of looking after a kid?"

"I look after forty dogs. I guess I can care for a child. How old is he?"

"Six. He's used to baby-sitters. You have to watch out for that pesky asthma of his. It's a real nuisance."

The brittle tone from the speaker did nothing to inspire Kelly's sympathy.

"I'll do my best."

The woman cut off the transmission without the slightest word of thanks. Kelly collapsed on the couch, her head buried in her hands.

Tyler! With a wife and a child? That explained his behavior. That explained why he didn't want to be tied down. He already was!

Shock gradually gave way to fury. She pounded her fists into the cushions. Damn the man for putting her through such emotional turmoil! Damn the man for making her fall in love with him!

Her fit of anger eventually ran out of steam. It gave way to worry over practical problems. She had committed herself to going to the capital tomorrow to meet this young boy. How to get there? Below a certain temperature, a truck engine simply refused to start unless it was kept warm by an electric heater. The motor might be fitted with one, but the cabin had no electricity. To seek advice, Kelly went to the radio and called Byron

"Byron, I need to start the truck. It's frozen."

"Use a tiger torch. Tyler is bound to have one."

"What's a tiger torch?"

"It's a... Look, hang on, I'll come up. See you shortly."

When she heard the whine of Byron's snowmobile, Kelly dressed and went out to meet him.

"Sorry to force you out on a cold evening."

"No problem. It doesn't bother me. There must be a tiger torch in the kennel room, plus a tank of propane."

Kelly used her flashlight to light the way. In one corner of the kennel room Byron found what he was looking for.

"This is a tiger torch. It's just a metal pipe with a handle on one end and a burner on the other. Connect the rubber hose to the propane cylinder and light the burner. When it's going properly, you crawl under the truck and heat up the oil pan. Simple."

"Isn't it dangerous?"

"Not as long as you don't touch any wires or fuel lines. Here, I'll light up and start that beast of a truck for you. So, you're taking me up on my offer to go and meet Tyler at Dawson?"

Fearfull of imposing on her friend, Kelly had hesitated to accept his offer to look after the dogs, but she'd love to be there to see Tyler and take care of the dogs for him while he rested. Now with the arrival of the child that was out of the question.

"I can't!"

"You can if I take care of the place while you're gone. This bad weather is slowing down the race. Tyler is still up front, but anything can happen on the final run to the finish line in Whitehorse. If you're in Dawson to help him that might be enough to give him the winning edge. He'd be able to get a good night's rest."

"You don't know the all of it, Byron. Tyler's wife just phoned. Their six-year-old son is arriving by plane tomorrow afternoon. I'm in shock. I didn't know he was even married."

Byron gave a low whistle. "He is? That comes as a surprise to me too, and I thought I was his buddy. He never told you?"

"Not a word."

"What are you going to do?"

"About the kid? I don't have any choice but to be at the airport to meet him."

"Then what will you do with him?"

"Keep him here with me, I guess. That's why Tyler's going to have to cope on his own in Dawson City."

"Just hang on a minute. We might just be able to do something. What if Vicky looked after him until you came back?"

"I can't ask Vicky to look after the kid. She's got her teaching job to do."

"It's mid-term break, Vicky is free, and I can take some time off work."

"That's really generous of you, Byron, but-"

"No buts! We'll do it."

Kelly detected the warmth in Byron's voice, though she also saw the hint of sadness in his eyes.

"Tyler's...wife said the boy has asthma. That's pretty serious. It can be life threatening."

"Yes, especially when he takes a few gulps of refrigerated Yukon air. I hope he has medication with him. Why don't you ask Vicky. She must have experience of asthma among her schoolkids."

"I'll do that."

"But first, we gotta get this truck warmed up."

Byron slid partly under the truck and trained the propane torch on the motor's oil pan. After a few minutes, he cut off the propane, climbed into the driver's seat and turned the ignition. The engine protested but cranked over and burst into life.

"There, you're all set. We'll just let it run for a while. It should start fine for you in the morning."

"Thanks."

"Call in at my place, and I'll follow you to Whitehorse in my truck. Vicky and I could fetch the brat on our own, but he's probably been told he's going to be met by you. Best not give the little guy too much of a shock. As it is, he's going to think he's dropped off the edge of the world. Hopefully, he'll agree to stay with Vicky."

"I hope so. Have you had dinner?"

"Not yet. When I received the damsel-in-distress call, I leapt on my black charger and came to the rescue."

"Thanks, Sir Knight. You're really great! Step this way for a frontier-style dinner."

"I've heard that the first mushers are expected in Dawson Sunday evening at the earliest. If you continue on tomorrow from Whitehorse, you'll get there Sunday morning. You've got to go."

"Tyler is not expecting me."

"Never mind that. There's plenty of time for you to get there. You don't mind driving through the night?"

"No. It doesn't make much difference since it's dark most of the day. Are you sure I'm not imposing on Vicky?"

"Up here, folks help one another out. We're all friends. You must have learnt that by now. I'm sure Vicky will be delighted to be able to do some shopping in the big city."

"Are you sure...?"

"I wouldn't offer if I wasn't. Don't worry we'll look after...What's his name?"

"Glenn."

"Shouldn't you send a message to Tyler that Glenn's here?"

"It might disturb him too much. He needs to concentrate on the race."

"You're the judge. Start the truck in the morning and let it run a bit. Call if you need help."

The tantalizing smell of dinner filled the cabin. Byron sprawled on the couch.

"D'you know Dawson?"

"No, I meant to read up about it, but I've been busy. It seems that the cold slows me down."

"It does. You're using more energy. Imagine the stampeders more than a century ago, during the Klondike Gold Rush. They didn't have the benefit of our high tech clothes." Byron laughed and affected the serious tone of a travelogue narrator. "In those days, Dawson's dusty streets echoed to the clamor of miners, prospectors and dance hall girls. Today, it's a sleepy town of a thousand souls, until it relives some of its former glory twice a year," he said.

"You sound like a travel brochure." She couldn't stop laughing. "Not twice a year. All the ads talk about the short summer and the hords of tourists who come to see the midnight sun."

"They're biased. They don't think life exists when the winter descend on the Klondike."

"We're going to change that with Boreal Sled Dog Adventures."

She spoke tongue-in-cheek.

Byron slowly nodded. "You could, especially since the Quest wakes everybody up and does bring people up. So on their way outside they could just drop by for a sled ride."

"Outside? Oh yes, the world outside the North, right?"

"Right. For us sourdoughs everywhere else is outside."

"Am I a sourdough?"

"You'll soon be. If you survive one winter up here you officially become a sourdough. But a bit of advice on the road to Dawson. There are few settlements or roadside facilities. Travelers have to be self-contained. So make sure you pack well."

"I'll do that."

"I'm off now. Dinner was great."

"You're welcome."

After Byron left, Kelly prepared food and camping equipment for her long drive to Dawson City. In addition to provisions, Kelly packed extra clothes for herself and Tyler, as well as a selection of spare harnesses and lines. The race was hard on men, dogs and equipment. She loaded additional frozen dog food in case Tyler was running low. Nothing could be taken for granted, nothing left to chance. In the event she'd need to bring back an exhausted or hurt dog, she checked the truck's dog transporter. The last thing she did was to replenish the soft spruce twigs that lined the individual compartments. There were enough to lay on the ground where the team would be resting, though they would probably be supplied with straw by the organizers.

Next morning she started the truck, and after letting the engine warm up in the sub-zero temperature, she drove to the capital to rendezvous with Vicky and Byron.

The airport was not large compared to others she'd passed through, but after the tranquility of her wilderness cabin, the noise and frantic activity assaulted Kelly's ears.

From the terminal window, she watched the arriving jet taxi to the apron. A female flight attendant, holding a young boy by the hand was one of the first to disembark. An adult's fur-trimmed parka was draped over his small shoulders. Kelly stood at the gate to greet them.

"Ms. Kelly Jefferies?" the flight attendant asked.

"Yes, that's me."

"Here is your charge. This pouch contains his medicine and instructions in case of an asthma attack."

"Thank you. I was wondering about that."

"He was fine on the plane. No symptoms of distress. The young woman crouched down and offered the boy her hand. "Goodbye, Glenn. I'll take my parka now, because I must go back to the plane." She turned to Kelly. "He's come from California. No one there had any idea how cold it would be up here."

The child clung to the woman's hand, looking at her with pleading eyes.

"This nice lady, Ms. Jefferies, is going to take care

of you now. 'Bye Glenn."

"Hello, Glenn. I'm Kelly. Did your mommy tell you about me?"

The youngster gave a shy nod. Kelly's heart missed a beat. The boy's gray eyes and dark hair, the shape of his chin and nose, were Tyler's in miniature. It was like looking at Tyler as a child. The boy reached for Kelly's hand. She gave his a squeeze. Glenn relaxed.

They waited for his baggage. "Did you like flying in the airplane?" she asked.

"Yes."

"That's good. Glenn, I want you to meet my friends, Byron and Vicky. Vicky is a schoolteacher."

Glenn looked at them timidly, but did not return their greeting.

"Do you go to school?" Vicky asked.

Glenn didn't answer. Instead, he lowered his gaze. "Where's my daddy?"

"He wanted to be here, but right now he's racing his dogs. That's why I came to pick you up." Kelly spoke gently.

"I want my daddy." Tears pearled at the corners of his eyes.

"He'll finish his race soon. Let's see how many fingers do you have?" Vicky said.

He didn't answer.

"There is one sleep for each finger on this one hand. That's when your daddy will come back."

Glenn looked down at his hand.

"For now, would you like to go with Vicky and Byron?" Kelly asked.

"No!"

The adults looked at each other in dismay. Byron raised his shoulders in a gesture of futility. "I'll tell you what. Let's get out of here and go and have a hamburger."

Kelly nodded. "Good idea."

Glenn kept his eyes lowered as, clutching Kelly's hand, they walked toward the exit.

At the door, Kelly said, "Just a minute. Do you

have a warm coat in your bag?"

Glenn stared at her. "I've got my coat on."

"Heck! The flight attendant just said he's from California. They don't need coats down there." Byron said.

"We can't take Glenn outside dressed like that!" Vicky sounded alarmed.

"I've got some warm things in the truck," Kelly said. "Glenn, you wait here with Byron and Vicky. I'll only be a minute."

Glenn shrieked and wrapped his arms about her hips.

"We're going about it the wrong way again," Vicky said. "Kelly, you and I stay here. Byron can get the coat."

"Bring the two blue bags," Kelly said. "Now, Glenn, let's sit on that bench out of the way of the people."

She tugged gently on his hand while Vicky picked up his luggage. Byron soon returned from the truck.

"Glenn, I'll need my hand to look for the clothes." Kelly said. She spoke in a soft voice, unsure of how to handle a six-year-old child.

Glenn accepted to let go of her hand. She pulled out her fleece jacket. It wasn't bulky, being designed to be worn under a coat. Glenn tried it on and giggled. The jacket fell to his ankles. When the sleeves were doubled back, they were of reasonable length.

"At least it will keep him warm," said Byron. "You look great, Glenn."

The child lifted his head from inspecting his strange new garment.

"This is your daddy's wooly toque," Kelly said.

That caught the boy's full attention.

"It's a one-size-fits-all, which is handy. And I have those miracle gloves which look so small a baby could wear them, yet stretch to a man's size."

"All he needs now is a parka," Byron said.

"I have a quilted anorak," Kelly said.

"Maybe he should wear my parka since I'm shorter," Vicky said. "And I'll wear yours."

"That might work. Let's try."

Glenn wrinkled his nose. "I don't want to wear pink."

Byron looked away to hide his amusement.

Kelly pressed her lips together. "Mine's blue. You'll wear it?"

"Yes."

The parka reached below his knees and gaped at the neck. By adjusting the drawstring of the hood and closing the tabs, Kelly and Vicky succeeded in making it more or less fit.

"His boots are only thin leather, but we won't have to walk far," Vicky said.

"I suggest we go and buy this young man some clothes. Then we can get that hamburger," Byron said.

"That the best idea so far. Don't you agree, Glenn? How about we buy you some warm clothes, first?"

He nodded and took her hand again. Byron and Vicky picked up the bags.

Outside, the boy stopped, his eyes round with astonishement.

"It's white!"

"It's the snow," Vicky said.

Glenn pulled his hand from Kelly's and rushed forward to snatch up two handful of snow. He looked at it before bring it to his mouth. With a cry of surprise and he threw the white stuff back on the ground.

The three friends chuckled.

"I guess he's never seen snow before except on Tv," Byron said.

"It's like ice-cream, but we don't usually eat it," Vicky said.

That satisfied the boy's curiosity. At the truck, Glenn eyed the dog box with interest. Each compartment had a door decorated with a dog silhouette.

"They're for my daddy's dogs?"

"Yes. When the race is over, they jump in and we bring them all home."

The shopping expedition was a success. Glenn came out of the store looking like a true northerner. At the fast-food restaurant, he stuck to Kelly's side.

"Glenn, you're going to go home with Byron and Vicky, because I have to go and help your daddy," Kelly said.

Glenn shook his head.

"It won't take long, then daddy'll be home."

Glenn burst into tears. The two women looked glumly at each other.

Byron handed Glenn a couple of paper napkins. "Here, son, cry your eyes. You don't want to drop tears on your smart new outfit. We'll think of something."

"Do you like school, Glenn?" Vicky asked.

Between sobs, Glenn nodded.

"Would you like to come and see my school?"

He shook his head again.

"Nice try, Vicky. I think he's traumatized. Leaving his mother, traveling alone to a cold place and being met by a bunch of strangers is a lot to ask," Kelly said.

"He seems to have taken to you, though," Vicky said.

"His mother must have told him Kelly'd look after him, so he hangs on to the only thing he knows," Byron said.

"You're probably right. Which means it would be better if I took him with me to Dawson."

Vicky gave her a smile. "I'm afraid so."

On the other hand, it might be safer to go home. Tyler can manage on his own since he was going to anyway. He's not expecting me."

"No, you must go," Byron said. It could make the difference in the outcome of the race. So, it's back to the store to get Glenn a sleeping bag."

"I'll have to use your credit card again, Byron-"

"It's an emergency. You can repay me out of the next sled ride."

Glenn stopped crying and dried his eyes. At the outfitter's, they equiped him with a sleeping bag and a bivy sac, as well as some thermal clothes. The boy was relaxed and fascinated by all the attention, but he still didn't want to go with Vicky and Byron.

Kelly said goodbye to her friends. Then she and

Glenn got into the truck. Half an hour later, they were on the Klondike Highway heading north toward Dawson City. It was not long before Glenn began asking questions about the rugged countryside he watched in fascination through the truck window, and about the dogs he would see when they arrived. Kelly described the pups back at the cabin. Night came, but he was still talking, even though he was practically falling asleep.

At Carmacks, they stopped for gas. When they set out again, Kelly had Glenn tucked comfortably into his sleeping bag on the truck's rear seat.

They rolled into Dawson City in the early hours of the morning. Glenn had woken up and was munching on nuts and raisins.

"First, we'll have a big breakfast. Then we'll go and check out the campground."

"We're going to camp? In a tent? In the snow?"

"That's right." That had been her plan. Glenn's appearance on the scene altered the picture. Should she camp with an asthmatic child in mid-winter? Tyler would be provided with a billet in town, though he probably intended to stay at the campground with his dogs. Now that she'd arrived, she'd insist he have a good night's rest in a warm bed. That meant she'd sleep in the tent.

"I want to sleep in the tent." Somewhere along the way, Glenn's shyness had vanished.

Kelly asked directions from the volunteers and drove over the quarter-mile-wide ice bridge over the Yukon River to the campground on the opposite bank. The site was deep in snow. Her first task, much to Glenn's amusement, was to put on snowshoes and flatten a space to picket the dogs. Glenn helped her shovel snow into a low wall.

"Are we building a fort like on the beach?" Glenn asked.

"Sort of. It's to protect the dogs. Now, let's put the spruce boughs down for their bed."

"Why do the people over there have a big tent?"

"They've made it out of a plastic sheet so that their

dogs are under cover. Your daddy's dogs prefer to sleep outside."

"But we'll sleep in our tent, right?"

"Yes. It's a bit small but it'll be warm."

Glenn was fascinated by the tent. He had to examine every layer of the bedrolls. His excitement rose when Kelly lit a fire to thaw meat and fat in advance of the team.

When the preparations were finished, Kelly drove back to town. A stuffed husky in a store window attracted her attention.

"Do you want a puppy, Glenn?"

"A real puppy?"

"Back home you'll have a real puppy, but right now, I was wondering whether you're too old to have one of those stuffed huskies?"

His eyes lit up. "I'm not old. I'm only six."

"Then let's go in."

Moments later, they came out, with Glenn clutching a gray and white husky pup with a red harness on.

They next visited the brightly-lit race headquarters where officials were huddled around a radiophone.

"The blizzard's dumped several feet of snow on the race trail," one of the men told her. "Now that the storm's over, we've sent out snowmobiles to flatten a track for the racers."

"Any news of the placing?"

Before he could answer, a voice came from the radio. "Hello, HQ? Ian Spencer of the Canadian Rangers here. We've just met Tyler Kade. He's carrying a media guy he found stranded in a snowdrift. My partner is transferring him to his machine and is heading back to Dawson. Kade must be in the lead because we haven't met anybody else. Over."

Kelly's eyes lit up with excitement. Tyler in the lead!

"What condition is he in? And his dogs?" the race marshal asked.

"They all look pretty frisky. Not badly affected by the weather. Some of the other racers are not so lucky.

Kade tells me he overtook several mushers waiting out the blizzard."

"What does he have pulling his sled, a snowcat?"

The Ranger's laugh crackled over the airwaves. "You might think so. They're big suckers with thick wooly coats. I've never seen dogs like them in all the years I've patrolled the Quest. Kade should reach you in a couple of hours. Over."

Hearing the man talk about Tyler and his dogs in that way sent a surge of pride through Kelly. Pride it was, certainly, and love too. It couldn't be, not love! She forbade herself to use the word. Tyler was married even though he and his wife weren't living together. He did go and see her at Christmas. Kelly thought it odd that she should be holding his son by the hand. Pain pinched her insides and brought tears to her eyes.

A short while later a commotion at the door attracted her attention. A tough-looking man dressed in military parka and fur hat came in. He supported a man, whose face was pinched with fatigue and white with frostbite.

The race marshal directed the man to a chair and gave him steaming coffee to drink.

"I'm Rob Larter," the man said, his speech slurring. "I've got to thank Tyler Kade for rescuing me in that storm. We traveled all night through the blizzard. That took some guts, particularly, since he risked his position in the race. Said I had hypothermia and made me drink all his thermos of hot broth. I nominate him for the Humanitarian Award."

"That's in the Iditarod. In the Quest's it's called Vets' Choice, the official said, "and it's for the musher who takes the best care of his dogs."

"What d'you mean? The guy risks everything to save my life and I can't vote him an award?"

"You're a journalist. Write him up in the press."

"Right! I will." Rob swayed but refused to check in the nursing station. He allowed himself to be helped to his hotel.

Broth? Kelly suppressed a laugh. It should have been hot chocolate. That's what the plan was, but she remembered Tyler had mentioned he's once drunk the dogs' broth. Her mirth was bubbling over.

"You're laughing?" Glenn's face puckered in a frown.

"Well, I think your Daddy gave that man some of the dogs' broth."

"Why?"

"Because the man was very cold."

It satisfied the boy's curiosity, and since Kelly was openly laughing, he laughed too.

Her spirits lifted by the praise heaped on Tyler, she joined the throng of officials and spectators on the high bank of the Yukon River to await his arrival.

A man with graying hair sticking out from underneath his toque, and a "volunteer" badge on his chest, bent over and began chatting with the child.

"Waiting for the big dogs?"

"My daddy's dogs."

"Your daddy's racing?"

"Yeah, with his dogs."

"You came to see him with your mom."

"With Kelly. She looks after my dad's dogs."

"Ah, she's a handler."

"That's what she said."

"What's your name?"

"Glenn Kade."

"Kade. Your daddy is Tyler Kade?"

"Yeah."

Kelly turned her head at the mention of the name, but seeing the official badge, just smiled.

"What's your name?" Glenn asked.

"Ben Kayson. Your dad is just about to arrive. Would you like to sit on my shoulders so you can see him?"

Glenn promptly stood and Ben hoisted him still clutching his stuffed husky, onto his shoulders. Kelly thanked him.

"Leave this little man to me, Kelly. You'll be busy for a while when Kade gets in. I'll stick right behind you."

"You're so kind."

"I'm only a grandfather."

Kelly pushed through the mill of spectators to the front and went down the snow-covered bank onto the river ice.

A wave of excitement rippled through the assembled crowd. Kelly strained her eyes and saw a black dot in the distance. As the dot took shape, she could distinguish a line of dogs and the figure of a man hunched over the sled.

The noise of the crowd rose as the team approached.

Darkness was closing in, but she could make out the steam rising from the dogs, and Tyler's familiar outline.

The lead dogs crossed the line to the cheers and shouts of the onlookers. Like any well-trained handler, Kelly ran forward to hold Capitor and Tekoone's lines and walk the team to the waiting race officials. Tyler jammed a snow hook into the frozen crust. A moment later he was engulfed by the crowd.

The officials opened his sled bag to check for the compulsory items all mushers have to carry. Everything was in order. Dawson City's mayor stepped forward to present him with four ounces of Klondike gold, the prize given by the city to the first musher to reach Dawson, the halfway point of the race.

A Canadian Customs officer asked the ritual question, "Do you have anything to declare?" to which Tyler jokingly replied, "Only these American icicles clinging to my nose since Eagle, Alaska."

"Icicles are duty free," came the deadpan reply.

Next, the Yukon Quest's vet examined the dogs. Kelly held Yanamiq's head as he pushed a cup mounted on a long handle under the dog's belly to collect a urine sample for the random drug test. She soothed Ekridi, who was reluctant to let anyone touch her feet. The vet declared the dogs' pads the toughest he'd ever seen.

Camera flashes highlighted the strain on Tyler's grim face as the media swarmed about him. He dealt patiently with the reporters' questions, and tried to ignore the Tv cameras and microphones thrust at him. He had spotted Kelly at the head of his team.

"Thank you everyone for that terrific welcome. Now, if you'll excuse me, I've got to take care of my dogs."

The crowd parted for him. He urged his team forward. Kelly turned to see Glenn, awestruck, watching his father and the dogs.

Sad that Tyler barely looked at her, she went up to him. "The camp is set up. It's on the left hand side toward the back. You'll recognize the tent. I'll get there in the truck in a moment."

"What on earth are you doing here?"

"This is the only checkpoint where your handler can help you. So I came."

Kelly watched him leave and went to Ben Kayson.

"Thanks so much, Ben."

"My pleasure, I guess you want this little one back."

"Thanks for holding him. We'll go to the campground now."

"I asked him if he wanted to get down and greet his dad, but he wisely said no. He'd have been mobbed."

"Word must have got around about how he saved the life of that photographer."

Glenn took Kelly's hand as she pushed her way to the truck. They made it to campground minutes before Tyler. Glenn ran into the tent with his stuffed dog then poked his head out.

When Tyler arrived in the campground, Kelly was waiting in front of the camp. Everything was ready, from the neatly laid picket chain to the tent and the stove with a big pan of snow on it to melt.

Several days' growth gave Tyler an outlawish appearance.

"We'd agreed you'd stay home." Tyler tried to keep a neutral face.

"I came to give you support. That's what a handler is supposed to do, isn't it?" She began unhitching the dogs, cooing at them.

"Who's looking after the kennel?" He knew the answer, but he had to hear it from her lips. Jealousy demanded it.

"Byron is. I'll tell you everything in a couple of minutes."

"So, Byron is looking after the dogs! That guy will do anything for you, won't he?" He grumbled something that Kelly didn't catch and went to unhitch Amiof and Ukiok.

Kelly excused his gruffness. She put it down to the stress of the race. "It's more complicated than that," she said in a calm voice.

At that moment, Glenn, wide-eyed, emerged from the refuge of the tent. Tyler was bending over a dog.

"Daddy!"

Tyler swung round. His face registered his disbelief.

"As I was saying..."

Tyler wasn't listening. Glenn threw himself into his open arms.

Kelly turned away and finished transferring the dogs to their pickets. She gave them the broth she'd prepared and warmed up their food over the fire.

Occasionally, she'd look and see the tenderness in Tyler's eyes as he held his son. Glenn was busy telling him about his trip.

The sight of a happy father and son getting reacquainted stabbed at Kelly's heart. A mixture of sadness and regret welled inside her. Love, too. No, she defended herself. He was married. She had no claim on him. Hating him might be easier, but she couldn't. He hadn't forced her to make love, those nights in the cabin. But, it was plain that it meant nothing much to him.

Tyler took Glenn by the hand and introduced him to his dogs. Somehow, Kelly was not surprised that the young boy showed no fear of the animals, even though they must have seemed huge to him. He laughed in hysterics when they licked his face.

"When you're ready, Tyler, I'll drive you to your billet in town."

"One problem. They're not expecting me to have a kid in tow.

"Glenn wants to sleep in the tent."

"But he can't. He's not used to camping, especially in this cold."

"I outfitted him in Whitehorse, courtesy of Byron's credit card."

A murderous look settled on Tyler's face.

Glenn looked up at the adults, a worried expression on his face. "Kelly said I could sleep in the tent."

"Don't you want to go with your daddy?" Kelly asked.

"I want to sleep in the tent." A stubborn furrow creased his brow.

A twinge of sorrow went through Kelly's heart. So much like his father.

"Then, I'll sleep in the tent too," Tyler said.

"The tent is not very big," Kelly said. "You're worn out. If you want to keep your lead position, you need all the rest you can get. Four hours lead isn't much when you're running against Alaskan Huskies. Now that the storm has ended, the other racers will be pushing to make up for lost time."

"Okay. You win. I'll leave the dogs and Glenn in your care."

Under his breath, he muttered a few words which Kelly interpreted as *will get a check to Byron*.

"This is your only chance for a hot shower and a comfortable bed. Make the most of it. I'll come and fetch you in the morning."

Glenn ran and climbed in the truck. Tyler caught Kelly's arm. "Before we go anywhere, I need an explanation. Why is Glenn here?"

"Your wife phoned."

"My wife. Is that what she called herself?"

"Yes. Your wife. She said she was taking a trip to New York. She needed you to take Glenn while she was away."

"She is my *ex*-wife. We've been divorced for five years."

His words stunned Kelly almost as much as the

shock of Gloria's disastrous phone call.

"I'm hungry," Glenn shouted.

"Let's go and eat in town," Tyler said.

Glenn's presence made it impossible to continue the conversation. Kelly's mind was swimming. A hundred questions clamored for answers that would have to wait.

During the Quest, Dawson City never slept. Bars, gambling casinos and Gold Rush era dance halls remained open around the clock. Tyler found a hotel restaurant that was not too crowded.

When they'd eaten they got back into the truck. Glenn was already asleep on Tyler's shoulder. "Tell me everything that happened after my *former* wife called you."

The stress on the word "former" was not lost on Kelly. In as dispassionate a voice as she could manage, she related the events following the woman's bombshell. Kelly was filled with a confusing mixture of relief and anger. He should have told her that he'd been married and that he had a young son! She would have been spared her heartache. At last, she had the reason for his angry moods and his avoidance of any mention of love and commitment, the discovery offered her little comfort.

Tyler ran his fingers over his stubbly chin. "Gloria was a model when I met her in L.A. I often wondered why she'd married me. We came from completely different backgrounds. She said she was attracted by the life up here, even though I made no secret of how I lived. We spent the summer in the South. I was committed to a speaking tour. We were very happy. When we came north for the race season, I soon realized she hated dogs even more than the isolation. She went to the city to have Glenn and never came back. I collected my son at the hospital. She ran off with another man. She sued for divorce. It was ugly, very ugly. She got herself a slick lawyer, and a year later got custody of Glenn. She and her fancy lawyer laid down impossible conditions for visitation. I'd have had to get rid of the dogs and move to California.

It was a nightmare. She had me over a barrel. Last Christmas was the first time she let me visit."

"Is that when your racing career went down the drain?"

"I was depressed and angry as hell. Besides, having a baby to raise wasn't helping me train the dogs."

Kelly covered his hand with hers. She felt him shiver. She fought the wave of troubling heat inside her and withdrew her hand.

"She's obviously mellowing. If she's relented, Glenn will be able to visit more often," she said.

"Did she say how long he'll be staying?"

"I didn't have time to ask."

"It doesn't matter even if she did. He's not going back to her."

"That's not reasonable, Tyler. It's not even legal."

"She can come and see him here." Fatigue sharpened the bitterness in his voice.

Kelly's heart sank. Although this other woman was no longer his wife, she still wielded enormous control over him. Kelly could imagined what Gloria looked like. The woman doubtless dressed in elegant designer fashions, wore long red fingernails and perfumed herself. Attractive for sure. Men are influenced by the visual image. With a glance at her own functional outdoor clothes, at her trimmed, unadorned nails, Kelly knew she could never compete.

Tyler and his ex-wife had something that would tie them forever. Their son. Maybe he could even be hankering after her in some way. It wouldn't be the first time a divorced couple got back together again, especially when a child was involved. Maybe he had always hoped she'd come. And if she did, he'd finish building the house for her. Winning the Yukon Quest would give him enough money to bring electricity to it. Kelly didn't doubt he could win the Iditarod too. Although he said Gloria hated dogs as much as the isolation.

"I can't leave you to look after my son. He's my responsibility."

"We hit it off. I'm anxious about him sleeping out because of his asthma. But he seems fine so far."

"Why are you going to all this trouble for me?"

"It's part of my job." She nearly added, *because I love you*, but the words stuck just in time in her throat. She'd die of embarrassment if she said something like that aloud.

"It isn't in your contract." He thought for a moment. "You're right. It's important I finish this race, even try to win it. The prize money would help. I'll be home in less than a week if I can keep up this pace."

"I heard that the trail is icy south of Bonanza Creek."

"The Yukon River was a mass of jagged ice and open water. It can't get much worse."

"Your team is strong. The dogs aren't even wearing booties."

"I check their paws at regular intervals. There's been no need to fit booties so far."

"The vet was impressed with your dogs."

Tyler's smile reflected his pride. Kelly realized that they had begun by talking about his wife and ended with dog talk.

She drove Tyler to his billet and returned to the campground. The presence of the child prevented her from dwelling on the new knowledge of Tyler's life. Excited and full of questions, Glenn finally fell asleep in the middle of a sentence.

The thirty-six-hour mandatory layover was up for Tyler. He drove his team at a brisk trot along Dawson City's Front Street toward the starting line. At four in the morning there were few spectators lining the route. The enthusiasm of those who turned out made up for the lack of numbers. Rob Larter was there taking pictures.

While the race officials made the obligatory departure check. Tyler pulled Kelly against him. "You're sure you'll be all right with Glenn? I could scratch here."

Kelly gave him a horrified look. "Scratch! What kind of an example would that be for him? I'm taking care of him."

"I know."

Two words softly spoken, and if she hadn't imagined it, tenderly spoken.

He took her lips with his. A short and sweet kiss that upset her fragile calm. He hugged his son. The timekeeper gave the signal to start. Tyler was off.

Kelly held Glenn's hand until Tyler had disappeared. There had been warmth in the kiss. Hope flooded her thoughts for an instant before dimming. Tyler was happy to have his son with him. His happiness even made him kindly-disposed to the reporters. Kelly dreaded to think what would happen when Glenn had to go back to his mother.

She began to wonder, too, what she would do at the end of the racing season. *You'll stay on and compromise your principles,* an inner voice whispered. Glenn tugged at her hand and interrupted her jumbled thoughts.

They joined the spectators waiting for the red lantern - the last team in the race. The young musher bringing up the rear finally arrived to the cheers of the few bystanders courageous enough to brave the cold.

Kelly tugged on Glenn's hand. "Let's go back to the campground and have breakfast. Then, we'll pack up and go home."

"My daddy's going to win the race."

"I hope so."

"I know he will."

She drove the short distance to camp.

"Can I go see those dogs under the tent?"

"Not on your own, you can't. Sled dogs are not pets. You must always ask the musher to show you his dogs. Right now, he's sleeping. It's still early in the morning."

"Okay."

Glenn devoured the hearty breakfast Kelly prepared. She saw their neighbors' truck head off to town to fetch the musher from his billet. It was not long before they were back. Glenn sidled up to them to watch them load the sled and hitch the dogs.

"He can't get enough of it," Kelly said. "We were up at two this morning."

"A future musher," the man said. "I'm Bill Stevens, by the way. I'm seven hours behind Kade. He'll win for sure. I'm dropping two dogs here."

"Hans Reesink is six hours behind. Can he catch up?" Kelly asked.

"Maybe, maybe not. A lot depends on the trail. Tyler's dogs are strong and his team is still intact. Reesink has had to drop another dog. He's down to eleven."

"They're faster, though."

"Not in this race. We're pulling three-hundred-pound sleds. I'd say that Tyler has the advantage. His Inuit dogs are born to pull heavy loads, unlike Alaskan Huskies. There's also the question of temperature. The light Alaskans can't stand the really cold conditions as well as Tyler's Inuit dogs."

"The sled gets lighter as you approach the next checkpoint in Carmacks."

"Yes, but it gets heavier again when we take on more supplies. Don't forget there's still over three hundred miles to go. Between here and Carmacks there are the Black Hills and the King Solomon Dome and the Eureka Dome to climb. Tough going all the way."

"How bad are they, really? I heard they take a toll on both dogs and mushers."

"Bleak, windswept, grueling. After Carmacks, there's a treacherous stretch down the length of Lake Laberge. We've got to watch for open water. There's ice fog, glare ice and biting cold winds. Anything could happen before the end of the race."

"It makes one wonder why people want to race it."

"Some people have it their blood. It's man against nature in a very primordial way. Mushers really depend on each other and on their dogs for survival, like in this last blizzard. But I love it!" An enthusiastic note crept into Bill's voice. A frostbite on the cheek distorted his smile. "We must be crazy!"

"It's enough to boggle the imagination. I hope Tyler keeps his lead."

"Why not go and take a look at Reesink's team? That'll give you an idea what Tyler is up against."

"I will before I leave. Good luck, Bill!"

After Bill's departure, and a visit to Reesink's team, Kelly set off for the long drive home. Glenn crawled into the back seat of the cab and fell asleep on the pile of coats and sleeping bags. In spite of the darkness, the freezing cold and the slippery roads, Kelly arrived safely at the cabin.

One of the first things she did was to circle on the calendar the day of Tyler's estimated arrival at the finish line. Glenn wanted to know exactly when his father would win the race.

Glenn adapted quickly to his new surroundings. He shadowed Kelly's daily routine. She was delighted to have his company. Every time she took a team out for an exercise run, he asked to ride in the sled. He had a naturally gentle way with the dogs, big and small. Kelly dubbed him the pups' manager. There was never a sign of the asthma she had been warned about, and he never complained about the cold. In the evening, he would carefully cross off another day on the calendar, impatient for the day of his father's arrival. And after hours in the open air, he fell asleep the moment his head touched the pillow.

On the evening before she was due to leave for Whitehorse, Byron and Vicky came to see her.

"Don't worry about the dogs," Byron said. "I'll take care of everything while you're gone."

"That's really good of you. If Tyler makes it in on time, I should be back on Saturday night."

"No, you won't. You're staying for the banquet. He'll have to be there, and you wouldn't want him to hitchhike back on his own, would you?"

"He didn't invite me."

"Nonsense. They said on the radio that he's still in the lead. Though Reesink is closing on him. It's fast becoming a tight race. At last report, Tyler was only two hours ahead."

"Reesink may narrow the gap even more tomorrow."

Gloom settled in the room for a while.

"He's pushing hard, but his dogs are tired," Vicky said.

Kelly had noticed the sadness in Vicky's eyes whenever the three of them were together, and wished she could shake some sense into Byron's head. He was blind to the way Vicky looked at him. The irony of the situation might have brought a smile to Kelly's lips if she hadn't felt like crying. Tyler was as equally unresponsive to her love for him as Byron was to his adoring admirer. Life was nothing if not unjust.

Once more, Kelly was driving to the capital, this time with Glenn who chatted away at her side. She'd packed the clothes Tyler would need for the banquet. In her own bag was her pretty green dress. In her present state of mind, Kelly was unsure whether he'd want her there. Nothing had been mentioned. The image of his glamorous ex-wife haunted her waking hours. One thing was certain, Tyler would want Glenn to see him cross the finish line. The love she had witnessed between the two moved her deeply.

In Whitehorse, she went to the race headquarters and identified herself as Tyler's handler. Bravely hiding her disappointment that he should have forgotten to invite her, Kelly bought tickets for herself and Glenn. She asked where she could make camp and was given directions to the park down by the river.

An official showed Glenn an electronic display panel that gave the latest placing of the race contestants. "Your dad's still out in front."

"Yippeee!"

While they drifted among the people in the room, Kelly overheard a race volunteer talking. "Tyler Kade seems to have made a comeback. Before he had that losing streak, he was my favorite. Lots of folks are rooting for him now."

Kelly couldn't take her eyes off the bulletin board. According to the latest update, Tyler would arrive midmorning. Glenn was falling asleep against her, so Kelly returned to the camp even though she'd prefer to stay to track the race results.

The thought of being on hand to greet Tyler as a winner prevented her from sleeping. When it was time to rise, she quickly rolled up her sleeping bag and prepared breakfast. She herself had no appetite but she had to think of Glenn.

A crowd had gathered at the finish line in spite of the relentless cold. Rumor had it that Reesink had made further gains on Tyler. The gap between them could now be measured in minutes. Providing Reesink's dogs still had some energy left in them, they could well make a dash for victory. A quick sprint would leave Tyler plodding along behind. Kelly had a leaden feeling in the pit of her stomach.

Glenn was chatting with a gray-haired woman standing next to them.

"Glenn, don't bother the lady."

"It's perfectly all right. I'm Ann Price. I've come to meet Tyler Kade. He's billeted at our house, and this young man here tells me Tyler is his father."

"That's right. I'm Kelly Jefferies, Tyler's handler."

"You'll be busy the moment Tyler gets in. Why don't you let me look after this youngster? I'll make sure he doesn't get run over by the crowd. All right, Glenn?"

"Yes, and I want to see my daddy when he gets here."

"Of course. I'll make sure of that."

Kelly thanked Mrs. Price and turned her attention back to the race. An idea born of desperation crossed her mind. She went to the truck and put on her old parka, the one she used for the kennel chores, now soiled by countless doggy paws. Remembering the unusually-keen noses of her Inuit dogs, she hoped they might scent her parka. Whenever they were out on the trail, their pace sped up when they were homeward bound. The same might happen here, particularly since she'd be standing upwind from their approach.

Her status as Tyler Kade's handler gave her a position at the front of the waiting crowd.

Finally, a loudspeaker announced that the lead team had been sighted. Lightheaded, Kelly waited and watched. A roar went up when a dog team entered the straight.

It was Tyler's!

About to jump for joy, she checked herself. Another team was right behind him and closing fast.

A tense hush fell over the spectators. Then as if on signal, pandemonium broke loose. Kelly felt a wave of fear travel from head to toe.

Tyler had to win! He mustn't let himself be beaten in the dying seconds of the race.

She crouched. She knew that at a distance, dogs recognize a person low on the ground but not standing. She willed the dogs on.

The intense concentration gave her a blinding headache. Had the dogs felt her presence? A barely perceptible whistle escaped her lips. Dogs' hearing is so acute, they might hear the familiar sound over the din and want to run to her. She saw Capitor's head lift a fraction. And then they did it. The whole team put on a last minute burst of speed as the final distance shrank to a matter of yards. Kelly dared not breathe. She saw the dogs reach inward to tap that deep source of willpower that makes their breed so endearing, and at times, so infuriating. Even above the wind and the crowd's tumult, she could hear Tyler singing to his dogs at the top of his lungs.

As the two evenly-matched teams fought for dominance, the line of spectators shrank back to allow them to pass. Reesink's team made a valiant bid to overtake. It was too little too late. Reesink, with a lame dog as passenger on the sled, lacked the reserve of power to defeat his arch-rival.

Tyler swept to victory by a clear length.

Once assured of his first place, Tyler called the dogs to stop and slammed his foot on the brake, which brought the sled to a spectacular halt amid a shower of ice crystals. Kelly ran forward. The dogs swarmed around her, each one eager to lick her face.

Tyler leapt off the runners and scooped Glenn into his arms. Together they hugged every dog on the team.

Won! Tyler had won! Kelly was in a daze as race officials, media and smiling fans flocked around the champion. The excitement reached fever pitch. Reesink and his loyal supporters put on a brave face. It had been a bitter pill to swallow. To come so close to winning, only to be forced to accept a second place.

Tyler, reeling from fatigue, answered as best as he could the questions put to him by the press. His eyes met Reesink's. Tyler's worthy opponent advanced through the crush and held out his hand.

"Congratulations, Tyler. The best team won. I have to thank you again for helping me back there during the blizzard. If you hadn't been so gracious, I wouldn't have been able to give you this final run for your money."

The two men shook hands. Their raw, sleep-deprived eyes shone from unshaven faces. Both men beamed with the satisfaction of a race honorably run.

Under the glare of floodlights, a woman television reporter monopolized Tyler. "Can you tell our viewers what makes you want to run this punishing sled dog race?"

Tyler thought for a moment. "A man alone with his dogs in the wilderness experiences the ultimate freedom. Nothing else compares with it."

Looking on with tears in her eyes, Kelly realized that in those few spoken words, Tyler had defined his life. His dogs, the wilderness and races formed his world. He'd make room for Glenn now that father and son had been reunited. Beyond that, nothing else mattered. There was no place for her in that closed circle.

Glenn twisted in his father's arms to be let down. The young woman interviewer in her rhinestone-studded parka probed Tyler for details. "You haven't run the Quest for several seasons. I understand you're also taking part in the Iditarod. What prompted the sudden comeback?"

"Because I've got an exceptional handler."

His eyes searched the crowd. Head down, Kelly busied herself with Kiki and Vanga, the two hyper females who didn't want to sit. Ukiok growled at them both, and the dogs obeyed.

The television camera turned on Kelly. She had no choice but stand and acknowledge Tyler's compliment. She shook her head at the invitation to join him on the podium and excused herself by saying she must drive the team to the campsite.

Ann stood watching father and son. Glenn left his father's side and took her hand. "Come and see my daddy's dogs." Giving the boy an indulgent smile, she allowed herself to be led into the midst of the panting team of dogs.

Glenn climbed on the sled and Ann went back to wait for Tyler. The media's attention switched to the third place winner, who was about to arrive.

***

Tyler made a move to run after Kelly and his retreating team, but exhausted as he was from the bone-numbing fatigue, he was unable to do anything except remain beside the track, watching the other teams cross the finish line. The image of Kelly standing among the dogs and laughing with Glenn was etched on his fogged brain.

An official came and slapped him on the back. "Kade, you'd better go and take a nap. You look done in."

He acknowledged the welcome advice with a wave and stumbled away. Mrs. Price hurried to his side and directed him to her car.

"Where's Kelly camped?"

Mrs. Price told him. "I'll drive you, but you're only allowed five minutes. You're asleep on your feet."

"If you don't mind. I'd like to spend a moment with my boy."

In no time, they reached the campsite. After kissing his beaming son, Tyler went into the tent to collect the bag Kelly had brought for him, and collapsed on the bedroll. Mrs. Price and Kelly waited for him, but hearing no sound, Kelly crawled in. She stuck her head out and laughed.

"He's sound asleep."

"Well, I guess we better leave him. I'll come back later. And Kelly, since your're busy with the dogs. you can leave Glenn at my place. We've got lots of room and plenty of food."

"Thanks so much. I'll see how it goes."

Kelly went back in the tent to pull off Tyler's boots and outerwear. She then covered him with a sleeping bag. After checking the heater, she and Glenn returned to the finish line to soak up the excitement.

***

Tyler slept for a full twenty hours. He eventually emerged, dishevelled and eyes puffed with sleep. The intense cold had eased its grip over the Yukon. A pale sun shone low in the sky.

"It's positively balmy," he said.

Kelly smiled at him. Unshaven, his clothes wrinkled, he certainly didn't look like a triumphant winner. She took a deep breath. "Did you sleep well?"

"I wasn't aware the world was still turning. How are the dogs?"

"All in order. The banquet is scheduled for tomorrow evening at seven. I brought you some good clothes."

"How thoughtful. Only, I'm not going. I never do. Pack up. We'll head home."

"It's not good for your image to skip the banquet. Everybody expects you to be there."

"Who's everybody?"

The former surliness was back. It showed in the arch of his brows and the caustic edge to his voice.

"Your public, for starters, the officials, the volunteers who give their time so that the race can run, the media, and your fellow competitors. Need anyone else? You'll also collect your winnings. It's part of the ritual."

"I don't go in for rituals. They can put my check in the mail."

"Well, Glenn and I are going. We bought our own tickets. I'll say you have a headache." Defiance flared in her eyes.

Tyler growled something impolite about official functions.

"You're not shy, are you?" It dawned on her that maybe he really was uncomfortable facing the cameras.

He pulled a face. "I don't like crowds and I hate ceremonies."

"It doesn't last long. Try to relax."

"Thanks, Dr. Jefferies."

Kelly burst out laughing. Tyler disappeared into the tent. When he came out, he was wearing his boots and carried his bag and parka.

"Ann Price is expecting you," Kelly said.

A tired smile stretched his mouth. "I'd like to shower. Will you drive me?"

***

Seated in the truck, with Glenn between them, Tyler kept his silence. His anger had vanished. He was intrigued by just how this petite, auburn-haired woman always managed to tally the score so neatly. He stole a glance at her over Glenn's head. Ever attentive to the traffic, her eyes scanned the road ahead. Her long eyelashes fluttered. Those lips he knew so well reflected her concentration. The heat in his lower belly made him acutely aware of his need. Raw desire boiled under his skin.

He recalled the earlier moments of shared intimacy. The loneliness of the uninhabited wilds of Alaska and the Yukon had been made worse by his longing for her. A musher constantly has to ponder his race strategy and the thousand and one details of team and trail. Yet there were long stretches when he imagined her next to him. He couldn't picture life in the cabin before her arrival. Damn! She'd look even more beautiful in summer. He tried to visualize her in shorts and top, with the cool breeze catching that magnificent hair of hers.

Glenn's insistent questions wiped the images from his mind. While he talked to Glenn, he noticed that from time to time, Kelly would smile at the boy. As if in a haze, he saw the three of them together, not simply driving side by side, as at that moment, but together in life. A family. He shook himself. The race must have taken more of a toll than he'd thought. He'd better quit dreaming if he wanted to keep his sanity. To add to the dilemma, was the unknown factor of what Gloria would do next.

The kindness with which they were received by Ann Price, one of the many people who opened their homes to the race participants, softened Tyler's agitated nerves.

"We'd love to have all three of you stay for dinner, Ann said.

"That's very kind of you," Kelly said. "Glenn will stay and so will his father. I have to go and look after the dogs."

Tyler dismissed Kelly's plan with a wave of the hand. "We'll both go and take care of the team. Then we'll come back here together."

"I'll agree only on the condition you come to the awards banquet."

He grinned. Turning to Ann, he said, "She always wins!"

Ann smiled. "While you attend to your dogs, Glenn can stay here and watch Tv or play computer games."

Glenn straightened his shoulders. "I want to go

and look after the dogs too."

"If you don't want to accept an invitation," Kelly explained to him, "you must always say thank you."

"Sorry. Thank you, Mrs. Price."

The motherly woman smiled down at the boy. "That's fine, Glenn. So, you want to be daddy's helper?"

"Yes. And when I grow up, I want to have lots of dogs of my own. I'll enter lots of races. Like that I can come and stay at your house and play your computer games."

Kelly joined in the laughter. She also detected a hefty measure of pride on Tyler's rugged face.

On the evening of the race banquet, Kelly accepted Ann Price's invitation to shower and dress in comfort.

"We'll drive you in our car, since we're going," Ann's husband Kevin said. "We can't let you clamber into your dog truck in your fine clothes."

Dressed in her green wool dress and heeled sandals, with her hair swept up, Kelly left the bedroom and walked into the Price's living room. Her entry brought a gasp of astonishment from Tyler.

"Kelly, you'll be the belle of the ball," Kevin Price said.

Tyler's smile creased his wind-weathered face. "You're a vision of loveliness."

Ann looked up from tucking Glenn's shirt into his pants and gave a knowing smile.

When Kelly reached for her parka, Ann placed a hand on her arm. "You can't wear a parka to the banquet. This the biggest event of the season. I'll lend you a coat." She rushed to her bedroom.

"I think I'm going to enjoy that banquet with such a beautiful escort on my arm." Tyler said.

Kelly blushed. At that moment Ann came back carrying an exquisite camel hair coat.

"It no longer fits me. Not since I acquired extra padding," Ann said.

"Thank you, Ann. It fits me beautifully."

"The fake-fur collar turns up to protect your ears

from the wind. And the insulated lining is a blessing in this part of the world. I want you to keep it."

"But, I can't. It's such a lovely coat."

"I'd sooner someone like you has it. You remind me of when I was a whole lot younger. Doesn't she, Kevin?"

Kevin chuckled with an approving nod. "I don't mind the padding."

"I'm so thrilled. Thank you, Ann."

"All right, let's go before the womenfolk start crying," Kevin said. He pulled on a jacket.

"Why would they cry?" Glenn asked.

The grown ups broke into laughter. Glenn joined in, though he was still confused.

"Sometimes people are so happy, they can't help crying," Tyler explained.

"Oh." Glenn frowned then smiled.

Chapter 9

The banquet was a boisterous and joyful affair. After the meal, came the speeches. The master of ceremonies called Tyler up to the platform to receive his winner's check and trophy. The next twenty racers each received prizes of lesser value. Cheers and good wishes were heaped on all participants. Next came the awards.

The Emcee called for quiet. "As you know, the race officials vote on the Challenge of the North Award. It goes to the musher who best exemplifies the spirit of the North. Ladies and gentlemen, I'm proud to announce that this year the award goes to...Tyler Kade!"

A deafening roar of applause erupted as all heads turned toward Tyler. Kelly smiled. For once, Tyler was at a loss for words. He stood and went to receive his prize of elegant crystal artwork and yet another check.

The Emcee retained Tyler by the arm. "While you're up here cleaning up on the prizes, Tyler, we're going to give you the Golden Harness Award for having the best lead dogs in the race. We're talking about two dogs with such noses they discovered a man lying off the trail in the deep snow. Their names, ladies and gentlemen, are... The man glanced down at his notes. "...Capitor and Tekoone, two of the finest Inuit sled dogs you'll find anywhere in the North."

The Emcee had trouble ending the deafening clapping. Other prizes were bestowed on various mushers.

"And our last but not least award tonight, folks, is

the Sportsmanship Award. The mushers themselves decide who gets this one. The Emcee looked at his assistant. "I hope everyone kept the secret."

A smiling young woman handed him an envelope.

"You will remember we asked all mushers not to reveal who they voted for." He waited a few seconds to allow the buzz of expectation to subside. With deliberate slowness the Emcee opened the envelope.

"The name that got forty-four votes out of a possible forty-five finishers is...hey, this is getting boring...Tyler Kade!"

The audience again broke into a flurry of cheers and whistles. The applause again brought Tyler to his feet. He was acutely embarrassed as he mounted the steps to the platform.

"Congratulations, Tyler. Here's a musher's hat and a check to keep the other ones company. Please tell us the true story of the incident on Lake Laberge."

"It was nothing, really. The weather was terrible. Ice fog hanging in clouds over the lake."

"So far so good. What about the open water?"

"There was some. A darn'd nuisance."

"So what did you do?"

"I detoured."

"Folks, if we wait until I drag the whole story out of him, we'll be here all night. Since my lady wife warned me I had to be home by midnight, I'll take up the tale. That night the temperature dipped to a numbing minus fifty below. Tyler discovered that the break in the ice had widened. Our trail markers were leading directly toward the open water. At the risk of losing his first place position, he backtracked several miles to reroute the markers, so that there was no danger of a musher losing his way and ending up in the drink. And that wasn't the first time in the race he'd done something that cost him precious time. There's a couple of mushers in this room who can vouch how he helped them out in the blizzard near the Yukon-Alaska border. It was during that snowstorm that Tyler saved Rob Larter's life..."

A standing ovation drowned out the last of the

Emcee's words.

Kelly stood and applauded with the others. Her eyes softened with the love she felt for the man. Tyler remained on the platform, shifting from one foot to the other and looking puzzled about all the fuss. He hadn't even mentioned the Lake Laberge incident to her.

In that breathless moment, she knew that she could never leave him. He did respect her. Their friendship was special. If he couldn't love her, they at least shared a love of dogs and the wild reaches of the North. If that's all she could lay claim to, she was willing to accept it. A nagging voice in her brain told her Tyler would reject her again. That she couldn't bear. From now on she'd have to pretend indifference. After all, she could still realize her dreams of racing. He couldn't object to his handler racing, and would just hire a second handler, now that he could afford it.

A commotion at her side shattered her daydreaming. An excited Glenn had climbed onto his chair. "That's my daddy! That's my daddy!"

The surrounding guests smiled at his exuberance. A press photographer snapped his picture.

"We didn't know Tyler Kade had a kid," the man said. "How come we never heard about it?" He pointed to Kelly. "Hey, young fella, is this your Mommy?"

Suddenly self-conscious, Glenn jumped down, ran to Kelly and flung his arms about her. At the same moment, Tyler came back to his seat.

"Quit bothering my son!" His bark made the press man flinch.

"Still as charming as ever with the media, eh, Kade? You never could take the heat."

Tyler was about to take a swing at the jeering photographer, when Rob Larter grabbed the man by his lapels. "Keep your questions and photos to the race, or clear out."

Faced by two angry and determined men, the disgruntled reporter snapped the lens cover back on his camera and slunk out of the room to the accompaniment of hoots of laughter.

Rob Larter came and sat at their table and related how Tyler had rescued him from near death in the snowbank. The band struck up a tune. Kevin Price led his wife onto the dance floor.

"Your turn, Tyler. Kelly's itching to dance," Rob said.

Kelly protested. "I can't leave Glenn alone.".

"Nonsense, I'll keep an eye on the young scamp."

Tyler hesitated. "I'm not much of a dancer."

Kelly raised her eyes. "Me neither. I really don't mind if we sit this one out."

"My only chance at babysitting a super-smart young guy! Say, Glenn, would you like to learn how to use a camera?"

"Yes, please."

"Tyler, is it okay if he comes round the room with me to take photos?"

"Daddy...please!"

"All right. But make sure you stick with Rob and do exactly what he tells you."

"Yippeee!"

The music started up again. Tyler turned to Kelly. "Shall we? No excuses this time."

Kelly felt a shiver of apprehension at the thought of being held in his arms. As he led her onto the floor, his hand burned an imprint on the skin of her back. When she faced him, his smile banished her fears. He didn't hold her close. He didn't need to. A vibrant current leapt between their swaying bodies. She tingled all over with excitement, conscious of every nerve-ending having come alive to his touch. Kelly's eyes held his. When he brushed against her, she became aware of his growing passion. A warm secret veil enveloped them, shutting out the other couples and the flash of cameras. In the midst of the crowd they were alone, lost in depths which only they could measure.

The spell ended with the music. Kelly and Tyler returned to their table. They found Glenn asleep on a chair, with his head on Rob's lap.

"I guess we better put Glenn to bed," Tyler said.

He carefully lifted his son in his arms. Kelly gathered up the trophies. At the door, Mr. and Mrs. Price were waiting for them.

"If you two would like to stay on, we could take the youngster home," Ann said.

"Thank you so much, Ann, but I've got to get up early in the morning. I have a team of hungry dogs waiting for me," Kelly said.

"We've got plenty of bedrooms. Why not stay with us? I hate to think of anyone camping out in winter."

"It's sweet of you to offer. I don't like leaving the dogs alone for too long in strange surroundings."

Back at the Price residence, Tyler fished the truck keys from his pocket. "I'm taking Kelly and Glenn back to the camp."

Kelly changed out of her dance dress. Glenn didn't even stir when Tyler picked him up.

"Why don't you leave him with us tonight?" Kevin said.

"That'd be great. Since he's so soundly asleep, it would be a shame to have to wake him to get him into his sleeping bag."

They settled the boy in the bedroom opposite Ann and Kevin's. He opened an eye and yawned.

"You're staying with Mrs. Price for tonight, okay?" Kelly spoke in a soft voice.

A grunt and a big sigh were the only reply Glenn made as he reclosed his eyes.

"I'll leave the doors open," Ann said. If he wakes up, I'll hear him."

"Thanks again, Ann," Kelly said.

Tyler climbed behind the wheel of the truck. At the camp, they checked that the dogs were comfortable. Tyler lit the tent heater and, carrying it in one hand, pulled back the tent flap to let Kelly go in.

"I'm happy that you won the Sportsmanship Award, as well as the Challenge of the North."

"It would never have happened without you. As for what happened on Lake Laberge, anyone would have done the same."

"Not many mushers would have jeopardized their race to go back and shift the trail markers the way you did."

"Don't be so sure. I just happened to be in the right place at the right time."

"And as a result, you risked losing your number one place."

"That's fate for you."

He fell silent. His hand slipped into auburn hair that fell in a soft mass to her shoulders. Kelly trembled. She mustn't let him caress her. His closeness made her weak. Tyler would never be satisfied with a simple kiss. He'd beg for more, and she would relent. She knew she would. She eased his hand aside. A tremulous wave of heat swept over her, sending exquisite tremors along her spine. The sensation centered between her hip, then scattered to her extremities.

Tyler leaned forward, his lids heavy with longing. Slowly, ever so slowly, his lips touched hers with infinite lightness. The result was inevitable. The tension she'd felt throughout the long evening resurfaced in a sudden explosion of fire. Her stern resolve melted like snow in summer. Tyler dragged her down onto the bedroll and held her close. The feverish pressure of his mouth on hers sent ecstatic quivers running over her burning skin.

Kelly pressed her eyes shut. Breathless, she broke free. Her sanity screamed to stop right there, yet her wanton fingers traced the firm line of his chin.

Again, Tyler hungrily pulled her to him. They both moaned.

"No, Tyler. We mustn't."

There was a long, silent pause.

"I know, dammit!" Tyler said.

With great reluctance, he drew away. For a full minute, he rested his chin in his hands, his eyes staring unseeingly at the red glow of the heater. As if emerging from a trance, he sprang to the tent door. "Sleep well, Kelly. See you in the morning." The flap fell back into place, and he was gone.

Kelly stared at the square of canvas long after the sound of his truck retreated into the night.

Next morning, Kelly had already exercised half the team by the time Tyler turned up with Glenn. Together they finished the task, walking each dog a little way.

"Have you two eaten?" Kelly asked. She strove to keep her tone even.

"Did you imagine Ann would let us go on an empty stomach?" Tyler replied.

"Lucky you! Then you won't mind waiting while I prepare something for myself?"

"How about having a bite in town? I could handle a second breakfast," Tyler said. "What about you, Glenn?"

"Oh, yeah, yummy!"

"Fine. Let's go. We'll strike camp when we come back."

They found a cosy diner that specialized in home-cooked meals. Over breakfast, Glenn talked nonstop about being the photographer's helper at the banquet. Both Kelly and Tyler listened, encouraging him from time to time with questions.

Kelly saw the friendly glances they were getting from the other customers. She colored, knowing they must think she and Tyler were two devoted parents accompanied by their bright young son.

Tyler swung by the bank to deposit his checks before driving back to the camp. Scores of curious children of all ages, wanting to see the dogs and talk to the mushers, already crowded the camp. When they saw Tyler, they rushed to him.

"Can we have your autograph, Mr. Kade?"

While Kelly and Glenn folded the tent, Tyler satisfied the insistant demands of his fans. Kelly came to his rescue by answering questions about the dogs. Finally, the throng dispersed. The packing complete, they lifted the dogs and placed them in their compartments. After that, nothing remained but to set off on the road home.

Several long miles later, a smiling Byron met them as they pulled into the yard. Kelly climbed out of the truck.

"My legs are so stiff, I don't think I'll ever walk again!"

"Congratulations, you two!" Byron said. "What a performance! I watched it on Tv. I just loved the way the team sped up at the last minute to clinch the title."

"Most of the credit goes to Kelly. She drew the dogs to her like a magnet. And I gotta thank you, too, Byron, for looking after things here."

"Don't mention it. Come on inside. I've got one of my gourmet stews ready on the stove."

"We must attend to the dogs first. Glenn is asleep in the truck."

Kelly had never seen Tyler so relaxed and happy. Success agreed with him. She didn't bother waking Glenn but put him straight onto his cot in her bedroom. The three adults sat down to dinner. As soon as it was over, Byron, ever the diplomat, took his leave.

Tyler wedged a cushion behind his head so he could watch Kelly put the dishes away. "When you're done, come and sit here with me."

"In the armchair? No thanks. Too dangerous. You know very well where that would lead. I haven't the slightest intention to tempt fate."

Tyler sighed. "I wouldn't dream of taking advantage of you, but I can't hide how much I need you."

Need. Desire. Fine talk, indeed! For her and Tyler there was no tomorrow. Since she'd promised herself to be happy just being in the same space as Tyler, she choked back her bitterness. The old saying that it was better to have loved and lost than never to have loved at all might have a grain of truth in it. But only if the love was shared. The fruit of one-sided love was only tears and grief.

She believed that for Tyler, making love, as opposed to *being in love*, was simply sexual gratification. To give in yet again would make the inevitable separation at the end of the race season that more painful, unless... Unless of course, he asked her to stay on as his handler. But how would she possibly live so close to him and not make love when her body almost overruled her mind? Merely to look at him, as at that moment, his long legs stretched out, his arm crooked over the backrest, was enough to deepen the confusion in her heart.

"I appreciate your being candid," Kelly said. "All the same, I don't intend to burden myself with a liaison. I want to be free to move."

That's not exactly what she had meant to say, but she felt powerless to correct it without making a fool of herself. What if they did make love? What harm could come of it? Something in her recoiled. She wanted more than mere physical excitement.

Tyler clenched his fists, a futile gesture of frustration. His face darkened.

"Be independent then."

For one moment, Kelly almost cried her love out loud, ready to throw caution to the winds and drag him onto the couch. Not that she'd need to drag him. He'd probably lift her up before she could move. When she spoke, she didn't know where her control had come from. "We must start planning the Iditarod." She pretended to be unaware of his inner turmoil.

"Time enough for that tomorrow," Tyler replied.

"Sure. If you don't need anything else, I'm off to bed."

"Okay. By the way, Kelly..."

She faced him.

There was no mistaking the tenderness in his voice. "Thanks...for everything."

As she retreated, Tyler grasped his head in both hands. He was going about it all the wrong way, unlike Byron who was always at hand, pleasant and courteous. It would come as no surprise if one fine day she and Byron announced they were getting married. Byron was young and inexperienced, and probably held absurd romantic notions about love and marriage. He'd soon find out, just as he, Tyler, had done, that rather than sharing troubles, a wife only doubled them. Though in that respect, Kelly was different.

The training routine resumed. Under Kelly's watchful eye, Tyler harnessed the team of Alaskan Huskies. She had trained them and knew them better than he did. He no longer questioned her judgement.

Although Glenn wanted to go with his father, Kelly persuaded him to remain with her. She patiently explained that Tyler would be returning late in the evening, long after the youngster's bedtime. The boy accepted Kelly's explanation.

After his training run, Tyler took Kelly in his arms and waltzed her around the living room. "Those dogs are incredible! They run like the wind. What did you do to them? I've never seen such obedient dogs."

"Nothing special. I took them out in small groups. As a result, I discovered several of them are natural leaders. With the full team, they react quickly to the commands. It's not a strictly orthodox method, though."

"Did you pick that up from your father?" His tone became gentle.

"No. I came up with it myself as a means of training them. You see, since at the beginning, I couldn't handle all twelve huskies together, I asked myself how would I behave if I was in their place."

"But dogs don't think like humans."

"No, not quite like we do, but they think, nevertheless. Just watch them carefully, without any preconceived notions and you'll see what I mean."

"Their intelligence is based on their ancestral instincts and what they learn from their trainer."

"In my opinion, their brain permits them to make a choice between actions. For me, that's the same as thinking."

Tyler looked thoughtful. "I reckon you must be

right. I recall times when I had the distinct impression that my dogs used logic. I simply put it down to an intelligent use of instinct."

Kelly smiled. "You have to try to understand their nature."

Tyler expressed his admiration. "You mean think along the same track as them. And, talking of tracks, tomorrow, I'm heading up to Wolf Lake and back. That will be my last big outing. In about a week's time, it's off to Anchorage and the Iditarod."

"I commend your enthusiasm."

He winked. "You're looking at a born again optimist. How can I not be with such an obedient team?" Tyler's smiling face reflected the self-confidence of his words.

"You'll win. I know you will. You'll be the first musher ever to place first in the two biggest races of the North."

"The Iditarod is every musher's dream."

Glenn came out of the bedroom. "What's the Iditarod?"

"You weren't sleeping?" Kelly asked.

"I woke up."

"The Iditarod is a really long sled dog race." Kelly said. "It helps us remember a real race years ago to save children's lives. Do you want to hear the story?"

"Yes, please."

"Sit next to your daddy and he'll tell you about it."

The little boy scrambled onto his father's lap.

"In Alaska, there's a village called Nome, a long way from anywhere," Tyler said, choosing his words with care. "In the old days, just like now, there was no road to it, and the only railroad was miles away in a place called Nenana. People used dog sleds to get around. One winter, in 1925, many of the kids got sick with a terrible disease known as diphtheria. Children don't get it nowadays because doctors give them a needle when they are just babies. Those kids had to have medicine or they would die, but there was no way of getting it up to them. Because it was January, the weather was very cold, with lots of big snowstorms.

The dog mushers in the area all got together and carried the medicine, called serum, from village to village by dog team. The serum arrived in Nome in time to save the sick children. The most famous of the mushers was a man called Leonard Seppala."

Tyler took a deep breath. Kelly chuckled as she guessed he'd found out how difficult it was to explain things at a child's level.

Glenn's thoughtful young face smiled up at him. "Was it a long way?"

"Over one thousand miles. That's a very long way to drive a team."

Tyler reached for a map from the drawer and spread it out on the table. "Here, I'll show you the route the mushers took."

Kelly stood back and watched father and son pore over the map. The sight warmed her heart. If only there was some way to keep Glenn here, where he belonged. Almost two weeks had gone by since his arrival, and not a word from the boy's mother. Kelly suddenly realized that in all that time, Glenn hadn't once mentioned his mother.

In the morning, Kelly and Glenn helped Tyler harness his team of twelve huskies.

"There's no need to take much food. I'll only be gone four hours at the most," Tyler said.

Kelly disregarded his words and stowed a package in the sled bag. "I thought we'd agreed we wouldn't go out without an emergency pack?"

"Okay. You're right. Somehow, I'd forgotten that clause in the contract!"

With Glenn at her side, Kelly watched him head out. Tyler turned and waved his hand.

His heart beat with a troubled emotion to see them together, two dark silhouettes against the brilliant white snow.

When they finally disappeared from view, he turned his attention to the trail ahead. At least, he tried to concentrate on the task of driving his team. The image of Glenn hand in hand with Kelly had imprinted itself on his mind's eye. The pair presented such a natural picture. Like him, the woman and child belonged here in this untamed wilderness. They belonged to him. Not true, he mentally corrected. Unlike every other woman Tyler had known, Kelly never spoke of love. In fact, she never used the word at all. It was as though it scared her, just as it scared him. Tyler hated the word. Behind it, there lurked the sinister word "marriage". He'd committed one big mistake in his life. He had no intention to repeat it.

He fondly remembered the passion with which Kelly had responded to his embrace. The thought made his loins contract with need. Later, she was the one that had refused. He had no idea why she should be so stubborn. The pleasure they experienced in one another's arms could in no way compromise her precious independence. Unless of course, she was saving herself for another man. The thought of Kelly in Byron's arms wrenched at his guts.

Perhaps because he was preoccupied with his thoughts, he failed to notice until the last minute the huge bull moose that loomed squarely in the middle of the trail ahead of him.

"Whoa!" Tyler yelled at his dogs and slammed his foot on the brake. The dogs jolted to a halt, their eyes fixed on the great beast. Low growls came from their throats. There was no doubt the moose was a fully grown adult. The right-hand side of its massive antlers had already fallen, the way they do in the winter. The moose snorted and pawed the snow. In defiance, he lowered his head at the dogs. Neither dogs nor moose backed away.

Tyler took care not to startle his ill-tempered adversary while he leaned forward to grasp the handle of his ax protuding from the sled bag.

The animal lunged in a feint but stopped several yards short of the lead dogs. Tyler leapt off the sled and ran forward. Oblivious to his personal safety, he shouted in an attempt to deflect the animal's attention from the team.

Moose have poor vision. The beast's eyes trained on the dogs had not yet seen the human.

Tyler calmed the team with a few soothing words. If the dogs chose to attack, mayhem would break loose. "Steady now. Sit." They didn't.

The bull moose shook his huge head in anger and sniffed the air, in an attempt to gauge the new threat. Tyler swung his ax. The sun glinted off the burnished metal, momentarily distracting the wild animal. The moose bellowed and made another charge. This time straight at Tyler.

Tyler expected it. With the agility of a bullfighter, he ducked and ran to the sled.

The moose ran at him, its single antler missing Tyler's head by a hair's breadth. Tyler had only enough time to yell, "Hike!" before he was struck by the moose's solid rump. The force of the blow pitched him into the sled. Confused and anxious, the huskies, felt the weight on the lines, and shot ahead at breakneck speed. Tyler vainly tried to hold on. A burning pain creased his side. Despite his efforts to hang on, he fell off and landed in the snow, still clutching his ax.

Tyler realized how vulnerable he was. Instinctively, he yelled, "Whoa! Whoa!" but the team paid scant heed to his cries. Again, "Itirit! Whoa!" Whether his faithful lead dog heard him or not, Tyler never knew. The team was in full flight. He could do nothing to stop them.

Shock almost made Tyler vomit. His dogs had disappeared into the distance. Alone with an enraged bull moose, his only weapon was a puny ax. The dogs risked injuring themselves in the trees. Worse still, they could plunge over the icy precipice of the escarpment. It was several hours trek back to the cabin. Without snowshoes, Tyler would have a tough time of it through the deep snow. The pain in his side spread to his back.

He had the faint hope that his trusty Nunii might slow the team and somehow urge them back to him.

If they didn't get hopelesly tangled in the bush. Given such a perilous situation, Tyler was fully aware he had no guarantee of getting back home in one piece.

Blood throbbed in his temples. He levered himself onto his hands and knees to determine the position of the moose. The beast had turned to watch the retreating sled, but now directed its short-sighted stare on Tyler. Its small eyes blinked and one or twice the animal appeared to frown.

Tyler took stock of his situation. He was in a shallow depression ringed by mature pines. On either side of the trail, dense brush and deep snow cut off any escape in that direction. If he could reach the spot where the trail entered the trees, he'd be safe. The heavy animal would be slowed down by the close-packed trunks and low-hanging branches. Tyler flexed his limbs to check if any bones were broken. Fortunately nothing was. He inched upwards, and drew himself into a standing position.

As if that was the signal it had been waiting for, the moose charged. With a superhuman effort, Tyler dashed for the trees.

He couldn't reach them before the moose gained on him. The ax gripped in his two hands, Tyler turned and swung at the animal's head. The flat of the ax struck the animal on the nose. Startled, the moose sank back on its hind legs.

Tyler took advantage of the momentary distraction to plunge into the forest. The enraged moose recovered and crashed through the brush after him. Tyler swerved but too late to avoid the deadly lunge of the single antler. One prong caught the fleshy part of Tyler's buttock. It tore his pants and lacerated his flesh.

Adrenalin surged through Tyler's veins. Blinded by his own rage and pain, he again lashed out. This time he landed a blow with the back of the ax on the beast's cheek. The moose stopped in his tracks, bellowed and shook his head. Tyler reached the limit of his strength. The effort of wielding the ax had brought him to his knees. Using the ax handle as a support, he got to his feet again.

For what seemed an age, Tyler lurched in a drunken dance with the stunned moose. The beast glowered at him, head hung low. Tyler knew this was his last chance to escape. Pine needles scratched his face. His leg throbbed in pain as he zigzagged deeper into the stand of tall timber.

Panting for breath and almost too weak to run any farther, Tyler glanced back. The moose was no longer in sight.

Chapter 10

Kelly looked up from pouring the last of the broth for the dogs and scanned the northern horizon for any sign of Tyler's return. He'd been gone for more than five hours. Although, the days were becoming longer, twilight was already settling over the landscape. She picked up the dog bowls and scratched Ukiok behind the ears.

"I'm going to play with the pups," Glenn said.

"All right. I'll be there in a moment to refill the heater."

She smiled and watched the youngster scamper over to the kennel house. A few minutes later, he and the pups crawled through the dog tunnel into the outdoor enclosure.

Worried, Kelly turned her attention to the deserted trail. *Come on, Tyler. This isn't reasonable. You're not equipped to spend the night outdoors. I know you can survive, but you said you'd be back in the afternoon. It's now evening.*

Whether in answer to her silent prayer, or purely by coincidence, Kelly saw a dark mass moving toward her in the distance.

"At last!" She breathed again. After putting away the bowls and broth pail, she looked again. All her anxiety came flooding back. What was Tyler up to? The sled was careening madly along the trail. Her heart sank when it came close enough to see that the dogs were there, so too was the sled. But there was no musher! Tyler was nowhere in sight.

The driverless team stormed into the yard. The dogs crowded around her, entangling themselves in the lines. A couple of dogs slipped their harnesses and raced around the compound.

In the midst of coping with the chaos, Kelly's eye fell on the open sled bag. The ax handle that normally stuck out from it was missing. She was sure something awful had happened to Tyler!

"Okay dogs! What have you done with your master?" She kept her voice level to calm the excited animals. In time, she succeeded in leading the dogs to their pickets in their enclosure. She hastily fed and watered them. Concern for Tyler made her clumsy.

While on her way to the cabin, Glenn looked up at her. "Can I stay and play a little longer?"

"That's fine, sweetheart. I've just got to go to the cabin and make a phone call."

Kelly dashed to the radiophone. "Hello, Byron? Omega Beta. Kelly here. Can you hear me? Over."

She waited. There was no reply.

"Hello, Byron. This is an emergency. Are you there? Over."

Again, nothing but the empty crackle of static.

In desperation, she dialed the number of the Wildlife Conservation Office. Conrad came on the line.

"Kelly! Is anything wrong? Over"

"I'm trying to get hold of Byron."

"You've just missed him. He's on his way home. Would you like me to call him on his truck radio and tell him you want to talk to him?"

"Yes, please, Conrad."

She gnawed at her fingernails, while she waited for Byron to phone. Through the window she saw the sky darkening. Glenn ought to come in. She went to the door and called him in.

"Daddy's back?"

"No, not yet." Kelly wondered what she should tell him. How to explain that the team and sled had returned, but his father was somewhere out there in the wilderness?

She decided that this was the time for a white lie as the child hadn't noticed the return of the driverless sled.

"Some of his dogs got loose and came back ahead of the others."

"And daddy?"

"He'll be here soon. He must be going slower now that he's short a few dogs. Go and wash up for dinner."

The radio crackled into life. "Hello, Byron here. Do you read me? Over."

Kelly yelled into the mike. "Byron! Look, I have Glenn with me. There's a bit of a problem. I can't explain fully. Tyler's T-E-A-M came back but not H.I.M. His ax is missing."

"Stay calm, Kelly. I have a hunch what might have happened. I'll be up as soon as I can. I'll call at Vicky's. She'll come along and look after the young'un."

"Thanks, Byron."

When Kelly stepped away from the set, she collided with Glenn. He stared up at her. There was a look of confusion in his eyes.

"Give me a hand to set the table for dinner. Byron and Vicky are on their way."

"Daddy's lost?"

"No, he's just been delayed."

"But he'll come?"

The trust she read in Glenn's eyes tweaked at her heart. The child sensed something was wrong, but she wasn't about to confirm his instinctive fear. Not until she knew.

Kelly let out a long breath when she heard the welcome sound of Byron's snowmobile.

"Glenn, open the door for Byron and Vicky, please."

They came in and brushed the snow off their suits. Vicky dropped a backpack onto a chair. "I've got enough things in there to keep a whole classroom of kids amused."

Kelly took Vicky's parka. "I can't express my gratitude for your help at a time like this."

"Don't mention it. We do what we've got to do to help each other."

"Dinner's ready. Glenn should eat."

"Leave everything to me," Vicky replied.

Kelly dragged Byron down to the far end of the room. In a low voice, she said, "Tyler's team arrived about forty minutes ago. Something must have happened. Itirit is very agitated. I had in mind to put a leash on her and let her guide me."

"You say the ax was missing?"

Kelly nodded.

"The most likely scenario is that Tyler encountered an animal, most likely a moose, on the trail. There's lots of them about right now. They're hungry and ornery. If it attacked, Tyler could have used the ax to defend himself. While he was doing so, his team could have bolted."

"Those dogs are usually most obedient."

"If they got scared, they'd panic. It's a good thing they got back here. They could just as well have gotten themselves tangled up someplace."

"I'm scared. He was on his way to Wolf Lake. What if he fell through the ice?"

"Relax. Wolf Lake is pretty shallow. With the kind of temperatures we've been having, it'll be frozen right to the bottom."

"Thank heaven for that!"

"Mushers have been known to lose their teams when they stop for a nature call. The missing ax, kinda rules that out."

"What are we going to do?"

"Organize a search party."

"How?"

"First, I'll get my buddy Conrad to come out with the search and rescue toboggan. You and I will scour the trail until he joins us."

"What can I do?"

"Hitch up your most reliable team and head along the trail Tyler would use on his return journey. I'll take the snowmachine and follow his outward route."

"He said he was sticking to his regular run. It was supposed to be just a short outing to keep the dogs in shape."

"Take Itirit along. She seems to know what

happened."

"She's good. I don't know if my teaching her search techniques will really do any good. I only did it for fun."

"This will be for real. I recall how she found Aqua."

Byron called Conrad on the radiophone. That was done, he said to Kelly, "You'll be happy to know that both Conrad and I are qualified in advanced first aid. Get some warm clothes on. I'll give you a hand to hitch up your dogs."

"I've got some dried fruit and nuts you can take with you. You've got to keep up your ernergy. This cold saps it."

"Have you got a first-aid kit?"

"Yes. It's in the sled every time I go out."

Glenn looked up from his play. "Where are you going?"

"We're going on a night training session, darling. Vicky is here to look after you until we get back."

Glenn was used to them leaving at odd hours, so he was not upset. Vicky made sure to keep his attention focused.

Kelly chose her team with care and took six sturdy Inuit dogs. Naturally, she put Itirit in the lead, and then decided to take Nunii along. The two worked better together. Although the dogs knew each other, there was a bit of growling from the Inuit sled dogs.

Kelly had an idea. "Byron, get Ukiok out of the pen for me. I'll let him run loose ahead of the team. He's bonded with Tyler."

"Okay. Sometimes, these dogs can surprise you with their sixth sense."

She gave the signal to go and they set off, Ukiok bounding ahead on his own. Noses to the ground, the dogs followed the fresh tracks of Tyler's incoming runaways. Now she was out searching, Itirit settled into a steady gait, which the others matched.

The first section of the trail was relatively hazard-free, so Kelly gave the lead dogs their head. Ukiok ran at the outer limit of her headlight. After a mile or two,

Kelly reined in the team, wanting to conserve their energy for carrying Tyler back home if she found him first.

Kelly was too absorbed in scouring the trail ahead to notice the full moon emerge from behind a thick bank of cloud, but she was thankful for the clearness of the night. If Tyler was walking home, at least he would be able to find his way. When examining the sled, she'd found his headlamp in the bag.

The dogs kept up their brisk pace for over an hour. There was not the slightest trace of Tyler. Not having had time to eat before setting out, she nibbled on dried bananas and nuts.

Soon the terrain gave way to the forested region. Had she not been burdened with fear and worry, Kelly might have enjoyed a moonlit ride through the magical landscape.

Without warning, Ukiok came to an abrupt halt. Even at a distance, Kelly saw the hackles rise on his neck.

"Steady! Whoa!" She kept her voice low to keep the dogs calm. Up in front, Itirit grew agitated. Kelly's eyes followed where Ukiok's nose was pointing. A huge shadow detached itself from the dark conifers and stepped out onto the trail. It was the largest bull moose she'd ever seen. Its sheer size shocked her. One half of his wide antlers was missing, which heightened the animal's fearsome appearance.

Ukiok gave a menacing growl and leapt forward. Kelly's pulse raced.

With an instinct born of many hours of rigorous training, she dropped the snow hook and drove it into the frozen crust with her heel. Willing herself to remain calm, she tied the snub rope to the base of a sturdy bush. Nothing would be achieved by getting panicky.

The moose was still some distance away, with Ukiok circling it. The dog let out a ferocious snarl, then leapt at the moose. From the moose's angry bellow, Kelly guessed the dog had sunk his teeth into its muzzle. Before the moose could lash out with his hooves, Ukiok sprang back and resumed his circling.

Again and again, Ukiok attacked and withdrew. The tactic enraged the huge animal. Seeing that her dog was keeping the moose at bay, Kelly released the sled and urged the leaders to pull into the brush, where she would be hidden from view.

She watched with bated breath as Ukiok harassed the moose the way she imagined a wolf might attack its quarry.

After making several attempts to gore the dog, the infuriated animal gave an earsplitting bellow and turned tail. Ukiok pursued it across a small clearing until the moose plunged into the trees and disappeared from view.

"Ukiok! Ukiok! Here, boy!"

The dog didn't obey right away. For several minutes he patrolled the edge of the trees, on the alert for any counterattack the moose might decide to launch.

Kelly was faced with a dilemma. If she left the relative security of her hiding place, she might encounter the disgruntled animal farther along the trail. But she couldn't stay where she was all night. Although it had been chased off by Ukiok, the moose could be lurking beyond the trees.

She'd heard stories of mushers being confronted by surly moose. The hard-packed snow of the trails was as attractive to the moose as it was practical for the dog teams.

It seemed certain that this was what had happened to Tyler, most likely with this same moose. But where was Tyler now? A sickening dread settled in her stomach. A man alone on foot was no match for such an animal.

A frantic series of short howls in the mid-distance brought all her faculties alert. Ukiok stood sideways across the trail. Between howls, he lifted his nose to test the air. Drawn by some instinct, Itirit tugged on the lines to join him.

Kelly fumbled with the lines to untangle the dogs that had become caught in the bushes. The team pulled ahead and she had just enough time to jump on the runners. Her dogs made the decision to go for her.

The trail skirted the dark stand of timber. Nerves on edge, Kelly scanned the shadows for movement. She breathed easier when she saw no sign of the moose. Though the danger to her and her team had lessened, she must still find Tyler. Itirit strained in her harness and Ukiok ran faster and faster, reluctant to wait for the rest of the team.

Almost an hour later, and just about to lose hope of finding a man alive in the middle of the wintery wasteland, she glimpsed a pinprick of light amid the trees. Ukiok and the lead dogs had seen it too, or smelled something, and were running toward it. Off the beaten trail, the going was difficult because of the deep drifts and scattered brush.

The light came from a campfire a few paces from the edge of the forest. In its ruddy glow, Kelly made out the figure of a man lying on his side.

"Tyler!"

She was greeted by Tyler's unmistakable voice. Kelly anchored the sled and ordered the dogs to sit. Itirit and Capitor didn't obey immediately. They first pulled to Tyler's side and sniffed him all over. Kelly patted the dogs and took them by the collar. She secured the sled and repeated the command to sit. This time Itirit sat and the others followed suit. Ukiok pawed his master.

"Gently, Ukiok. Sit!" She held him back by his collar.

The dog sat on his haunches. Kelly dropped to her knees beside Tyler.

"Are you hurt?"

"I had an argument with a bull moose. He wasn't very polite."

"We figured as much. It must have been the same one I met farther back along the trail."

"Did it attack you too?"

"Fortunately no. Ukiok chased it off."

"He did!"

"How badly hurt are you?"

"It got me with his antler."

"Any bones broken?"

"I don't really know. I don't think so. When I escaped from the moose, I hid here until I felt safe. Then I lit the fire. Thanks for stuffing those waterproof matches in my pocket. When I heard you coming, I thought it was my team returning. They ran off on me."

"That's how we knew you were in trouble. The dogs arrived back on their own."

"Not hurt?"

She shook her head.

"That's a relief."

"Now, what about you?"

"I packed snow against the wound. The bleeding has more or less stopped." Tyler shifted to one side. Kelly saw blood stains on the snow.

"Don't move. I'll get the first-aid kit." She ran to the sled and dug out the box.

Kelly laid a folded thermal blanket in front of the fire. "If I help you, can you ease yourself onto the blanket?"

Tyler winced and slid himself onto the makeshift bed. Kelly wrapped the spare parka around him. He didn't complain, but she could see he was suffering. She took a rolled sleeping bag from the sled and placed it under his head as a pillow.

Once she'd got him as comfortable as possible, she picked up the ax and waded through the snow to cut enough dead branches to keep a bigger fire going. Fueled with dry wood and pine cones, the flames gave off a comforting warmth. Kelly hoped that the fire would also make the moose think twice about causing more trouble.

She filled a stainless steel dog bowl with snow and put in on the fire to melt.

"Conrad and Byron are on their way with snowmobiles. It shouldn't take them long to find us. If you've warmed up a little, I want to examine your wound."

"Best wait for the men to arrive. The cut is on my

backside. Right where I sit down."

"Come on, Tyler! I've already seen your backside. This examination is strictly for medical purposes."

Tyler burst out laughing. "Oh, hell! It hurts when I laugh."

"See, you need attention. Don't move while I unzip you. There. Now, raise yourself on your arms so that I can ease your pants over the affected area."

Tyler gritted his teeth and let himself be undressed.

"Damn! It's cold!"

She put his good leg inside the second sleeping bag she'd brought and covered as much as she could of his other leg.

"It'd be best if you lay on your side. Good. Now you can relax. It's a mess down here. You've got a nasty gash across your buttock cheek. Luckily the antler missed your kidneys."

Kelly opened the first-aid kit and busied herself with the injury.

"It feels like it's bleeding again," Tyler said.

"Yes, it is. That's because I had to cut away your underpants. The cloth was sticking to the wound. I'm going to clean it up. Don't yell. It may hurt a bit."

Using the melt water from the bowl, Kelly washed the gash. "I'm putting on antiseptic powder. It'll sting, so be prepared."

Tyler stiffened when she dabbed the raw flesh, but other than a few grunts, he didn't complain.

"I'll put a dressing on it. That's all I can do for the moment. It's going to require stitches."

"Stitches? Won't it heal up on it's own?"

"What's the matter? Is the great Tyler Kade scared of being sewn up?" Although she meant it in jest, Kelly immediately regretted her mocking remark. Tyler had no need to prove his courage, either physical or moral. She eased him in the sleeping bag and zipped it up.

At that moment the dogs began to grow restless. Kelly knew their keen sense of hearing had detected something, so she moved out of range of the crackling fire and listened. From far away, came the unmistakable whine of a snowmobile engine.

"Tyler, I think they must be coming. If they stick to the trail, they're bound to see the fire."

"Kelly?"

"Yes?"

"Before they get here, I just want to say I knew somehow you'd find me."

"Did you expect me not to be worried when you failed to return?"

"No. Even if the team hadn't made it back, I had the feeling you'd know that I wasn't just dawdling around, and that something had gone wrong."

"I admit that when I finished the chores, I intended setting out with a team to look for you. I would have had to bring Glenn along too."

"Glenn, yes. Where's he?"

"Byron had the foresight to ask Vicky to come and take care of him, so I could join the search."

"Byron..." Tyler closed his eyes and sank back on the makeshift pillow.

The brilliant glare of a snowmobile headlight sliced the darkness. Seconds later, Conrad was with them.

"You've found the old guy! How badly hurt is he?"

"The good news is that there are no broken bones or internal injuries, as far as I can tell. The bad news is that the moose caught him with his antler. He's got a nasty cut."

"Where?"

"On my rear end." Tyler grinned despite the discomfort.

"Okay. You'd better let me take a look at that butt of yours."

"Forget it, Windett. My butt is private. Besides, Kelly's done a great job cleaning it up and applying a dressing."

Conrad laughed. "You lucky swine! Lucky for you that Florence Nightingale got to you first. You'd wouldn't have received that level of TLC from me or Byron."

"Cut that out, you sadist! You're making me laugh and it hurts like hell."

Conrad stopped the joking. "I've got something for the pain, if you need it."

"Thanks. I'll be okay."

"Just lie put for a while longer. I'll call up Byron and tell him where we are. As soon as he gets here, we'll settle you on the toboggan. You'll be at the nursing station in no time." Conrad returned to his snowmobile and picked up the portable radio.

Tyler raised his head and smiled at Kelly. "Knowing how people around here monitor the air waves, we're likely to have the entire community of Fletcher Creek arrive at any moment."

"Tyler, talking is going to tire you out. Try to relax. We'll take care of everything from now on," Kelly said.

"You're great, you know that?"

"Only doing my job, Mr. Kade. Now shut up and rest."

***

"I tell you, I'm leaving as planned!" Tyler shifted uncomfortably in the armchair and threw Kelly a defiant glance.

"That's out of the question, and you know it. You can't even sit properly, let alone bend down to deal with the dogs."

"What a damned waste of time and money this has been! All that good training for the Iditarod in vain." Tyler's face reflected his intense frustration

Kelly put the last of the dinner dishes in the cupboard and turned to him. A smile softened her lips. "There is one solution."

"What's that?"

"I take your place."

"That's a crazy idea! You know nothing about running the Iditarod! It's not at all like the Yukon Quest. Besides, you've never even run in a big race."

"True. But tell me who trained this Iditarod team of yours? Think of the time we've spent discussing the details. I can recite the strategy word for word."

"Okay. I'll grant you that. But how can you compete against those seasoned racers? A rookie stands no chance of coming in first. Lucky if you finished the race."

"My personal ambition tells me otherwise. I could at least place in the top few finishers. That would be better than just dropping out."

"If only we had more time."

"Listen! That's a snowmobile coming up the slope."

Tyler grimaced. "More visitors! I'm beginning to prefer the old times better. Back then, nobody ever bothered me."

"They only want to wish you well. Tyler Kade is the local superstar again."

"It's probably Byron. He comes to see how I'm doing, but it's really an excuse to see you."

"You're an old cynic."

Byron's noisy arrival drowned out Tyler's reply.

"Excuse me," Byron said. "I forgot Glenn must be in bed."

"Don't worry. When he's asleep, nothing disturbs him," Kelly replied.

She smiled a welcome. Her eyes sparkled as she spoke to Byron, but she didn't miss the somber expression that darkened Tyler's face.

Byron took a seat next to Tyler. "You don't look altogether happy."

"Neither would you be, buddy, if you were leaving for the Iditarod in seven short days and you were still virtually bedridden."

"Then send Kelly in your place."

"Are you two in cahoots?"

"Did she suggested replacing you too? It makes sense. She certainly knows dogs."

Kelly's voice softened to a whisper. "I did offer to take his place. Only, he doubts I'm capable enough."

"No, no. That's not exactly what I said." Tyler threw up his hands. "I said you lacked the necessary preparation."

Kelly leaned toward him. "In which case, tell me everything I need to know. I could write up my race strategy according to your instructions."

"She's right, Tyler, old pal. All the technical stuff about handling the sled and the team she knows already. Between the two of you, there's no reason why she can't compete in the damn race."

"It's an awful lot to ask of anyone," Tyler replied.

"I'm not just anyone." Kelly's eyes sparkled. "If I don't try, we'll never know. To succeed, you must take risks."

Tyler rubbed his chin. A reflective mood settled in his eyes. "It's not certain that the race committee will allow a last minute change of mushers."

"I'm beginning to hope I can convince you," she said.

Byron got to his feet and reached for his parka. "I'm really glad the patient is back to his old, grouchy self. I tell you what I am going to do. I'll phone the head of the Iditarod Committee and plead your case. You might have to pay a late entry fee."

"That's alright," Tyler said.

"Do you think you can?" Kelly asked. "Convince him to bend the rules, that is?"

"I don't even think they have rules for a case like this. But you're already registered, so it's only matter of a name change on the papers."

"Even though I haven't done any of the qualifying races?"

Byron crammed his fur hat on his head and gave her and Tyler a broad smile. "We'll see. I'll call you just as soon as I have a reply. G'night, folks."

The sound of Byron's snowmobile faded.

Tyler looked at Kelly. "Hand me that stack of old log books, please."

She made him more comfortable by placing a cushion at his back. She then perched herself on the armrest, and together they studied the race logs.

Tyler held up an open notebook. "This page describes the last checkpoint before Nome..." His sentence hung unfinished on the air. He glanced at her. "Something wrong?"

His leg had brushed hers and sent a shiver through her body. She fought the waves of longing that engulfed her and tried to concentrate. As she leaned over to read the entry, an auburn curl caressed his hand. With deliberate slowness, his fingers closed on the silken lock of hair and brought it to his lips.

Oblivious to the soreness of his wound, he drew her down to him. He pressed his lips against the cool skin of her temple. The throbbing pulse fluttered under his touch. His ardor stripped the few remaining restraints from her crumbling resistance. His arms encircled her waist and tipped her into his lap.

Quivering with want, Kelly parted moistened lips, a silent invitation he could only accept. Successive waves of ferment silenced her clamoring voice of reason.

With breathless impatience she abandoned all pretense of caution, and leaned against the muscled shield of his chest. Time stood still while they forgot the mundane reality of the cabin and lost themselves in a turbulent sea of rapture.

Kelly took a deep gulp of air and came to her senses. Gently, so as not to aggravate Tyler's injury, she freed herself from his embrace.

"You'll hurt yourself, Tyler."

"Your sweet lips will heal me."

"Be reasonable. That's a deep wound you have."

"It's nothing compared to the one in my heart."

"This is not the time to wax poetic. Do you need anything?"

"Yes, you."

"I was speaking of more material things."

"Me too."

"How about using my shoulder to help you to the bathroom?"

"Thanks. If you push the kitchen chair over here, I'll use it as a support. I'd better learn to fend for myself, since you're threatening to leave at the end of the week."

"It's not 'if' I leave, but 'when'," Kelly replied.

"Seriously, you can take all my equipment. Have you all the clothes you'll need? If not, you'd better drive to Whitehorse tomorrow and buy whatever you want."

"I'll go to the village. I saw that Mary had some nice native-made mukluks. I'd like to have a pair. My boots are almost worn through. A couple of spare toques and gloves are the only other things I need. Mary will have those in the store."

"You can charge it to my account."

"I have my credit card."

"Take mine. You'll need gas and meals on the road."

"It's fine, Tyler, I'll-"

"Take mine. That's an order!"

"Sure thing, boss." Her laughing eyes mocked his severity.

As punishment, he seized her about the hips and looked into her eyes imploringly. She kissed him lightly on the mouth. Then, taking advantage of his distraction, she wriggled free and ran to her room.

Sleep did not come immediately. Part of her was distressed to see Tyler injured, yet she could not quell her excitement. On the one hand, Tyler's mood was happy like it was before Christmas, on the other, she was being handed a wonderful opportunity to take part in the race of her dreams.

Two days later, Byron called on the radio. "Tyler, you'll be happy to hear that everything is in order. Kelly has been given permission to replace you under special circumstances. The only condition is that she attends the meeting for rookies in two days' time in Anchorage. I assured them she'd be there."

"That's great news! Kelly is out with the dogs right now. She's going to be overjoyed."

"I'm glad to have been of help. It pays to cultivate old friendships."

"I owe you."

"I phoned Marcia last night and told her about your mishap. She sends her sympathy and says to get well soon."

"You rat! There was no need to publicize my misfortune. I'm not particularly proud of my exploits with that stupid moose."

"Don't fret. Marcia would have found out soon enough, anyway. Once she heard that Kelly was running the Iditarod, she immediately said she'd set out for Anchorage to be there to help. Her boss has agreed to do without her for a few days."

"That takes a weight off my mind. Entering the Iditarod for the very first time is tough enough for anyone, but to do it with no backup…"

"Yeah, I agree. It takes grit. But we both know that Kelly has that. I'm off now. While she's away, I'll come up and take care of the dogs until you're fit enough to handle them."

True to his word, Byron was at the cabin early in the morning. He helped Kelly load the dogs into the truck.

After breakfast, Kelly stood up to clear away the dishes.

Byron held up his hand. "Leave them! Don't waste time getting on the road. It's a long drive to Anchorage."

"I can at least wash the dishes before I go. You've got enough to do with the dogs."

"Quit fighting, you two. I'm doing the dishes," Tyler said.

Byron took a stern pose. "You have to rest.".

"I'm able to stand up. That's all a guy needs to wash a bunch of dumb plates."

Glenn sprang from his chair. "I wash the dishes."

"Bravo! Spoken like a true northerner." Byron stifled his smile.

"With all my gallant gentlemen to take care of things here, I can see I'm not needed. Goodbye then, everyone. Be good, Glenn."

Byron took down his coat. "Get dressed, Glenn. Come and help me warm up the truck for Kelly. It'll only take a couple of minutes."

Glenn scrambled into his outside clothes and dashed outside in Byron's wake.

Kelly watched them go and silently thanked Byron. How considerate to want to give the *lovers* a few moments alone to say farewell. How was he to know that Tyler stubbornly refused to love her? Kelly tugged on her woolen gloves.

Tyler stood beside her, using the back of a chair for support. His free arm snaked around her waist. His mouth descended on hers. Despite her determination not to weaken, the pressure of his lips sent a fiery current directly to the very center of her feminine being.

Kelly took an uncertain step backward.

He lowered his voice to a throaty whisper. "That was only a good luck kiss."

"Is that all?"

"Isn't that enough?"

For a split second, she hoped he might say something else, something akin to a declaration of love.

"I'll bring you back the winner's Golden Harness Award."

"Complete the course and bring back the team in one piece. I'll settle for that."

His reminder of the grueling race ahead cast a shadow over her joy. In spite of the top-rate veterinary attention the dogs received during the race, there were always unexplained deaths. The thought of losing one of her precious dogs made her cringe. At that minute, she might have backed out had she been pressed.

"I put the welfare of the dogs above everything. If they get tired, we'll stop, no matter what."

"And take equal care of yourself."

His sudden tenderness made her quiver. It was genuine. She could hear it. At the same time, she told herself it was only the friendship inspired by their common interest in dogs.

"You take care of yourself too." She had the irresistible urge to kiss him, but she held herself back.

She gave him a quick final smile and went outside. Byron was waiting for her at the door of the truck. The racing sled was firmly secured on top. The excited dogs poked their noses through the vents of the transporter.

Byron opened the door for her. "All set?"

Before she could climb into the cab, he brushed the veil of hair that the breeze blew in her face, and pressed a light kiss, so laden with regret, on the corner of her mouth.

"Good luck," he whispered.

"Thanks, Byron...for everything."

***

Tyler listened to the sound of the truck fade away, unaware that his nails dug painfully into the palm of his hand. Sadness constricted his heart. He threw himself onto the couch. His tortured mind pictured those last tender moments outside, with Kelly saying goodbye to Byron. He'd guessed right. Kelly was enamored with him.

After those few nights of delirious passion, she now kept her distance. Tyler was convinced that he had been mistaken. They'd established a working relationship, a friendship even. Nothing more. And that was as far was it went. Byron, on the other hand, could offer her love and commitment. How could a surly musher compete against that combination? In a mixture of anger and disgust, he hurled a cushion across the room.

Love! What a farce! Love was merely a figment of people's romantic imaginations. Once, as a young racer, fresh from winning his third Iditarod victory, he'd been naive enough to believe he was in love. He'd been dazzled by the adulation of the fans, the lavish offers of corporate sponsorships and speaking engagements. When he'd met Gloria at a glitzy cocktail party, he'd fallen head-over-heels. At that time, he had it all. The future belonged to him.

It was not long before the life that had once smiled on him turned sour. Love ceased to exist for him. What reason had he to resent Kelly seeking happiness in another man's arms? Did a few nights of blissful sex give him any special hold over her? He found he was unable to answer his questions.

"It all boils down to a matter of hormones," he muttered. But he wasn't entirely convinced by his own explanation.

"What's hormones?"

The childish voice startled Tyler. "Huh... It's... about the dogs when they're going to make babies."

Fortunately Glenn was still at the age when simple explanations satisfied him. To watch him happily getting wet in the overabundant soapsuds made Tyler smile. He switched his thoughts to the race ahead.

He chided himself for not having spent more time explaining the difficulties she'd encounter. There was the appalling weather in the mountains, winds that could topple a loaded sled, and blowing snow that blotted out every landmark along the wide sweep of Norton Bay.

On the lower reaches of the Yukon River she'd meet treacherous overflows, the frightening undercurrents that spilled over onto the surface ice. If he could have forewarned her a little more of these dangers, she'd have a better chance of realizing her dream of winning. There he was talking about winning as if he really believed she would. It was not impossible, but racing had become a highly sophisticated sport and rookies didn't have much of a chance against veteran racers. Kelly might just make history though.

He laughed. She had spunk. Glenn scooted to the armchair, climbed on his lap and joined in the laughter.

Chapter 11

Kelly brought the truck to a halt in the service station parking lot and cut the motor. Stiff from wrestling the tight grades over Tahneta Pass, she flexed her shoulders to ease the pain. The mountains were behind her now. Ahead lay the easy descent to Anchorage. This would be her last stop to exercise and water the dogs.

She'd been there some thirty minutes when a red and white truck, similarly laden with sleds and dogs, drew alongside. A slim woman got out, accompanied by a young man. The pair came over to Kelly.

"Hi there!" The woman smiled and held out her hand. "I'm Lauren Kains. This is my handler Tonio Vargas."

Kelly was impressed. Lauren's reputation as a top racer was well known. She shook the woman's hand. "Pleased to meet you. I'm Kelly Jefferies."

"Is the late Guy Jefferies your father?"

"Yes. And I'm Tyler Kade's handler."

"I thought you must be. I recognized the truck. I'm looking forward to competing against him again."

"Unfortunately, Tyler isn't running the Iditarod."

"No?"

"I'm taking his place. He had an accident just recently and injured himself."

"Badly?"

"Enough to stop him entering the race. Luckily, they agreed to let me step in at the last moment."

Kelly's joy was written on her face.

"That's great! Then this is your first Iditarod?"

"My first long distance race. The committee made

a big exception for me."

"The combination of your name and Tyler's is a pretty powerful one."

"I hope to live up to everyone's expectations."

"You will, I'm sure. So, Kelly, if you stick close to me I'll do my best to steer you in the right direction. If I can be of any assistance, don't hesitate to ask. You have no handler? The most important thing is not to screw up at the beginning of the race. We'll find you a volunteer to help with the dogs."

"My cousin Marcia is supposed to meet me."

"Great, but an extra pair of hands is always a good thing."

"I'll welcome any advice you can give me."

"We women mushers have to stick together, no? We'll both help. Tonio, you've finished with the dogs? We gotta roll. Follow me, Kelly. I know the way."

Enchanted at finding a friend in Lauren, Kelly took to the road behind the red and white truck. By some miracle, her weariness had vanished. Everything seemed too good to be true. Lauren had placed second several times in the Iditarod. To get help from her was more than Kelly could have dreamed of.

On her arrival at the campground reserved for the race participants, Kelly searched for her cousin. She didn't need to look far. Marcia came running up and threw her arms around her. Kelly was pleased to see that she and Lauren had been allocated neighboring campsite. It didn't take long for an easygoing friendship to blossom among the young racers.

Kelly sailed through the necessary registration formalities and attended the rookie seminar. Unabashed, she had no hesitation in asking questions. She drew the twenty-ninth starting position, a placing that suited her just fine. Having other teams ahead of her meant she'd have no problem finding the trail. The start took place along Fourth Avenue in the town center.

"Departures make me nervous," Kelly confided to Lauren. "My dogs are not used to crowds, let alone streets and houses."

"Most of the mushers here are in the same boat.

Trails of the Heart

We live away from towns. Don't let it worry you. Dogs are smart. Once we're beyond the city limits, it's wilderness all the way. That's where the real race begins."

Some distance back from the starting line, amid the frantic bustle of cameras and microphones, Kelly waited for her turn. The announcement that Tyler Kade was being replaced by his handler, a rookie, created a considerable stir. Tyler's success in the Yukon Quest had heightened interest among the racegoers. Kelly was encouraged by the kindness of the other mushers and the behavior of the media. The cheers of the spectators helped her overcome her jitters.

The actual start proved less of an ordeal than she'd feared. Her spirits were boosted by the banner suspended over the starting line that proclaimed the race covered no less than 1,049 miles. Although actually seeing the figure gave her the shivers. It was an incredible distance.

Number One was called out, but no one appeared. The number was reserved for the memory of Leonard Seppala. A sled was then driven up to honor a particularly deserving musher. Emotion ran high when it was announced it would honor the memory of Peter Farson who went through lake ice with his team while training. Finally, number twenty-nine came up. All sleds had to carry a passenger or drag another sled behind for the first few miles. In hers, she carried no less than the Iditarod Race Committee president. He wanted to see for himself how capable she was. Her dogs, still bewildered by the noise and confusion, stood silent. Then lay down. Already, she heard comments in the crowd that her dogs wouldn't go far. Other teams were straining forward, barking and jumping three feet in the air against the harness. Enough to make Kelly nervous.

Two hours later, after a faultless start, Kelly was in Eagle River. There, she met Marcia, along with Nick, a dashing young volunteer. Together they loaded the dogs into the truck for the ride to Lake Lucille in Wasilla. The ice on the Knik and Matanuska rivers wasn't safe, and the organizers opted for trucking the dogs around the hazard.

"Why don't they start the race here for good?" Marcia asked.

"I guess starting in Anchorage draws more spectators and more media attention."

"Don't forget the sponsors' publicity," said Nick, who was driving.

The race proper started again that afternoon.

Not long afterwards, Kelly's team was toiling up the impressive slopes of the Alaska Range. She concentrated on finding the best pace for the dogs. To her surprise, even on some of the steepest sections, they didn't show signs of undue fatigue. Earlier, her confidence had been tested at the sight of strings of sixteen dogs hitched to sleds alongside her own lightweight contingent of twelve. This show of stamina by her dogs helped restore some of her confidence.

Several teams had already overtaken hers, and she too had taken the lead over some slower competitors.

At her last rest stop, she'd consulted her notes. In her head, Tyler's voice reminded her to take it slow and easy through the mountains. *The Dalzell Gorges are dangerous, so when you reach them you want to have your dogs in good condition. Take them slowly. Never mind the clock. Go slow.* Those gorges now lay ahead of her. After that, it was the Rohn checkpoint, where a good many mushers took their compulsory twenty-four-hour layover.

Once again, Tyler was on her mind. This was not the time to anguish about the love she carried in her heart, a love he'd spurned. Instead, she dwelt on his advice. It was as if he were there with her, riding on the runners. Thanks to him, she tackled the gorges and their notorious switchbacks during daylight hours. The thorough training enabled her to negotiate the difficulties with the full mastery of her team.

With a deep sigh of relief, she pulled into Rohn. Lauren was already there.

"Your dogs look in great shape," Lauren said. "Keep going. When you see them flagging, that's the time to give them a long rest."

"I found the mountains pretty tough going."

"That's because you chose not to ride the runners. I saw you pedaling back there to help them. You've got a great team of dogs. Trust them. I've not made up my mind about pushing on or not. My team is quite strong, but I see signs of fatigue in a couple of dogs. I might drop them here and head out again."

Kelly had no such hesitation. She pushed on.

The race trail was unrelenting, a never-ending routine of eating, sleeping, examining dogs' paws, checkpoint stops and fresh departures.

In spite of the monotony, Kelly never grew discouraged, never failed to pat her dogs to instill them with her own enthusiasm.

"Tyler is expecting you to do a good job, dogs. So, let's go!"

With seven hundred and ninety-six miles still to be covered, Kelly reached the village of Nikolai just in time to wave farewell to Lauren, who was pulling out. Kelly finally decided to take the required long rest, and so set about organizing her camp.

That night the temperature took a steep dip. Next day, while waiting for the departure time, she noticed the wind had picked up. Each time a team left the village, her own dogs showed impatience to be off too. The exception was Tioralak. He lay utterly relaxed on his back, with all four paws in the air. In contrast, Itirit, anxiously raised her muzzle each time Kelly took a step.

At last Kelly was able to leave. She signed the official's time sheet and resumed the trail. By now the wind was driving the snow horizontally over the ground. Snow clung to the dogs' fur. Deep drifts rendered the going painfully slow. To keep up her spirits, Kelly sang to the dogs.

They trotted with renewed vigor and made good time into the McGrath checkpoint. Kelly had no intention of stopping there longer than was necessary, but she did ask a race official what time had Lauren come through.

"She's here still, taking her twenty-four hours."

Kelly was surprised that her new friend was not making better time, unless it was part of her strategy.

In the Kuskokwin Mountains, blowing snow reduced visibility down to a few yeards. The wind shrieked through the high valleys. More than once, Kelly felt the sled tip sideways. But the dogs plodded onward, nose down, shoulders hunched. After many weary hours, Kelly arrived at Iditarod, the mining ghost-town that gave its name to both the trail and the race.

To her astonishment, she discovered she was among the frontrunners. Three of the veteran racers were taking their long rest. Not daring to hope she was gaining on them, she halted only long enough to water her team. Six days running, another four or five to Nome depending on the trail conditions. The excitement kept a smile on her slightly frostbitten face.

Tradition had it that the first musher to reach the Anvik checkpoint was regaled with a gourmet banquet prepared by a cordon bleu chef from the Regal Alaskan tourist hotel on the banks of the Yukon River. Phil Richter was that lucky musher.

Of more immediate concern to Kelly were the reports of a fierce blizzard raging along the Alaskan coast. Praying that it would end before she found herself engulfed by it, she set up camp in Anvik to take the eight hours required rest. At what exact spot along the Yukon River to rest was left to the discretion of the musher. At first, Kelly was tempted to postpone the layover until later. Then she realized that a good rest would permit the dogs to travel faster over the frozen river, where the going was smoother. Perhaps by that time the blizzard would have blown itself out.

While she was getting ready to leave, her assurance was shattered when she found that light snow had obliterated the well-marked trail. There were now only a few mushers ahead of her, and for the first time since starting the race, she saw a faint possibility of winning. Present standings meant little because the race was only half over. Until now, Kelly had not made any great demands on her dogs. She could always push them harder.

Okay, Tyler, what would you do in my place? As much rest as hours of running. No compromising on rest for the dogs. Right?

She took her time in hitching up her team before she signaled her readiness to depart.

The race marshal grinned over his clipboard. "You're in luck, Kelly. The trail-breaker is going out ahead of you. You'll think you're sledding down Main Street."

The man's news boosted her morale. Although battling high winds all the way, she kept up a brisk pace to Kaltag. From there, the route quit the Yukon River and struck out toward the coast.

On the way, she passed a musher resting on the side of the trail. He might still overtake her later. The White Mountain checkpoint was a compulsory stopover. When she got there, the only musher she saw was Phil Richter. He'd been leading the race for the past five hundred miles. There was no question he was a strong contender for the first place.

Kelly felt a tinge of disappointment. She thought of Tyler. Did he really expect her to win? If he were here now, he would know how to place himself in a strong position to win. She was sure of that. Her lack of experience prevented her from snatching the fruits of victory. Or was her refusal to push her dogs to the limit the deciding factor? Even favoring her team the way she did, she'd made it to the very front of the pack. And she still had her full complement of twelve huskies.

Three other leading mushers arrived at race control minutes after her. Being experienced racers, they could easily overtake her. Kelly had one big advantage. Already, they'd been obliged to drop off dogs along the way and were down to eleven apiece. The finish line at Nome still lay more than seventy miles to the north.

Resigned to a fourth place, Kelly went outside to massage the shoulders of her dogs. Thinking they were about to set off, they jumped to their feet, full of vigor.

"Okay, my darlings. We're not doing so badly. Thanks to you I'm going to finish this race with a respectable placing."

A man's cheerful voice behind her added, "For a rookie, Kelly, you're doing just great!"

She glanced over her shoulder. Phil was busy fitting booties to the feet of several of his dogs. In Kelly's sled bag, she too had a supply of booties, all unused. Her dogs' feet remained in perfect condition.

"Thanks for your vote of confidence."

Phil pointed with his chin at the resting mushers. "You'll have to drive your team flat out, Kelly, if you intend to stay ahead of those guys."

"But I'll be behind you."

"I leave first. I'll be first over the line. Good luck to you!"

"Break a leg!" she shouted as he sped off. The silly logic of the traditional wish of the theater world made her smile. But in the best sporting spirit, she'd meant it as a sincere expression of goodwill.

Kelly gave her own dogs the signal to start. The remaining mushers gathered to see her off. They shouted good-natured promises to catch up to her later. Although tired beyond belief, she felt her excitement rise now that the end of the race was so close. When she began to sing, Itirit, out in front with Nunii, quickened the pace.

Darkness fell. Kelly looked behind. Nowhere in the inky void could she see the telltale flicker of a musher's headlamp. That was nothing to draw any comfort from. Her pursuers would doubtless catch up to her sooner or later, but she was determined to make them sweat first.

"Keep going, dogs. At the end of this trail you'll get all the food and rest you want." As if they understood, the team broke into a gallop.

Lulled by the unrelenting pace, Kelly half-dozed. All of a sudden, something in the beam of her headlamp jerked her to full consciousness. At the end of the dancing beam, the light caught a reflection. Kelly peered into the darkness. Whatever it was, the team was closing in on it fast.

Kelly pressed her foot on the brake. "A man!" As she drew closer, she recognized the dark green parka of a man walking on the trail. It was Phil Richter, her arch-rival.

As if resenting having to break their rhythm, the dogs took a long time to come to a full stop.

"Phil! What happened?"

"Damned dogs! They didn't listen to me. I fell off the sled."

"Climb up behind me. We'll catch up with them."

In one bound Phil was on the runners. He snaked one hand around her to grip the sled's handlebar.

"Thanks. This is really good of you. You know you're under no obligation to give me a ride? You could simply sled on by and anchor my team when you catch up with it."

"I know. But it could be another twenty miles before that happens. You're not going to hoof it for that distance, are you?"

"I'm dropping from lack of sleep."

"Nobody gets much shut-eye during this race."

"I must have fallen asleep on the runners." Phil's tone was gloomy. "And now, I'm slowing you down. Those guys behind are catching up. No, this is no good! Let me get off here. My team can't be far ahead now."

"Phil, I think you're having hallucinations. Stay where you are."

Kelly knew from the way the light from Phil's lamp bobbed up and down over her shoulder that he was getting woozy. In stark contrast, she was fully alert thanks to the adrenalin pumping through her veins. If she could maintain her lead over the others, there was a chance for her yet.

Several miles along the trail, they came across Phil's team. The dogs had been fighting and the lines were tangled.

"Thanks, Kelly. Get on your way."

"I can lend you a hand."
"Go! I'll manage. And Kelly?"
"Yes?"
"You're going to win if you don't slow down from now on. Your dogs can do it."

In a state close to shock, Kelly realized that she was out in front. Nome lay no more than thirty miles ahead. Hardly three hours sledding! But fatigue was taking its toll.

"Hike! Hike!" The energy in her voice communicated itself to the dogs. They needed no urging. Lighter now without the passenger, the sled skimmed over iron-hard snow whipped clean by the off the Bering Sea.

An unexpected burst of applause greeted her as she stopped at the last checkpoint village of Safety. She remained only long enough to check in and tell the officials about Phil's mishap.

It was with a pounding heart that she set out once more. The team sensed her urgency. They ran proud, their heads high, bushy plumed tails curled over their backs.

Soon the lights of Nome glittered on the horizon. More ominous, though, were the headlamps closing in behind her. Using her foot to pedal the sled, she put all her effort to get the most from her dogs. She tried to forget what was behind. Her eyes were fixed in front. Her approach had been spotted. The clamor of shouts reached her ears when she neared the town's limits. She burst into a song and her dogs responded by running ever faster.

She hit the brilliantly lit Front Street at full speed. Her laughter brought tears to her eyes. She and her team streaked toward the burled arch that marked the finish line.

The finish line! She couldn't believe she had actually won! Kelly Jefferies, the rookie of the Iditarod, had won! Eleven days on the trail and now, it was over.

A delirious crowd swarmed about her. Helping hands grasped the sled lines and brought the team to a halt. She jumped from the runners and dashed forward to hug her lead dogs, Itirit et Nunii, then all the others. Oblivious to the flash of cameras, she let the tears of joy and relief stream down her cheeks.

Her blurred vision prevented her from seeing a tall figure pushing through the crowd toward her.

"Kelly!"

She rubbed her eyes.

"Tyler!"

Tyler opened his arms wide. The next instant Kelly hurled herself into them, hugging him, not believing that any of this was actually happening. Tyler swept her off the ground. Her feverish lips found his. In that passionate kiss, the crowd melted away, the rest of the world ceased to exist.

Tyler set her on her feet and helped her up to the winner's podium, and led Itirit and Nunii on either side of her. Race officials and reporters pressed forward. The race marshal placed a garland of silk flowers over the heads of her two gallant lead dogs.

Being the focus of so much attention from television cameras and reporters' questions made Kelly's head spin.

Her eyes met Tyler's. A radiant smile lit his face. She noticed that the officials were moving her team aside to make way for the next arrival.

Kelly stood and waved a greeting to the second place winner as he crossed the line. The man raised his mittened-hand to acknowledge her greeting. No words were needed. His face showed the chagrin of losing to a rookie, a woman rookie at that!

"I must take care of my dogs," Kelly said.

Tyler placed a restraining hand on her shoulder. "Stay. You're the celebrity. I'll take care of them with Marcia. She's here too."

Kelly heard the tenderness in his voice. Her heart was filled with renewed hope. Tyler had come to her.

"Can you? Your wound..."

"It's fine. The stitches are out. I'm almost back to normal."

Kelly saw pride fill his eyes. There was something else too, something undefinable but wonderful. A tremor agitated her. How she longed to tell him she loved him, but he was all too soon swallowed up by the sea of people.

He returned. Arms linked, she and Tyler greeted the third place winner to cross the finish line. Phil Richter came in a close fourth.

Phil had no reservations about her achievement. In front of the assembled spectators and media, he announced, "More than simply winning hands down, Kelly Jefferies showed great sporting spirit by giving me a ride for several miles to catch up with my runaway team. She and her dogs deserved to win. They're magnificent."

His short but fiery speech whipped up the crowd's fervor even more. Eventually, Tyler was able to lead Kelly through the smiling and cheering throng.

In the lobby of the finest hotel Nome possessed, she and Tyler were greeted by the staff. With great pomp, they showed her to her room.

"Knowing from experience what you must feel like, I guess your wish right now is for a hot bath and a soft bed, in that order." He threw his fur hat and parka onto a chair.

"Your guess is right."

With infinite gentleness, he undressed her down to her silk underwear. Breathless, she waited. Tyler was unable to resist. He took her in his arms. Their lips met in a fervent kiss. She pressed her trail weary body to him and crushed herself against his muscled frame. Tired as she was, she sensed his growing need.

Tyler straightened. His strong hands turned her and firmly propelled her toward the bathroom.

"Go and take care of yourself, while I'm still in control of myself."

"Tyler..." She hesitated part way across the room. "The bath can wait."

"No, sweetheart. Take care of yourself, first." He carried her bag and placed it on the bathroom vanity.

When the door closed behind him, Kelly traced her nail over lips still tingling from the imprint of his kiss. He had called her "sweetheart". Did that signify anything? Probably not. It was the same as Byron calling her "honey". A mere pleasantry offered in the heat of the moment.

There was no mistaking his joy of her win. With a sigh of delight, she ran a steaming bath and lay back to savor its luxury.

Dressed in a satin robe, Kelly came from the bathroom to find Tyler seated in an armchair.

"I've never seen you look so beautiful!"

Color suffused her cheeks.

"I'd better go before I tire you further," he murmured.

"I feel better now, after the bath."

"Your eyelids are drooping. I'll be back this evening."

"Where's Glenn?"

"He's staying with Vicky. Good news! Gloria finally broke down and phoned. The dear gal is getting married again. Glenn stays with me. She gets him for vacations."

His rugged face shone with a new-found happiness. Kelly was too tired to grasp the full significance of what he was saying. Her mind vaguely registered that all his happiness was because his son was staying with him. Nothing to do with her. But exhaustion prevented her from elaborating.

"You must rest now."

A soft touch on her cheek woke Kelly from her deep sleep. Without moving, she opened her eyes. For several seconds, she had no idea where she was.

"Time to wake up, beautiful." Tyler leaned over and helped her into a sitting position. Her hair tumbled about her shoulders in splendid disarray. He put his arms about her and held her close.

Hungrily, he took her trembling lips. Hers responded with even greater fervor. He trailed a path downward to tease the fragrant softness of her neck.

Kelly's laughter echoed in the room. She pulled

him down into the pillows, and began a voyage of discovery. The flux of her craving carried forward by her breathless impatience emboldened her now that their mutual passion was released.

Teasingly she trapped his mouth with hers, while he struggled free of the incumbrance of his garments. He stripped off her nightdress in one fluid sweep of the hand. Unhindered at last, she arched to him, reveling in the feel of her naked skin against his.

Slowly, he possessed her.

As he did so, she let a long, pent-up sigh escape her parted lips. His consummate lovemaking was measured and gentle. Nothing seemed more right at that moment than the wish to give themselves fully to each other.

Deep down, bolts of silent lightening exploded in a paroxysm of sensual joy. Tyler sealed her rising tide of happiness with a kiss.

They lay as one, delighting in the exquisitely fading euphoria. With the tenderest of movements, Tyler rolled to her side. He cupped his chin in his hand. "You must be hungry."

" Hungry for...?"

"For food, of course. What did you think? Shall we go and eat?"

"I'd like to take a short walk first. I need some fresh air."

Tyler smiled. "I need to cool down too. Let's go, or we'll never get off this bed."

With stolen kisses and much silly laughter, they dressed.

The festive air along the busy street intimidated Kelly after eleven whole days of utter wilderness silence. Back on the frozen trails, alone with her dogs, she'd felt part of another time. Indeed, the Iditarod trail belonged to a world apart. Tyler guided her to where the ground sloped down to the edge of the frozen sea, well removed from the noise and lights behind them.

"Tyler, look!" Kelly motioned upward. Immense veils of emerald green hung in giant curtains against the night sky. Across the vast heavens the aurora borealis undulated with breathtaking beauty.

"Some call it the sky's lover," Tyler murmured.

Kelly nodded, spellbound by the sight. Tyler crooked an arm about her shoulder and turned her to face him.

"Now that you've proved yourself, you must continue. There are other races to be won."

Her tone became serious. "I intend to. Next summer I'll put together a team of my own."

"No. I mean continue as of now. This season. I spoke to Lauren Kains while you were resting. That lady is full of praise for how you ran the race. You'll get all the help you need from her."

"What about you? Don't you want to help me?"

"Me? I want to love you." His warm lips grazed her forehead.

Her heart skipped several beats.

"One doesn't preclude the other, does it?" All she could manage was a faint whisper.

"Not if you marry me. There, I've said it."

Kelly could feel his heart pound wildly against his chest. He waited for her answer before releasing his breath.

Kelly's mind swirled in a warm mist. Had she heard correctly? it was some time before emotion let her speak again. "Marry you...? You mean you want me to be your wife?"

Tyler gave her a confused look. "Forget it! I must be babbling. Just forget what I said."

He released his hold on her and took a small step backward. Kelly's hand shot out and grabbed the front of his parka, as usual, open to the wind.

"Tyler, wait a minute, you want me to become your wife? Wife, as in marriage?"

"Yes, that was my idea but I know how much you cherish your freedom. So, let's forget it. I should never have-"

She didn't allow him to finish his sentence before closing her mouth over his in a long, unhurried kiss that left them both gasping for air.

"Yes, Tyler. I do want to be your wife."

"Do you love me?" he asked.

"I love you with a passion that knows no bound. And have done from the very beginning. And you?"

"I'm hopelessly in love with you. I must have been all along, but was too stupid to admit the truth. I was so scared. I didn't know how to handle all those feelings. I must have been such a boorish guy, but you put up with me."

Kelly chuckled. "Let's remember only the good times."

In the starlit sky, the northern lights worked their silent magic over the heads of the couple, secure in each other's arms and bound by their enduring love.

Some exciting romance novels from Whippoorwill Press

Awakening Dreams by renowned romance author Vanessa Grant.
Take off in a float plane with Crystal, and pilot Jesse. Crash in the wilds of British Columbia, survive with them and fall in love with them.

Midnight Hour by well-known romance author Jillian Dagg.
Serena tries to prove herself by running the show. She doesn't want overpowering Nick to take over. The set buzzes with tension. Will they put their differences aside and find love?

And more....

Red Phoenix Rising by Marie Carroll.
The Vietnam War tore lives apart. Follow reporter Alaina when she goes after the truth. Meet Col. Blackhart who refuses to talk to journalists. These are dangerous times. Will their love survive?

A Dance for Two
by Geneviève Montcombroux
Tanya on a leave of absence from the New York Ballet Company to look after her ailing father, opens a dance school. She dreams of a return to the stage.
Brach, a former NHL player, hankers after the excitement of the game.
She knows nothing about hockey. He knows nothing about dance. Will love bridge the gap?